PRISONER'S CINEMA

A Novel

ADAM JAMES JONES

Black Rose Writing | Texas

ISBN: 978-1-68433-671-5
PUBLISHED BY BLACK ROSE WRITING
www.blackrosewriting.com

Printed in the United States of America
Suggested Retail Price (SRP) $19.95

Prisoner's Cinema is printed in Book Antiqua

*As a planet-friendly publisher, Black Rose Writing does its best to eliminate
unnecessary waste to reduce paper usage and energy costs, while never
compromising the reading experience. As a result, the final word count vs. page count
may not meet common expectations.

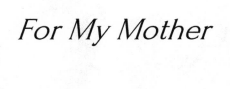

For My Mother

PRISONER'S
CINEMA

PSYCHONAUTWIKI

Page Discussion   Read View source   More   Search

 Donate   IRC

 Main page
Site map
Effects
Substances
Experiences
Tutorials
Replications
Responsible use
Random article

Prisoner's cinema

The **prisoner's cinema phenomenon** is a term used to describe the entoptic occurrence in which an individual, deprived of light or visual stimuli for extended periods of time, subject to solitary isolationism, sensory deprivation, or in extended trances of meditation, experiences hallucinations or "light show" style imagery both with their eyes open and closed.

It has been suggested that the hallucinations are a result of high levels of phosphene production and there is anecdotal proof suggesting that the shapes of these hallucinations may take on that of geometrical form constants. Additionally, it is quite possible that the hallucinations can take on other more abstract or nebulous forms including (but not limited to) shapes, faces, figures, places, or even the entire production of full on imaginary scenarios.

"The world is a beautiful place and I am no longer afraid to die."

This page was last modified on 11 August 2015, at 04:00.

1

Savannah lay sprawled on her bed, shameless in the murky light seeping from the blinds, when her social worker pulled into the drive. She heard the tires groaning through snow, the ratchet of a transmission. She knew without even having to look that it must be Miss Jill — or, as Grandma called her, "The State" — come for a visit. If not "The State," then why the panicked whispers in the kitchen, the footsteps padding quickly down the hallway? Who, besides Miss Jill, even knew Savannah and her family existed?

It felt early, barely dawn judging by the dim light. Then again, it took Savannah a long time to fall asleep last night, and maybe she'd slept straight through dawn and into dusk. She was fourteen years old and, as of last week, no longer going to school. Savannah had no more control over how long she slept than she did any other part of her life.

She knelt on her mattress and peeked between the blinds to see the front yard blanketed with snow. A row of red gas jugs lined against the family's mobile home were all but buried under what had slid from the roof, their nozzles snorkeling to the surface. The trailer park sat atop a low mesa overlooking town. From her vantage point Savannah could see the chimney smoke of the houses below dispel in the gray sky, the winking lights and concrete towers of the coal plants in the distance. Dime-sized flakes drifted down, stacking onto the hood of Grandma's pickup. A black sedan sat in the driveway next to the truck, a red flasher bulb on the dash.

Savannah didn't think Miss Jill, or any other social worker for that matter, drove with a flasher bulb. Two sets of footprints led from the sedan around the side of the trailer toward the front porch. Savannah could see where one of the prints' owners had stopped to wipe the snow from a rusty BB gun propped against a cinderblock.

Someone pounded on the front door, rattling the walls.

"Mía," Savannah said, turning around.

But the bed across from Savannah's was empty, the sheets open, pillow on the floor. Savannah and her sister had argued last night. The memory of it settled into her like a stomachache.

She heard the front door open, followed by her grandmother's greeting, muffled and curt. A man's voice responded, and then that of a woman. For a long moment, Savannah sat at the edge of her bed, holding her breath.

The door closed, and the conversation continued on the porch. Savannah exhaled. She couldn't make out the words being uttered outside, but she recognized all too well the agitation in her grandma's tone.

"*Girls?*"

Savannah jumped, standing now. The voice had come from inside the living room. She listened to the sound of boots being stomped, their wet squeaking as they wiped along the rubber doormat. The feet grew still.

"Hello?" the woman called out. "Savannah? Mía?"

Savannah relaxed. She hadn't recognized Miss Jill's voice at first. She also hadn't realized the woman had been let inside. Savannah pictured her standing out there in the living room, absorbing the state of the mobile home, its silence.

"Where are you two?" Miss Jill asked. Her footsteps thudded into the hallway, approaching the bedroom door. Savannah flopped back down on the bed and pulled the sheets up over her head.

Fingernails tapped on the plastic bedroom door.

"Girls?"

Savannah sat up slowly, rubbing her eyes. "Hmm?"

The door groaned open. Miss Jill stood in the doorway, heavy-set with a black and white blouse and nametag, cream-colored ponytail so thick it could haul a wagon. She held a three-ring binder fat with papers.

"Did I wake you, Savannah?"

Savannah squinted at her.

"We tried calling, but your grandma never answers her phone. She's saying she lost her phone, but I'm not really buying it. She used to say you guys didn't get service out here, but then I told her everyone gets service out here, so obviously she's just...."

Miss Jill checked herself, pinched her nametag, found her center. She closed her eyes for a second, opened them back up and smiled. "Savannah, are you wearing anything underneath that shirt?"

Savannah looked down at the San Juan Community College t-shirt pulled over her legs — something she'd salvaged from her mom's old clothes before Grandma had given the rest away. She lifted the shirt's hem to reveal her boxer shorts.

Miss Jill looked away, shielding her eyes. It made Savannah suddenly embarrassed — not for her body but because it seemed she didn't know any better than to show this woman her underwear. Things like this were part of the reason why Savannah kept more and more secrets from Miss Jill.

"Okay, no problem. Savannah, I'm going to step back into the hallway and shut the door. Do you think you could get dressed and let me know when you're done?"

Savannah shrugged, and Miss Jill left the room. Savannah slipped into jeans and pulled on a hoodie Grandma had won last summer at the stock show. Looking down at the big Coors Silver Bullet logo across the chest, she thought better of it and ditched the hoodie.

She was about to call the woman back in but hesitated. Under the faint conversation between Grandma and the man on the porch, she listened to Miss Jill creeping down the hallway toward the back bedroom. Savannah looked around for something to hide, not knowing what, only that this might be her last opportunity to do such a thing. She settled on the two Marlboros she had stashed in her backpack. She shook the cigarettes free, mushed them between her fingers and tossed them under the pile of clothes in her closet.

"Miss Jill?"

The door to the master bedroom clacked shut, footsteps returning.

"All good, Savannah?"

"Yeah."

Miss Jill came in and took a knee before Savannah. "Okay, Savannah, I need you to listen to me for a second, okay? The man talking to your grandma out there is an officer with the New Mexico State Police. You're not in any trouble, understand? We're only here to check on you and Mía. How come she's in your grandma's bed?"

"Amelia."

"What's that?"

"It's Amelia, not Mía."

It was both, but only Savannah called her Mía. She'd reminded Miss Jill of this before. Even Grandma called her Amelia.

"Right. Well, why is it she's sleeping back there? She looks sick."

This was news to Savannah.

"She's pale as can be, poor thing. How about you, Savannah? How are you feeling?"

"Fine."

"I hope you're not sick too. Do you usually sleep this late?"

"I don't know. What time is it?"

"It's after ten. That's good you're getting sleep. Teenagers need lots of sleep. But there is such a thing as too much. Have you been staying up late?"

Through the walls Savannah heard her grandmother blurt out, "Horseshit!" Savannah sniffed. The air in the house was thick, tangy with the scent of vinegar, which meant that Grandma had been canning more food in the kitchen.

Miss Jill opened the three-ring binder on her knee and started to write. Without lifting her gaze from the paper she asked, "Are you liking the new house?"

Savannah leaned forward, trying to read the upside-down scribbles streaming from the woman's pen.

"The house, Savannah. You like it?" She stopped writing and inventoried the bedroom: the matted carpet, twin oak dressers and matching vanity crammed together, faux wood paneling decorated

4

with cut-out pictures of animals on Mía's side and award ribbons on Savannah's.

Savannah shrugged. "The house is okay. It's small."

Miss Jill snorted. "Yeah well, at least it's in better shape than the old one. Plus, it's closer to town, so I bet it's easier to see your friends. I'm sorry you don't have space for horses, though. I remember that was important to you."

"Not really."

"No?" The woman's eyes went to the rows of blue ribbons on the wall above Savannah's bed.

"I stopped riding before the horses were gone."

"How about your cat? Did you ever find him? What was his name, something like—"

"He died," Savannah said.

"Oh."

Miss Jill seemed to swish this information around in her mouth as if trying to decide its flavor. She went back to her notes, tapping the pen a moment before writing something down. Savannah pictured a tiny sketch of a cat with X's for eyes.

"Savannah, you ever hear the saying, 'when you get bucked off, get back in the saddle'?"

Savannah rolled her eyes.

"I know, but it's true. You get bucked off in life. Things like moving to a new house or losing a parent. But eventually you have to get back in that saddle. That means returning to school. Your freshman year's a big one, same with fourth for your sister. Those are fun grades, and I'm sure your friends are missing you."

"My sister's in third grade." Savannah didn't bother adding that none of her friends were missing her. Or that Sarah Atkinson—the only real friend she'd ever had besides her sister—entered high school prettier and boobier than most upper-class girls and had thus ditched plain-and-thin Savannah for a rut of senior boys. But whatever. At least now Sarah didn't have any real friends either.

"Third, that's right," Miss Jill said. "So why haven't the two of you been going to school?"

"We're being homeschooled. Grandma teaches us."

The tone on the front porch had turned ugly. Grandma was all but yelling now, and Savannah could hear the officer repeating, "*Ms. Unser—, Ms. Unser—*"

It occurred to Savannah then how hot the room had become, the air stuffy and dank with the pickle juice wafting in from the kitchen, as well as the stale scent of Savannah's own sleep. The tiny bedroom and its bulky furniture seemed to suddenly *squeeze* Savannah. Her heart began to pound, her lungs pumping for air.

Miss Jill's face tightened. Concern? No, not quite. *Suspicion.* "Savannah, is anyone else living here besides you, your sister, and grandma?"

Savannah's gaze flicked toward the doorway.

"Savannah?"

"No."

"No one at all?"

"No."

"Not even your father?"

On the porch Grandma was demanding the officer leave. Miss Jill snapped the binder closed. She put two fingers on Savannah's cheek and gently turned her so that Savannah had nowhere to look but at the face inches from her own—the coatings of makeup around her eyes, the face powder so thick Savannah could smell it.

"Savannah, is there a reason your grandma won't let the officer inside?"

"She doesn't like cops."

As if to verify this statement the living room door burst open, Grandma audibly cursing the officer on the doorstep before slamming the door closed again. Both Savannah and Miss Jill stiffened at the sound of her barging through the living room and yanking out cabinet drawers.

This time Savannah shoved the social worker, ready to step right over her for the door should she topple over. But against Savannah's slight build Miss Jill took the shove like a pile of bricks, and it was Savannah who bounced backwards. Miss Jill stood up.

"Let me out," Savannah said.

"I don't see why you're so panicky. It's just me."

"I'm getting claustrophobic."

"Do you feel unsafe living here?"

"I need to check on my sister."

"Savannah, listen to me."

"Get out of my way"

"Have you spent any nights alone here?"

Savannah paused, backed away.

"Why are you afraid to answer me, Savannah?"

Footsteps thundered down the hallway toward them. Miss Jill jumped away from the door just in time for it to bang open, buzzing on its hinges. There stood Grandma, peering over her glasses at the cameraphone aimed at the two of them. She wore cowboy boots, jeans, and a tucked white t-shirt through which two dark nipples protruded. A couple months ago she'd shaved her head, and her white hair had grown back just enough since then to curl and fluff a little, reminding Savannah of poodle hair. There was a glistening of sweat in the white roots of her temple, and for a split second Savannah thought she saw the rainbow in it.

Grandma swung the phone onto Miss Jill. "And tell us your name! Tell us your name one more time, ma'am!"

At first Miss Jill only stood there, wincing slightly under the fathomless eye of the camera lens.

"Ma'am, your name please."

"You know my name. Will you please—"

"Again, it's ten-eighteen AM on Tuesday, November fourteenth. My name is Judith Unser and this is Jill Russell, who is in my house and as you can see is *not* wearing a body camera."

"I'm not a police officer," Miss Jill said. "I don't need to wear—"

"She has been speaking to my daughter *without* my supervision," Grandma said, turning the phone to Savannah for a moment before going back to Miss Jill. "And now she is being recorded to provide evidence which I *will* be submitting in my lawsuit unless she leaves my house within the next ten seconds. Ten... nine..."

"She's not your daughter, Ms. Unser. It's the law I check in with her, and besides you let me in. The girls can't keep missing school. That's also law."

Grandma stepped closer to her. "I called the school and said I was teaching them here. I can produce phone records to prove it."

"It's not that easy, Ms. Unser."

"You didn't come out here because of my kids' truancy. Why'd you bring a cop then?"

Miss Jill glanced at the cameraphone and kept silent. Savannah grew increasingly aware of how dizzy she was, how cold her face felt, the tiny flashes of light at the edges of her vision.

"There are sheets and a pillow on your living room sofa, Ms. Unser. Is someone else staying here?"

Grandma spread her thumb and forefinger across the screen, zooming in. "That hardly seems like any of your business."

"It's my business to make sure these girls are living in a safe environment. That includes knowing everyone they might be staying with. These are all things you agreed to in the custody —"

"I slept there. Amelia's sick. She came crying to me in the middle of the night so I gave her some ibuprofen and let her sleep in my bed while I took the couch."

Miss Jill turned to Savannah and Savannah stared at the floor. She concentrated on a swimming patch of carpet, little floaties dancing at the corners of her left eye. The bad eye. The damaged one. The eye she didn't trust like she did the other.

Miss Jill continued with Grandma. "You haven't seen or heard from your son?"

"No. I already told that to your friend outside."

"You understand their father is not to have any contact with the girls? Again, it is my job to know if the girls might be in danger or —"

"The hell I just say? Haven't seen him. None of us have."

Both women were quiet. Savannah felt their minds lock onto her at the exact same time. The back of her knees trembled against the bed frame. She rested a hand on the mattress.

The silence was broken by a tiny moaning coming from the other end of the house. A second moan followed it, louder than the first.

Grandma scowled at Miss Jill. "*And now* you're disturbing my youngest one while she tries to rest. You are keeping her sick by not letting her sleep. I'm asking you one more time to —"

"I need to see her before I go," Miss Jill said.

"Out of the question. Not while she's sick."

"SAVANNAAAAH!" Mía shrieked from down the hall, the walls humming. Savannah blinked, pushed herself away from the bed and moved toward the doorway. Grandma thrust an arm out, barring her path.

"Just let me see her, that's all," Miss Jill said. "After that I'm gone. We both are, the officer too. I swear it."

For a moment Grandma only stood there, the phone drooping in her hand as she considered. Mía continued to cry.

Grandma pressed the stop button and set the phone on the dresser. Keeping her eyes on Miss Jill, she called out: "What's wrong, Amelia?"

After a moment: "I threw up on myself!"

Grandma looked from Savannah to Miss Jill. Then: "Okay, hold on, Amelia. We're coming." She lowered her arm and Savannah glided past, the two women instantly at her heels. The hall was dark at the far end, and Mía could be heard whimpering behind a closed door.

"We're coming, sweetheart," Grandma said, her hand falling on the back of Savannah's neck to control their pace. "All three of us are coming to check on you."

Savannah opened the door. Mía sat upright, her tiny figure afloat amongst the blankets of the queen-sized bed. Yellow vomit stained the pillow behind her and streaked down her chin. She was on the verge of another big sob, but she caught it in her throat the moment they entered. She held the breath there a moment before letting it out in a long sigh, her whole body slumping.

Grandma turned to Miss Jill and held a hand out to the child. "There, you happy? Is this what you came to see? Sick girl barely slept last night, you barge in, wake her up and get her sick all over again. Boy I bet you just *live* for this stuff. That you can't wait to go home tonight and tell everyone around the dinner table how bad some people got it, how bad some people is, how thankful everyone around that table should feel. You'll tell 'em you don't know how you do this job sometimes, only that you *have* to. *Fuuuuuck*, like your own don't get the flu."

"You might want to get her to a doctor."

"You think I wasn't? How can I when I been dealing with you all morning?"

"And you need to start sending these girls back to school. Or, if you're going to homeschool, you've got to submit the right papers. It's not a deal you simply call in."

"I'll take care of it."

"This isn't something that's going to go away."

"We'll see about that."

"I'll be coming back."

"I don't doubt it."

Miss Jill pursed her lips. She took one more look at Mía, then turned her attention to Savannah. Savannah met and held the woman's gaze. At least that much was owed. But she gave nothing more, and finally—sad, like an apology—Miss Jill said goodbye to Savannah and left.

"Look to your sister," Grandma said, disappearing after Miss Jill down the hallway.

Savannah stared dreamily at the scene before her: the thick green curtains of the window filtering a pea-colored light over piles of musky laundry, the sour reek of hot vomit, the Sprite can-turned-ashtray on Grandma's nightstand, the scattered perfume and medicine bottles. The hundreds of long, amoeba-looking floaties multiplying in her left eye. Reproducing. Clogging her periphery in an effort to suffocate her sight.

Savannah braced her hands against the doorframe and sank to the floor. She put her head between her knees and concentrated on the floor.

"Savannah?"

"Give me a second."

"I threw up."

"I know. I know. Just give me a second."

"What did Miss Jill... What's happening?"

"I'm not sure, but it's all okay."

"I don't feel good, Savannah." Her voice cracked when she said her sister's name, and she started huffing again.

The front door slammed, followed by the tinkling of blinds. Savannah, her cheekbones on her kneecaps, swayed gently to the sound of her sister's whimpers, the faded blue carpet undulating in her vision like wind on water. Grandma ran back down the hall and nearly tripped over Savannah in the doorway. "What are you doing? Get up."

Savannah climbed to her feet, planting one hand against the doorframe. But Grandma didn't step past her. Instead she leaned her head in and said, "They're gone. Just us."

Something rustled under the bed. A socked foot darted into view before disappearing back under. There was a light clunk as the foot's owner banged his head against the bed's wooden frame. The mattress lifted and Mía squealed in surprise.

Teddy Unser crawled out from under the foot of the bed, the top of his shaved head oily and glinting. The nails of one hand clawed into the carpet while the other gripped a large, heavy-looking black handgun. Savannah watched as her father spat, picked something off his tongue, and brushed a few clinging bits of lint from his beard.

"You okay?" Grandma said.

He craned his head up at her. "If we're going to do this, we got to do it now."

2

Savannah put her sister into a bath. When she returned to her bedroom she found her grandma waiting for her and holding two aluminum-frame backpacks.

"Pack up everything you and your sister can't live without," Grandma said. "It's all got to fit in these two packs."

"Where are we going?"

"You'll see when we get there. We leave in thirty minutes. And I'm serious, pack only what you need."

"What, like food and water?"

"Like things you'd really, really miss."

"I'd really, really miss food and water."

"Or take nothing at all. I don't care. Either way, thirty minutes."

Grandma went outside. Savannah watched through the bedroom window as Grandma started the truck and began work scraping the ice from the windshield. Her father paced in the kitchen, talking low and fast into a cellphone.

Savannah looked at the packs. She didn't know where to start except with her iPod and headphones. Most teenagers listened to music on their phones now, but Savannah didn't have a phone. She had a scratched-up, eight-year-old iPod that she cherished. It was one of the few items of value she'd managed to hold onto following the bankruptcy. Savannah remembered standing on the big deck of Grandma's old house in the country while men in overalls and ball caps filed past her, loading the family's belongings into trucks. She still recalled the awful curses Grandma had showered upon the men that day, the police officer who more than once had to physically restrain her. And yet, Savannah had felt no sorrow watching the house be emptied, only an irrational fear that one of the men was going to check some list and all of a sudden ask about the iPod. That any second one of them was going to march up to her and demand she empty her pockets. But none of them ever did, and when the house was finally gutted Savannah, Mía, and Grandma had nothing left to do but follow the police escort to their new trailer on the edge of town.

She slipped the iPod into her pocket and listened to the soft sounds of splashing coming from the bathroom. With the backpacks propped against the wall, Savannah looked around for things to pack for her sister. The day her grandma bought Savannah the iPod was the same day she'd won custody of the girls. On the drive back from the courthouse, they'd stopped at Wal-Mart. There, Grandma told Savannah and Mía they could have anything in the store. Savannah went wild, scooping into her cart the iPod, dozens of CDs, a laptop and many more things now gone. Mía on the other hand had settled on a simple stuffed lion that she later named Mauricio. Seeing Mía hold the lion next to her own overflowing shopping cart had both shamed Savannah and made her love her sister more than ever.

Living in Grandma's run-down house in the country — where the ancient potbelly stove barely kept the inside temperature above see-your-own-breath degrees, and where leaks in the roof were solved with buckets on the floor — Savannah felt even guiltier when she realized her grandmother had never been in a position to afford the splurge at Wal-Mart. It'd been her attempt at spoiling her granddaughters — with money she didn't have.

Savannah searched through the toys and stuffed animals in the closet until she found her sister's stuffed lion. She fit it into one of the packs.

From outside came the steady rumble of the idling pickup, the *shrrnk shrrnk* of the ice scraper. Savannah opened the drawers and pulled out socks, underwear, shirts, jeans — every article rolled small and tight then stuffed into a backpack. She moved over to Mía's dresser and did the same for her.

She carried a bundle of sweats into the hallway and knocked on the bathroom door.

"Mía, you almost done?"

A light splash of water.

"Mía?"

"Leave me alone."

"We have to get going. I'm packing your stuff. Can I come in and get our toothbrushes?"

"Go away. I don't feel good at all."

Savannah opened the door a crack and slipped inside, a warm fog greeting her. Mía's head was a dark and swirling silhouette behind the tub's curtain. Savannah reached her hand through and flipped the stopper to let the water drain.

"*Savannaaah*." Mía started to cry again.

"I don't understand what's wrong with you, Mía. You were fine last night. Fine enough to keep…." She didn't want to say arguing. "Talking. Did you wake up feeling this way? When did you change beds?"

But Mía didn't answer, merely sank a little farther below the receding water.

"Grandma's going to be mad if you don't hurry. She's already got the truck warmed up."

"I don't want to go anywhere. I don't feel good."

"I think we're moving."

"I don't want to move again."

"I'm leaving you some clothes here on the sink." Savannah set the clothes down, grabbed a hairbrush, both their toothbrushes and a tube of toothpaste. As she closed the medicine cabinet she caught a glimpse of her reflection in the mirror. She wiped the mirror with a forearm to see a great big whitehead on her nostril.

Gross. How fucking *embarrassing.* She'd been face-to-face with Miss Jill the whole time with that thing floating there. How had the woman been able to concentrate on anything else? Maybe she hadn't. Maybe that's all she'd been writing about in that binder of hers, like, *Patient exhibits what appears to be a second head, albino, sprouting from nose. Wonder if sentient? Recommending transfer to volcanologist.*

Is that how Miss Jill thought of her, a patient? Whatever the case, Savannah felt it should be common courtesy to notify one another of these things, of whiteheads or lettuce shards in teeth, so that one could politely excuse oneself and take care of it, rather than obliviously grossing everyone out.

The drain in the tub gurgled. Savannah wiped at the mirror again, ripped off a piece of toilet paper, leaned close and took care of the whitehead. She washed her face, turned off the faucet but remained hunched over. She watched the water drip from her skin into the pink plastic sink—cruddy with old toothpaste like pigeon droppings.

She looked back up at her reflection, already fogging over, and in that softened image thought she saw the hints of something attractive. She knew she wasn't beautiful—at least not Sarah *Atkinson* beautiful— but she wasn't ugly, either. Both she and her sister had inherited their mother's petite figure, which wasn't mousey but dainty and feminine. For Savannah, the curves were still in their early stages, but if she continued like her mother those curves would turn out complimentary yet never distracting. And she liked to think that her mother's Colombian descent mixed with her father's German lent her a quality both exotic and sophisticated, as if her almost-but-not-quite-black hair and mocha eyes hinted at someone neither belonging to nor above any one world. Mía on the other hand was darker, and when Savannah thought back to her own experiences in school, she hoped her sister never found herself categorized.

The tub sucked empty. Savannah wiped her face with a towel, opened the shower curtain. Her sister lay fetus-like on one side, shivering. Savannah wrapped her in the towel, took a seat on the edge of the tub and held her. She held her for a long time, wishing as she did that acne was the only thing she had to worry about.

"Meet you out there," she said at last, standing up and putting the rolled-up sweats in her sister's hands. She picked up the toothbrushes, toothpaste, a hairbrush and, before she forgot, some face wash.

She stepped into the hallway. A shadow stretched over the carpet, and Savannah turned cold. She looked up to see her father.

"You're a good big sister, aren't you?"

The handgun was holstered now against his hip and he had changed into army boots, camo pants, and a camo vest with what looked like three-hundred different pockets. Under the vest he wore a beige turtleneck that bulged with his muscles. In one hand he held a puffed-out garbage bag, in the other the cellphone Grandma had used to film Miss Jill.

"You are, aren't you? A good big sister?"

Savannah shrugged.

Teddy dropped the bag and pushed past her into the bathroom. He reached one of his giant hands out toward Mía, still wrapped in her towel and seated on the edge of the tub. But instead of Mía his hand reached to the toilet lid. He grabbed it, flipped it open, and dropped the cellphone inside. He stepped out of the bathroom without even trying to flush, closing the door behind him.

"You almost done with your bug-out bags?" he asked Savannah, hefting the garbage bag.

"Is that what we're doing, *bugging out*?"

"And not a second too soon. Come on, better let me take a look."

She turned around and led him to her room. The back of Savannah's neck prickled with him behind her, the garbage bag crinkling. He was a big man, not just thick but tall to the point his bald head barely missed the top of the doorframe as he set the bag down beside it. Savannah watched him paw through the backpacks. She noticed what looked to be a tattoo veiled through the shirtsleeve over his upper arm. She didn't recall a tatto....

He pulled out the stuffed lion, looked at her and cocked his head.

"I don't know," she said. "I thought it'd be good. His name's Mauricio."

He tossed the lion into a corner. "The turtle's better. Let's bring him instead."

"What turtle?"

His eyes darted to the other toys spilling out of the closet. He went over and began to rummage through them. "That stuffed turtle I gave you, where is it?"

Savannah sat down on the edge of her bed. The last three days had left her reeling. It all felt like a dream, everything from the moment she and Mía had walked in from the bus to find him sitting on the couch. He'd stood up and spread his arms wide, and when they didn't rush up to him it was he who closed the gap, wrapping both girls in a giant bear hug. The smell of sweat and smoke pressed into their faces. Grandma smiled and wrung her hands behind him, shifting her anxiety from one foot to another. He asked them how their day was — as if it had been mere hours and not two years since last they'd seen him. As if neither girl knew the police were looking for him.

Yet here he was, digging through the girls' closet, searching for some stupid stuffed animal.

"We don't have it," Savannah said.

He backed out of the closet. "You threw it away?"

"I'm not sure. Yeah, maybe. I don't really remember it. Mía likes the lion though."

He rose to his feet, looking hurt. Savannah didn't know what to say. Out in the driveway the scraping of ice had stopped, and the truck's door slam shut. Teddy returned to the backpacks, crossed one arm over his chest and combed his fingers through his beard. The beard was so brown it was almost red. So long and scraggly that birds could live in it.

"This everything then?" he asked, packing the lion back in.

"I guess so. I'd rather just have a suitcase."

"Suitcases are no good where we're going. Or did your grandma not tell you we'd be riding horses before this day is over?"

"Horses? Where'd you get horses? And why a backpack then and not saddlebags or —"

"These horses I got are not exactly prize-winning thoroughbreds. You'll understand when you see them. We're going to have to hike if they run out of steam. That's why the backpacks."

"You're coming too?"

"That a problem?"

Savannah looked at her feet. "No."

"You don't need to be nervous around me. I don't understand why you are."

Savannah only nodded.

He moved over to Mía's bed and lay down on his side. He propped his head on an elbow, the soles of his oil-stained boots tapping the dresser. He ran a hand along the sheets, picked up a corner and smelled it. "This packing job you got going... You need warmer clothes."

Savannah's chest grew tight with whatever she seemed to be agreeing to. "How warm?"

"Like, really warm. Long johns, thick hunting socks, flannel, sweats. Don't you still have your combat gear?"

He was referring to the bags, boxes, and oftentimes savage-looking contraptions he used to bring home from General Cody's Army-Navy surplus store: nylon flight jackets, boots three sizes too big tied together by their laces, folding shovels, space blankets and green tactical helmets. Knives. Savannah was always confused by the presents; disappointed and a little embarrassed by her father's excitement at giving them. As far back as she could remember he was always "prepping" for what he vaguely referred to as "The Event." This process included not only stocking up on books and survival manuals, gadgets and gear, but also conducting "field tests." Savannah recalled her amazement the time he started a campfire in their backyard by rubbing steel wool against a 9-volt battery. She never did see much use in any of it, though she wondered if today that was about to change.

"Do we need our sleeping bags?" she asked, going to her closet and pulling out clothes.

"You'll be surprised how much I already got taken care of. Right now worry about what to wear."

Teddy dug into a pocket and produced a giant folding knife with a webbed-steel handle. He flipped out a blade the size of a dollar bill and began cleaning his fingernails with it. "I worry about your sister. She's so... *dependent*. She's a lot like her mother. I'm glad you're not."

Savannah focused on the clothes. She knew he said it as a compliment, even if it felt like an accusation.

"That social worker," he said. "You two had a talk in here?"

"I didn't say anything."

"Why? What'd she ask?"

"Pretty much just why I was missing school."

"She say anything about me?"

"Yeah, but I said I haven't seen you."

"That's what she asked, if you'd seen me?"

"Pretty much."

"Anything else?"

"No, other than like I said, that we need to start going back to school."

Savannah had her back half-turned to him as she pulled clothes off their hangers and draped them over her arm. She saw see him splayed out in the corner of her vision, the blade still out but no longer picking at his nails. She folded the clothes and stuffed them into the backpacks, keeping her hands busy.

"What else did she ask?"

Savannah felt her legs shaking. She knelt in front of the packs. "That's all I remember."

"What if I told you I heard *every*thing?"

She was stuffing a handful of socks into a backpack when he said it. But she pushed at a wrong angle and the pack fell to its side. She looked at him and he winked.

"She asked if we'd spent any nights here alone, Mía and me. We talked about living in this house. Other things I guess, I don't know —"

"Relax, Savannah. I believe you. She was only trying to trick you into giving something up. They're thinking about taking you, you realize? You and your sister. But I won't let them without a fight. We've been kept apart way too long, you and me. And neither of us deserved it. From now on I'm taking care of you. Given everything that... well, given everything that happened, I understand that could be hard to believe. But believe it. From now on you're my number one concern. You're all I've got, I'm all you've got, and that's all we need."

Savannah wondered if that was true, whether what she was missing — had always been missing — was in fact the steady presence of her father. She could offer herself a hundred reasons for her despair, why not this one too? There was a lot about him she didn't know, and a lot of what she did know about him scared her. But she also felt weirdly empowered around him — power having become another stranger of sorts in her young life. It crossed her mind that perhaps those two things—fear and power—always operated together. His muscles, the years in prison, the things she heard he did. Even the big handgun strapped to his waist. He was a half-tamed Rottweiler, loyal only to his family.

And Savannah supposed she was loyal to him, too. Why else would she spend the last three days forbidding her sister to tell anyone he was back?

"What did you say when she asked about spending nights here alone?" he asked.

"I didn't tell her anything. That was right when Grandma came in with the camera."

He laughed. "Mom and her home movies. Cops love it when you shove a camera in their faces. I taught her that, about filming cops." He flipped the knife closed. "Something I need to ask of you before we go. Something important."

"Okay."

"And you need to be truthful with me on this, because once we go...."

She didn't prompt him to finish, really didn't want him to.

"Here is what I want from you, to give me your trust. You can think and feel for me as you like, but at the very least trust me. Can you do that?"

She fiddled with a strap on one of the backpacks. She wasn't sure if she could summon something like trust. Then again, there was an appealing opportunity in this, in how she chose to answer. Because if she couldn't trust him, she needn't be truthful with him, either.

"Savannah?"

"Yes, I can."

He smiled. His eyes went to the garbage bag he'd left by the bedroom door. "Oh, I almost forgot." He got to his feet, snatched up the bag and pulled out a puffy camouflage coat with matching pants. He tossed the outfit over to Savannah who was unready for it as the jacket flopped over her head. The pants hit the floor in front of her.

"Try it on," he said. "It's all brand new."

Savannah held the suit up in front of her. Hot with self-consciousness, she put the jacket on. It was comfy enough, but she felt like some kind of astronaut soldier.

"I got them special ordered," he said, reaching back into the bag and pulling out a second camo outfit, this one smaller. "Even have one for your sister. Now I'm almost wondering if I shouldn't have gotten them in white. Once we get in the trees you'll appreciate the woodland pattern. We'll see. Anyway, you're welcome."

"Thanks," Savannah said.

He looked meaningfully at her now. "I will do anything to protect you. Like I said, from now on we look out for one another, you and me. It's not going to work otherwise. And don't worry if your grandma ever comes off as, I don't know, *erratic*. Is that the word for her? In any case, I have her under control."

He came over and set one of his heavy palms down on her head. Savannah had a vision of a giant starfish plopping down up there. She heard her grandmother come back in and start banging around in the kitchen, humming what sounded like a Christmas song. Savannah thought she recognized it. Didn't Mía sing it once in a school musical? What was it called, "Good King Wenceslas?"

Savannah wasn't sure if she wanted to laugh or cry the moment was so surreal.

Power and fear.

3

Grandma's pickup chugged and shuddered in the driveway. The truck had a bench seat. Grandma got behind the wheel while. Mía and Savannah slid in from the other side, followed by Teddy. It had stopped snowing by the time they swung out of the driveway, but the county road was slippery. Grandma kept the truck under thirty all the way to the highway, but going up the onramp she accelerated too hard and for a second the truck slid sideways. She eased on the gas and pulled the vehicle back in line.

"Christ," Teddy said, "watch you botch the whole the whole job before it even gets started."

"Road's slick," Grandma said, merging onto the highway. "What do you want me to do?"

"For one, use your turn signal. All they need is one stupid excuse like that to stop us. And if that happens your slick road isn't going to make for a quick getaway."

Mía was already drifting in and out of sleep next to Savannah. Bundled in her new miniature camo outfit with the hood up, her head dipped up and down, her eyelids drooping only to snap back open. Savannah felt the heat radiating off her sister, could smell her sickness. She thought back to the spaghetti they had for dinner the night before. All of them had eaten it, including Savannah. She tried to think of any other way Mía might've gotten sick, whether she'd been out in the cold too long or around someone else with symptoms. She couldn't think of anything.

The heater on the dash blew full blast, their breaths fogging up the edges of the windshield. Savannah struggled out of her jacket and stuffed it down by her feet. Her father wore a new coat, too, a black duster that hung past his bootlaces. From one of its deep pockets he produced a can of Skoal and stuck a plug beneath his bottom lip. He grabbed an empty Mountain Dew can on the floor and used his thumb to peel the aluminum mouth wider for a spitter. Savannah caught a hard whiff of earthy wintergreen. She watched his fingers as he closed the Skoal can and slipped it back into his pocket, the black band inked around his ring finger. He had opted for the tattoo—a tribal design extending nearly from the knuckle to the lower joint—over any piece of jewelry. During that brief period between military prison and the state penitentiary she remembered his explaining that in his line of work a ring could get your finger ripped off, and that, besides, what's the point of wearing a wedding band if not permanently? Grandma had rolled her eyes when he said this, whether because he had no particular line of work, or because technically he hadn't been married for years, Savannah didn't know.

In twenty minutes they were in the heart of San Juan. They exited the highway, turning a sharp one-eighty downward before pulling to a stop beneath the overpass. Grandma shifted into park and turned on the hazards.

"Be quick," Grandma said.

Teddy opened the passenger door and stepped out, the cold air and rumble of the highway filling the cab. Savannah slid across the seat and hopped down to the icy street beside him.

"What about Mía?" she asked. Her sister was sound asleep with her head tilted back against the seat.

"Better let her rest," Grandma said.

Teddy nodded and spat. "She's not old enough to appreciate it anyhow."

Savannah thought that unfair and untrue, but she closed the door anyway. Teddy leaned into to the bed of the truck and grabbed one of the four backpacks stored inside. The pack clinked, the main compartment bulging with Grandma's jarred vegetables. He unzipped a side pouch and pulled out a bouquet of polyester flowers entwined in red ribbon.

Semis thundered overhead, the entire overpass shuddering as Savannah scaled the paved embankment behind her father. A biting wind funneled in, whistling past her ears and numbing her hands as they hiked out from under the bridge. Through the soles of her boots she felt the pavement turn to sharp, melon-sized rocks netted beneath chickenwire. Shortly below the guardrail, Teddy stopped.

"Mother*fuckers*...."

Two white crosses protruded side-by-side, a blue and yellow wreath draped over each. Half-buried under the snow, scattered on the ground around the crosses or leaning against the bases were more flowers—their petals shriveled, faded, frozen. Stapled at the center of one cross was a small photograph of a young Hispanic man in a red sweater, grinning.

Teddy whirled on Savannah. "Has this been here the whole time?" He jabbed a finger down at the cross and picture as if Savannah were a dog who'd just shat the carpet. "How long have they been coming up here?"

"I've only been here the one time."

"Driving by you must've noticed."

Savannah rarely got to come this far into town, let alone down this particular road. But the few times she had, yes, she had noticed. And yes, both crosses had been there.

"This is the first I've seen them," she said.

"They probably figured I was out, that's why they came up here so recently." He wrapped his hands around the top of the cross and began rocking it free. "It's just like them, too. Disrespectful." He pried the cross loose and carried it a few steps down the embankment before chucking it sidearm over the road below. The cross spun—curving like a boomerang, hovering before the gray skyline—until clattering finally onto the asphalt a little before the idling truck.

"Help me clean up the rest," he said. Savannah crouched and started rounding up the stiff flowers. Vehicles roared past a dozen yards away, whipping up Teddy's duster in billowing gusts. Savannah watched as her father picked up a folded note lying where the second cross used to be. He unfolded it and read, shaking his head before crumpling the note and tossing it over his shoulder. He removed the wreath from the remaining cross, and Savannah handed him her share of the flowers. He smushed them between his hands and let the pieces scatter in the wind.

Teddy removed the polyester bouquet from the pocket of his duster and propped them against the lone cross. He stood peering over the two items, frowning with his hands on his hips. "I thought we'd have time to say a little something, but not now. I'm too upset anyway."

He made his way back down to the truck. Savannah stayed where she was a moment, eyeing the small dark hole where the second cross used to be. Finally she turned and followed after her father.

Savannah got in the truck and slid up against her sister. Mía looked to be in a sort of delirium with her eyes half-open and her head lolling above on her shoulders. Savannah shivered. The passenger side door was still open as Teddy rummaged once more through the blue pack in the truck bed. When he climbed back in he held in his hands a Mason jar filled to the lid with what looked like water.

Grandma shifted into drive and steered the truck toward the onramp, rejoining the highway and heading south. Teddy set the jar on the floor and held it upright between his boots. He rolled the window down a crack, reached into his mouth and removed the plug of tobacco. He let it fly out the window in in bursting particles before cranking the window back up.

It was quiet in the cab then, save for the truck's defogger blowing against the windshield and the faint hum of static on the radio. Teddy unbuttoned his coat and opened it to reveal the handgun still holstered against his hip. He popped open the holster, drew out the gun and set it on his thigh. It was a revolver, and there must've been well more than a foot of it extending from the handle to the end of the barrel. Engraved in red, italicized lettering down the barrel were the words, *WRATHFUL JUDGE.*

Teddy looked up and locked eyes with Savannah, who turned away and blushed.

"Pretty cool, huh?" Teddy said, flipping the gun over onto its other side. Showing it off. "Five hundred magnum. This thing can drop a rhino. Especially when loaded with these bad dudes." He opened the cylinder. "Here, hold out your hand."

"No thanks," Savannah said. "I believe you."

"Just hold it out. You'll like this."

Savannah opened her hand and let her father shake one of the bullets into it. It landed with a light smack against her palm. It was so heavy she almost dropped it. The cartridge was bigger than her middle finger. It looked like something designed for a rifle, except for the flat tip of the bullet itself, which was strangely green.

"Why's the tip green?" she asked.

"You don't know?"

If there was one thing her father had tried to teach Savannah during his short presence in her life, it was guns. But a green-tipped bullet was new to her. She shook her head.

"They're incendiary," he said. "Meaning that when they make impact, they sort of... *ignite*. I got a guy to custom make them for me. Expensive as shit, although just one of these will get the job done and then some."

"Neat," she said, giving the bullet back to him and returning her attention to the road ahead. She noticed his face fall a little before she turned, apparently hurt by her lack of interest. But Savannah possessed only bad memories of guns, nothing but painful associations, not to mention blurred vision in one eye. It baffled her how this hadn't occurred to her father. After everything that had happened.

He slid the cartridge back in the cylinder, snapped it shut and reholstered the gun. He turned and watched the guardrail flicker past outside the window.

Savannah leaned back, retrieved the iPod from her pocket and unwound the headphones. In the months following her mother's death, there was a song she used to listen to over and over—usually in bed before falling asleep. It was a sad country song called "If I Die Young" and even at the time—eight years old with her whole life turned upside down by tragedy—she'd recognized the melodrama in her ritual. Not only because of the sentimental lyrics or melancholy mood of the song, but because every time she listened to it the song made her cry. For a while it never failed, and before long she listened to the song to do exactly that: cry.

But time and repetition glazing memory and emotion, eventually the power of the song began to fade. This worried her. She had yearned to be numb, but she never wanted to lose the ability to cry over her mother — even if the only trigger was a mushy pop song. She recalled a school assembly years ago. The guest speaker was a man whose son had died of an overdose. The man had wept during his presentation. From what Savannah understood, this man gave these presentations fairly often. It might've even been his job. So when he started to well up Savannah couldn't help but wonder how many other listeners in how many more audiences around the country he'd done this in front of. Hundreds? She wondered at what point — after so many performances, after so much time — the tears would finally elude the father.

And so, in order to preserve the song's effect, Savannah placed a moratorium on "If I Die Young."

Until now. Squeezing the buds into her ears, she unlocked the hold button and the screen flashed to life. She scrolled through her playlists.

"Whoa, hold on," Teddy said. "Is that a cellphone?"

Savannah looked up to see him transfixed on the device. "No, it only plays music."

"Does it connect to the internet?"

"No, not this one."

"Let me see it." Now it was his turn to hold out his palm. Savannah appealed with her gaze to Grandma, but Grandma kept quiet with her eyes on the road.

Savannah set the iPod in her father's hand. He tapped through the various icons on the screen, his thumb stamping down as if squashing flies.

"It's fine," Grandma said. "Just a music player."

"It's got radio on it," Teddy said. "I bet it has data access, too. Is that what you call it, 'data access?'"

He knew what data access was. Teddy often liked to pretend ignorance. This included talking like he was less intelligent than he really was. Savannah could think of certain boys she knew who did the same thing, treat intelligence like a vulnerability.

"It has a radio and that's it," Grandma said. "No internet or anything like that. C'mon give it back to her."

Teddy put one earbud in his ear and Savannah, her heart pounding, watched him open the radio feature and scroll through the frequencies.

Abruptly he unplugged the earbuds and shoved them in a pocket. Then, looking over his shoulder, he rolled down the window. Savannah clutched at his one arm and lunged for the other, but she was too late. Teddy flung the iPod into the wind. It clanked against the truck bed before being swallowed under the roar of the highway.

"It was going to die on you anyway," he said, rolling the window back up. "And besides, we've already got a radio—a much better one that doesn't have to be plugged in to charge."

"But that was mine and had all my songs! It wasn't hurting anything!" She heard the hitch in her voice, felt her eyes brimming with tears.

"We have a radio, a better one. And I *did* have to do it. You may not understand that now, but pretty soon you will. Trust me."

"But you didn't have to—"

"Drop it, Savannah. I don't want to hear another thing about it. Look, you're upsetting your sister."

Mía squirmed and mumbled something under her breath. Teddy patted the top of her head, but Savannah knew he didn't really care. What he cared about were his stupid green bullets, and how she hadn't. Who would have thought that after all this time her cherished iPod would still end up being taken from her? And for what, because of how she'd reacted to a bullet in her palm?

Savannah gazed into the rearview mirror. A tiny light glinted from a bit of roadway behind them. It might've been ice. It might've been imagined. Savannah envisioned her iPod—still warm from being inside her pocket—lying faceup on a patch of ruddy blacktop. She could read the text on the screen, the song she had just selected. And in the vision the song title was at the same time the name of something inside her own body, something like an organ. According to the screen, the song was playing. But whether it was because she knew there were no headphones attached or because this was only a vision, Savannah heard no sound.

4

They joined Route 550 leading further south into New Mexico. The desert opened before them, dry riverbeds and marooned gas stations. It was a road Savannah knew well, the feel of the truck dipping through arroyos and swelling over yucca-dotted hillocks. She knew the sage and rabbitbrush, the billboards urging passersby to report human trafficking. Off the road to either side, pumpjacks—or "nodding donkeys" as Grandma called them—dipped their heads robotically up and down, siphoning the gases below. Dozens and dozens of them scattered across the landscape like steel dinosaurs grazing.

They drove past the empty corrals and white barns of the fairground where Savannah had participated in countless events, from barrel racing to breakaway roping to mutton busting. It was in the dirt parking lot, vacant now but packed that autumn day of her ninth year when she kissed Travis Swanson. The other kids had formed a circle around them as Savannah and Travis wordlessly approached one another. His cowboy hat jabbed her in the forehead on the first attempt and everyone laughed. But he lifted it up, came in again slower, sideways, and his lips found hers. His tongue surprised her, a not unpleasant taste of the orange Gatorade she'd seen him give his buddy to hold. When they came apart, she saw moisture in his eyes.

Beyond the fairground was the small adobe diner called The Mustard Seed. The diner used to serve breakfast and lunch on weekends, or else every day during hunting season. It was where

Savannah and Mía used to pop the little plastic cups of half-and-half into their mouths until their grandmother demanded they stop. The Mustard Seed, closed now, condemned and abandoned. The windows were boarded over with plywood. A yellowing marquee still out front by the side of the road read:

FOT THE GD FITE
THANKS FR MEMRIES
F U MWR

Teddy laughed. "'F U Mountain West Refining'. Amen to that! You gotta love the Mustard Seed. Surprised the sign hasn't gotten taken down yet."

"It was only a few weeks ago they actually left," Grandma said. "But the whole thing will be torn down here any day. Ray and Linda really did fight hard, and folks got behind them. They held an eat-in where everyone got to dine for free as long as they never stepped foot outside the building. People were sleeping on the floor under the tables. It was on the news and everything. They finally had to arrest Ray and Linda, plus a few more who refused to leave."

"I wish I could've been here for it," Teddy said, swiveling around to watch the old restaurant pass and kicking the mason jar at his feet in the process. He lunged forward and picked it up, holding it in front of his face, checking the lid.

"What is that, vinegar?" Grandma asked.

"No, but it'll make a helluva mess all the same."

"What is it?" Grandma persisted.

"Just something to be careful with," Teddy said, setting the jar back down between his feet. "Damn though, how I wish I could've been here for that eat-in thing. Good for Ray and Linda."

Grandma kept eyeing the jar on the floor but said nothing. She reached into the breast pocket of her denim coat, removed a pack of cigarettes and lit one. She rolled the window down a crack and focused on the road. Teddy reached into another pocket inside his coat and pulled a book out—a dog-eared paperback titled, *Apocalypse Law*. The book had a picture of a man riding a motorcycle—a rifle strapped to his back and what appeared to be a giant mushroom cloud in the horizon behind him. Savannah wasn't surprised her father had a book in his pocket. When she was little her father always carried a book around with him and seemed capable of reading anywhere. For a while she'd been the same way. One proud summer she read Mía no less than twelve *Lemony Snickets*. But reading was something Savannah associated with Teddy, and because she came to doubt her father she couldn't help also second-guessing his qualities. The things he passed on to her. It hurt Savannah to scrutinize everything she loved. Some of her earliest and best memories were of her father reading to her.

The hills extended in the distance, their tops flattening into mesas. The only trees were the occasional round junipers floating alone on the desert floor. More jacks. Every so often they passed another abandoned structure, usually a home boarded over and covered in black graffiti. Some of the houses, however, still looked lived-in, with cars parked out front and white plastic chairs scattered about the patios — all this despite a jack rarely being more than a stone's throw away, pumping away unconcerned. Savannah realized the people in these homes were considered the lucky ones, though she wondered how they ever got any sleep with all the whirring and creaking outside their windows.

Savannah focused her attention on the familiar row of telephone poles running along the right side of the highway; the roadside reflectors, tree clusters, and other indistinct landmarks she used to know so well. If she didn't pay attention she'd miss it. The old driveway always crept up on her. There were so many more drives like it branching ninety degrees from the highway that Grandma had to tie pink fluorescent streamers on the fenceposts to make it easier to spot. Before the streamers — right around the time Teddy had enlisted in the army but taken down a few months after — it'd been miniature American flags.

And then, suddenly, there it was. The truck slowed as they drove past, and all heads except Mía's turned to look. A long gravel drive bridged over two steel culvert pipes before extending into the sage. The girls had lived most of their lives up that road. Same with their grandmother and Teddy. Even the girls' mother had lived there for a time, moving with Teddy into his mother's home after Savannah was born. Savannah remembered walking hand-in-hand with her mother to the end of the drive where they'd ting rocks down the two culvert pipes. Years later Savannah would steal her first cigarette from her grandmother's purse and sneak down to the same culvert to smoke it. A swath of dirt slowly being reclaimed by brush marked where the family used to corral their horses near the end of the drive. Savannah remembered jogging back and forth along that driveway after joining the girls' basketball team in the seventh grade. Ten times equaled a mile, give or take.

It was along the driveway out the window that Grandma's own parents built the home. As Grandma told it, they came with everything they had in a Pontiac Streamliner that they lived in until construction of the house was complete. It turned into a sound house, given the time and circumstances, and Savannah picked up enough to know it was only after her grandmother came into possession that the house fell into disrepair. But Savannah didn't hold this against her. Teddy's father — a local cowboy named Rick Unser who got Grandma pregnant one year out of high school — died trying to install a tv antenna on the roof of the house. A gust of wind struck him and he fell thirty feet onto the wooden deck. Grandma rarely talked about the incident, but Teddy said that after it happened she got to believing the house was cursed. He said he and Grandma were standing on the deck when Rick fell, that he still felt the impact in his legs. Teddy was ten years old at the time. When Savannah imagined her father as a young boy witnessing his father fall to his death, she wondered how he could grow up feeling anything else but cursed.

Of course, the house was long gone now. The old road had been expanded and smoothed. Now the driveway led to a big circular pad of gravel on which three towering jacks bobbed up and down — sucking up minerals and any Unser family roots still lingering, severed and dead.

Grandma flicked the rest of her cigarette out and rolled up the window. Savannah waited for someone to say something, but no one did.

It was late afternoon by the time they reached the town of Conchos, the sun setting pale in the steely horizon. The snow thinned as they drove farther south until it was little more than an inch deep. Nonetheless, the plows were at work, carving low barriers of brown slush on each side of the road. Paths were shoveled between the snow banks leading to the parking lots of diners, motels, liquor stores and Family Dollars. A Navajo town set between the Jemez Mountains to the east and sweeping desert to the west, Conchos teemed with life. Even in the cold men leaned against ramshackle storefronts smoking cigarettes. Women thrust strollers down icy sidewalks, two or three more young children scampering along behind. Near the edge of town, Savannah observed an older man wearing only jeans and a t-shirt, jogging on the side of the road. His arms were tucked inside his shirt and he moved with a limp in one leg, but when their truck neared him the man shook one arm free and held out a thumb. Grandma drove past. Savannah watched in the rearview mirror as the man drew the arm back in and resumed his jog.

About ten minutes outside of town they turned right onto a dirt road, the truck rattling over a cattle guard. Mía coughed and opened her eyes. "Where are we?"

"We're on our way to our new place," Teddy said, putting his book away inside his coat. "Got to run a couple errands first, but then we'll be going straight there. Aren't you excited?"

But Mía simply lay her head back against the seat and watched with half-closed eyelids. The road before them grew fainter until it was visible only as a doubletrack split by sage. Savannah felt the brush scraping the undercarriage beneath her feet. The land was high desert with limitless expanses of dry washes and sandstone bluffs in any direction. Every so often the truck pitched down into a depression and bounced all four of them in their seats. A few miles along this path Savannah observed a shadowy row of structures in the far distance to her left.

Teddy pointed at the structures. "That used to be a town out there called La Gloria. The Penitentes still hold mass in the old church during Holy Week, but other than that the town is deserted. It had a good run for a while starting in the 1870s. The post office was still operating until forty-eight, forty-nine, something like that. Same with the trading post. La Gloria was where all the farmers and ranchers for hundreds of miles around would go to stock up on supplies, get their mail, communion, booze, whores. I'm pretty sure there was an old dance hall or two. A lot of contradiction in some of these old southwest towns, what between the Penitentes and the dancehallers. Lot of one side trying to blackball the other. In the end though, the droughts hit, and God, Mother Nature, whoever, decided to kick all sides out.". He squinted at the icy horizon, and Savannah wondered whether he looked for something or rather wished to conceal some emotion in his face. "Just as well. Every town will be a ghost town someday. La Gloria just got it over with quick, and I respect that."

Savannah peered out and tried to make some shape out of the buildings, but even with her good eye the old town remained little more than a dull mirage in the grim light.

They continued along the rough doubletrack for close to an hour, veering steadily toward an outcropping of tall mesas. Teddy pointed to something and without warning Grandma steered the truck off the road and drove in the direction Teddy had indicated. At first there appeared to be nothing marking their path as they plowed through sage and bounced over rocks, but soon Savannah noticed the faint tracks of another vehicle trailing off in front of them. They followed this seemingly directionless set of tire tracks all the way to a barbwire fence. A makeshift gate had been inserted into the fence by connecting the strands in one section to a loose post that was in turn hooked against another post set in the earth.

Grandma pulled to a stop before the fence. Teddy hopped out, unhooked the gate and tossed it into a mess of coils by the side of the road.

"Where are we?" Savannah asked.

"We're picking something up," Grandma said.

"Yeah but whose land is this?"

"BLM."

"*BLM?*"

"Bureau of Land Management. Meaning it's everyone's land."

Teddy opened the door and slid back in. "*Woowee*, it's cold out there! Might be in the negatives later tonight." He leaned across the seat and play-punched Mía on the shoulder.

Grandma bit her lip, accelerating the truck forward. "I'm kind of worried about her, to tell the truth. Thinking that I might wannna take her in real quick? Like to urgent care or something. There's one back in Conchos."

"For the flu? What, she never had a bug before? All they're going to do is give her Tylenol and soup—both of which we've already got up there. Trust me, if I thought we had time and wouldn't have six million questions dumped on us, we'd see a doctor. But there are way too many wheels in motion now. Not worth the risk."

As they crested a low rise, two parked vehicles appeared before them. One was a small, flatbed truck, spray-painted black, with livestock fencing arched over the back. Except instead of sheep or pigs or whatever else the fencing used to contain, a rusted-out camper now sat snug on the truck bed. The camper was boxy, and its narrow slot windows were curtained over from the inside with what looked like t-shirts. The second vehicle was much bigger, and at first Savannah thought it might be a semi—its cargo hidden beneath a bungeed patchwork of blue and brown tarps. But the tarps covered only so much, and Savannah glimpsed the aqua green plastic of the huge cylindrical container underneath.

Grandma pulled to a stop. "That's what you got, a water truck? I thought we'd decided a U-Haul."

"This is better," Teddy said. "Ever since Oklahoma City they keep an eye out for moving trucks and things like that. But a water truck is perfect. Nobody's going to look twice at one around here. Plus, look how big that mother is, almost thirty thousand liters."

There came the sound of horses whinnying and Savannah followed the sound to where two horses stood tethered to a dead cottonwood tree. A five-gallon bucket hung by its handle from a branch between the horses. Both animals were saddled, and they jostled anxiously next to one another as they strained to better face the newcomers. Even from a distance Savannah could tell the horses were bony and underfed. One appeared to be keeping weight off one of its front legs.

"Rez horses," Teddy said, following Savannah's gaze. "There's a million of them wandering this area. They may not be much to look at, but those two there at least know the taste of a bit. It didn't take much to catch them either, basically just had to shake an oat bag." His fingers paused from zipping up his jacket and he gestured his chin toward the smaller truck with the camper in the back. "Uh oh, check it out. I think we woke him up."

Savannah looked to where a long, furry creature appeared to be birthing itself from the back of the vehicle's camper. It looked like a weasel at first, slender as it squeezed farther and farther out from the camper's rear door. It pushed out backward, arms and legs extending as if from a chrysalis, lengthening into the form of a man who stood up and turned around to reveal not one but two faces—one on top the other. The lower face was half-concealed by a pair of visor-like sunglasses that Savannah associated with baseball players. The skin around his mouth though was dark, Native perhaps—Navajo most likely. The second face, the one on top, was raggedy, pointy-eared and slit-eyed—the dead face of a coyote, drawn out into a rich pelt that hung from the man's head past his hamstrings.

Both horses whinnied now, yanking so hard at the tree they were tied to bits of dead branches rained down.

"Goddamn, listen to that!" Teddy laughed. "Shiloh sure has a way with animals, doesn't he?"

The man outside waved, reached inside the camper, pulled out a backpack and slung it over his shoulder. He was tall and spindly in red flannel and jeans, a few strands of jet-black hair visible below the coyote pelt. He took off at a jog for the water truck.

"At least I'm not the only one excited," Teddy said. He patted his pockets, slid out the door and slammed it shut. He took off at a jog toward the other man who'd already started removing the tarps from the water truck.

"Who is that man?" Savannah asked.

Grandma scratched her temple, watching as Teddy approached the stranger. The two stood and faced each other but did not shake hands. "His name's Shiloh," Grandma said. "Someone your dad met." She stared at him a moment, squinting, then reached over and rubbed the back of Savannah's neck. "He's not coming with us."

The two men unhooked the bungees from the water truck and pulled off the tarps. Shiloh opened the driver's side door, climbed in and turned the ignition. The engine growled to life, a burst of exhaust spouting from the chimney-like pipe extending above the cab. It was only then that Savannah noticed how full the truck's tank was, the water level quivering near the top of the green plastic container. Shiloh left the truck running and leapt to the ground.

"What are we doing?" Savannah asked.

"What do you mean?"

"You know what I mean. I have a feeling they're going to do something...*bad*. That *we* are."

Grandma put both her hands back on the steering wheel. She stared out the windshield, tapping the wheel with her thumbs.

"Grandma...."

"You don't always need to know everything all the time, Savannah. *You* are going to be fine as long as you listen to your dad and me. You're just going to have to trust me on that."

Outside, Teddy appeared to be explaining something to Shiloh, gesturing toward the three of them in the cab and shaking his head with what Savannah could tell without even hearing it was a forced laugh. But when Shiloh abruptly turned and began marching toward the three of them in the pickup Teddy's smile dropped. He lunged after the man, grabbing him by the shoulder and stepping in front. The two men began to argue. Shiloh pushed past Teddy and resumed his march to the pickup, making his way to Savannah, her sister and grandmother.

He reached for the passenger door and Savannah slid as far across the seat, pressing into Mía. Shiloh yanked the door open, and Savannah was instantly overcome by the smell of gasoline. Beneath those chemical fumes she sensed something coppery, like the gutted corpse of an animal, as well as another scent altogether more mysterious: the lonely perfume of wind, campfires, and fine dirt. The smell of the desert.

Shiloh peered at the three of them from behind his black visors, his narrow body somehow filling the opened door.

Teddy ran up behind him. "Okay, okay, just to see and only for a second. She needs to keep sleeping, and it's not good we wake her. They still have a long night ahead of them and—"

"Quiet," the man said, his voice low and halting, hiccupping over the vowels. *Kwi. Et.* He reached for Savannah, and she tried to dodge him—pressing away from his outstretched hand and into her sister. But suddenly the pressure went slack behind Savannah and both she and Mía flopped onto their sides. Grandma had hopped out the driver's side door.

Shiloh thrust his body inside the cab. Savannah shrieked, shrinking into the seat as the hand reached over her—reaching not for her, she realized, but for Mía.

He snatched the girl by the scruff of her coat and hauled her across Savannah's lap. Savannah shoved at his arm, clawed it, no longer afraid but angry. Violent. Teddy meanwhile talked a mile a minute, telling the girls not to worry—that the man was only checking Mía's temperature.

Savannah bit into the arm, the flannel sleeve oddly crusty and tasting of salt. Shiloh ripped it free and thrust his forearm against her chest, pinning Savannah against the seat as he snaked his fingers through Mía's hood to the side of her neck.

Savannah froze. The man's fingers against her sister's throat, she made no sudden movements. She could only watch, heart thudding, as for what felt like minutes the cold overtook the cab and the man's breath jetted from his nostrils—dissolving around his porous nose, the craters of acne scars on his cheeks, the dark whips of a goatee and mustache around his mouth. Savannah noticed a knife tucked into his belt, the blade serrated and attached to a handle made of what looked to be deer antler. Mía's mouth fell slack, her eyelids fluttering. From the corner of her vision Savannah saw her grandmother retreating across the ground outside the truck. Cowering.

Shiloh removed his fingers and held his palm across Mía's forehead. He clucked his tongue and released her. He backed out of the cab and turned to face Teddy. "*Ts'íjh niidóóh.*"

"No, just a cold," Teddy said. "A fever. She's getting better."

"Go to a doctor," Shiloh said.

"No doctor. You already agreed on today. They're looking for me as it is, and everything's ready to go."

Shiloh pursed his lips.

"Kids get sick, man," Teddy said, shrugging. "They get sick and then they get better, that's how it works. I'm not worried. Now you made a promise."

Shiloh folded his arms, glanced behind him then back at Teddy. *"Jiníyá it shí"*

"What? We never said that!"

Shiloh kept his arms crossed.

Teddy shook his head in disgust. "Whatever. But I'm driving."

Savannah held Mia and watched the two men. Whatever exactly her father had just compromised, she got the feeling he'd anticipated it.

Also, since when did Teddy speak Navajo?

Shiloh returned to the water truck. Teddy spat, his eyes venturing up to Savannah's only to immediately fall away.

Grandma was still standing outside the pickup. "What do we do?"

Teddy sighed and moved to the still-open passenger side door. "Get back behind the wheel for one. Then you follow us, not too close but not too far. Keep me in your sights, because once we get there things are going to move fast."

He took the Mason jar from the floor and slipped it into his duster's inner pocket. He turned his back, hesitated, then turned back around. Teddy gave Savannah a weak smile and squeezed her leg. Then he closed the door and made his way to the rumbling water truck.

An apology, she supposed.

5

They continued farther south along the highway, toward Albuquerque. The light faded into a shrinking hue of gray at the bottom of the western horizon. Grandma kept a steady distance behind the water truck, which traveled below the speed limit, its liquid cargo dark and sloshing. A line of cars formed behind them. Every time the road straightened and one or two of the cars pulled out to pass, Savannah stared at the drivers, imploring them through the power of her gaze to turn their heads and look at her. Just for a moment, she thought, to lock eyes for even one second. That's all it would take. But the drivers paid no attention, their annoyed expressions fixed farther ahead, on the tanker responsible for this slight delay in their lives.

After a while though, she did get the feeling of being watched. In the side mirror of the vehicle ahead of her she noticed a tiny face being reflected. He had his sunglasses on despite the fading light. Savannah slid as close to her sister as possible, out of view. Mía slept, wheezing against Savannah's chest. Savannah kept an arm around her, the little body hot against her own. Grandma had so far kept her face screwed up tight and said nothing. Savannah sensed the uneasiness radiating off her, stifling the air like paint fumes.

"Can't you just tell us where we're going?" Savannah said.

Grandma squinted behind her glasses, the road sucking under the hood.

"I thought we were moving. So why do we have a water truck? And how come—"

"You heard your father say it was okay, that it was all right to let him check her temperature. Those were *his* instructions, and I have to respect that, you know? He's your father. Otherwise I wouldn't let *anyone* touch her."

Savannah saw doubt in her grandmother's face, heard it in her voice.

"What are we doing, Grandma? Why can't you tell us?"

Grandma chewed on her bottom lip. "Your dad, ever since he got here, has he said anything to you about me?"

Savannah felt a chill. It was the thought of her father and grandmother withholding information not only from her, but from each other as well. "What do you mean?"

"I mean, is there anything he told you that he said not to tell me?"

"No, not that I can remember."

"If he did you need to tell me. Legally I'm the one in charge of looking out for you, and I take that very seriously. I love your dad, it's only that sometimes… Sometimes I worry he's been through so much, seen so many rotten things and been penned in with so many rotten people that he's had no choice but to, I don't know, *adapt*. He's gotten so good at telling stories, including to me. Except half the time I can tell that the story he's telling me has got a whole 'nother one behind it. His heart is still good. It's his head that…." She stopped herself, squeezed the steering wheel and rolled her palms over it. "So that's a no? He didn't say anything to you?"

"No one's told me anything. But I wish they would."

"We agreed we'd explain everything to you after. Otherwise you wouldn't understand. Tonight's going to be…heavy. But you're going to be brave, and in twenty-four hours everything's going to make so much sense, Savannah. I promise."

Heavy. The word floated in the air, drifting down like the snowflakes Savannah had observed through her window that morning. The morning that felt like so very long ago now. The morning that felt irretrievable, like everything in it—her room, her things, the life she'd known — gone for good. And for what, she didn't know. *Heavy.*

It was almost completely dark now. The brake lights flashed on the tanker, washing the cab of Grandma's pickup in a reddish glow. The tanker continued to slow as they approached a sign with an airplane symbol on it. The left turn signal began to blink and Grandma flipped hers, steering behind the water truck onto a paved county road.

Savannah had been down this road only once before, now more than three years ago when they'd taken it on their way to pick Teddy up at the small regional airport. Along the way she had tried to imagine what he'd look like. She wondered if he would look the same as he did in the pictures hanging in Grandma's house: boyish, bright-eyed and handsome in a brooding, action-star kind of way. But when he emerged from the terminal escorted by a uniformed soldier — his shaved head down, a thick beard all but swallowing the little blue tie he had on, the white dress shirt that was too small as it squeezed around his barrel chest — all Savannah saw in her father was a dejected outlaw.

"Are we flying somewhere?" Savannah asked.

"Not going to the airport," Grandma said.

"Where then?"

"Be patient. Wait a minute here and you'll see."

The county road was nearly empty; they passed only one car traveling in the opposite direction. Standing on either side of the road were signs for sand and gravel pits, tractor sales and service, welding shops, self-storage. The silos and strewn-about machinery of the various businesses shined in the headlights. Savannah looked at them with dread in her stomach, imagining herself in a submarine beaming its lights on the carcass of a sunken ship. Knowing she was somewhere she shouldn't be.

The road curved and there suddenly appeared a towering structure of light. It loomed six stories tall with floor-to-ceiling office windows. Twinkling light poles presided over a large parking lot, the whole area surrounded by pine trees planted evenly apart. Savannah didn't recall the place and guessed it to be new. If not for the trees, the scene looked like it could have been plucked from another city's downtown and dropped here amid the tractor parts and sage. The building stuck out like a big, shiny, too-modern-for-these-parts blue thumb.

The water truck braked to a stop in front. Savannah's pulse quickened. The building's floodlit sign came into view near the parking lot's entrance, and it occurred to Savannah the structure wasn't out of place around here at all. In fact, dominating the sign was a logo she'd seen stamped like a brand all across this part of the country. The logo consisted of three interlocked letters: MWR.

Mountain West Refining.

The driver's side window rolled down on the stalled water truck. Teddy stuck his arm out and waved them forward. Grandma veered even with the water truck in the other lane and told Savannah to roll down her window. Savannah did as instructed. Teddy pointed to a spot on the side of the road near the building and said, "Pull in there and stay where you can see us. Keep the engine on but no headlights."

Grandma eyed the road—empty and dark. "Be quick," she said, and without another word accelerated, flipped a U-turn and guided the pickup onto the designated shoulder. She jammed the transmission into park and switched off the headlights. About twenty yards straight in front of Savannah lay the entrance with its MWR sign. To her right stood the wall of pines, and beyond that the parking lot and glass building.

"Put the window back up," Grandma said.

Savannah rolled it up. The water truck revved and curved into the entrance, crawling slowly through the parking lot, weaving between a handful of compact cars and trucks with logos on their doors.

A memory flashed through her mind: a boy, many years ago, tip-toeing behind a much smaller boy dangling his feet in a swimming pool. In the seconds before he was pushed, she wondered whether the small boy could swim.

The feeling now was like that. Only so much worse.

"That's not water," Savannah said. Her grandmother continued to squeeze the steering wheel with both hands, the lights of the parking lot flaring off her glasses and the sweat on her forehead. "Grandma, what's in that container?"

"Shush."

"Grandma…"

"Turn around. Look."

The water truck hooked around now, sidling up close to the building. Very close. It bounced over the concrete parking barriers, mounting the sidewalk until a metallic screeching noise sounded as the passenger side of the tanker ground against the building. The truck came to a stop. Something moved high above it, and Savannah looked up to see two figures standing side-by-side at one of the windows. Their hands were cupped around their faces to see whatever was happening below.

"There are people inside," Savannah said.

Grandma's eyes drifted up, but she didn't respond.

"Grandma there are people inside!"

"Shh, stop talking." Grandma said, leaning forward to see past Savannah.

The two figures remained at the window, gazing down at the water truck wedged against the bottom floor.

Run, Savannah thought.

Get out of there.

She cranked the window down, stuck her head out and screamed.

Grandma clasped a hand around her mouth and ripped her back. Savannah writhed, trying to break free, but her grandmother held her grasp tight. Savannah's fingernails raked into the cloth of the seat as she was hauled over her sister into her grandmother's arms, the oily palm clamped tight over her mouth. It was all she could do to breathe, sucking in and out through her nostrils as she watched the horror unfold.

The door of the water truck flew open. A pair of boots hit the asphalt, the long black duster whipping wide as Teddy whirled on the man who, with the passenger side scrunched against the building, had no choice but to follow him out the driver's side. Teddy held something in his hand. Something shiny. And in the split second it took for him to raise it in the air and then smash it down on top the other man's head, Savannah recognized the glass jar.

The jar burst, an eruption of glimmering liquid and glass. Shiloh collapsed into the parking lot.

Teddy spun around and ran, his face screwed up in pain. He shook one hand at the wrist while the other fumbled inside his coat.

Then, back near the truck, movement. The man crumpled on the ground, Shiloh....

He was getting up.

Teddy was almost to the sign at the edge of the parking lot. A little farther and he'd be at the pickup. Back by the water truck Shiloh pushed himself to his feet. He brought his hands up to his face and let loose a scream so loud and thick with agony that Savannah felt it in her body, her bones.

Teddy skidded to a stop, yanked his revolver free, pivoted back around and dropped to one knee. Shiloh staggered forward, hands splayed across his face. Teddy raised the gun.

"Close your eyes!" Grandma said, squeezing Savannah even harder, sinking deeper into the seat. But Savannah wasn't fast enough. That or she'd already seen too much not to see it all.

Two bucks of the Wrathful Judge—twin jets of flame spitting from the barrel—followed by an explosion of light bigger, hotter and more powerful than anything Savannah had ever known. The water truck appeared to split at the seams, a bursting bellyful of pure fire. The shockwave smashed into the pickup. Savannah heard glass break, felt it spray across her body in a blast of heat that lifted the pickup up on two wheels before dropping back down. Grandma's hand loosened around Savannah's mouth and Savnnah gasped, breathing in a chemical-tasting air that made her choke. Her eyes stung and she squeezed them shut only to see an image, seared into her brain, of two shadows standing behind a tall window, wrapped in flames.

Coughing, blinded by light, Savannah felt around for her sister and experienced a surge of panic when she didn't find her. She wriggled out of her grandmother's grasp and rolled onto the floor of the truck... directly on top of Mía. The heat gusted in through the broken side window like a furnace as Savannah draped herself over her sister's body. She didn't know how long she lay like this, half-deaf and with flames seared across her vision, feeling Mía's body trembling below her. It couldn't have been long, for suddenly the truck's door was jerked open and she heard Teddy's distant, distorted voice echoing in her head.

He was saying *go*.

Go go go go go.

6

But seconds after Teddy jumped into the cab and ordered them to go, he shouted for them to stop. Grandma slammed on the brakes, Savannah rocking forward and smacking her head on the dash.

"Did you see that?" Teddy said, craning his head out the broken window and scanning the inferno outside. Fire crackled and licked from the pines. Blazing chunks of debris littered the parking lot. Tiny flames rained down from the sky. The building itself, or what was left of it, looked like it had been gutted with a giant ice cream scoop. Only a smoldering, C-shaped section remained standing, dangling its twisted steel innards.

"What?" Grandma said.

Teddy pointed to the far back corner of the property. "Someone's running out there. Right behind—"

He was cut short by a deafening boom, an eruption of fire in the parking lot—one of the cars exploding, somersaulting in the air before crashing down on its side. Teddy ducked and grimaced, sucking air through his teeth. The skin on one side of his face, as well as that on the back of his right hand, was pink and bubbly.

"We're going," Grandma said.

"Wait! Look over there," he said, squinting. "Shit that's him!"

Savannah saw it, whatever or whoever—a shadowy form darting through the sage, away from the flaming wreckage. Teddy wrenched the door open, leapt to the ground and took aim with the revolver.

"There's nothing out there!" Grandma said. "Get ba—"

He fired — another deep bang thundering in the night — then again, and again. He followed the fleeing shadow with the barrel. Savannah saw a tiny burst of fire where one bullet struck a tree trunk.

Grandma smashed down the horn. "Get in the truck, Ted! We're going! NOW!"

Teddy lowered the gun, peering in the direction of the disappearing shadow. He got in the truck.

"I missed," he said.

Grandma peeled out, the truck's back end fishtailing. "No, you didn't 'cause there's nothing out there."

"Someone was."

"Probably just a deer," Grandma said.

"That was no deer," Teddy said. "That was you-know-who."

The freezing night air streamed into the cab through the broken side window. Mía began to wail — delirious but aware of some great trauma that'd just occurred. Teddy seethed in pain, clutching at his acid-burnt hand and the flame-roasted side of his face. Grandma yelled for both of them to be quiet as she strained to keep the truck between the lines. Sirens sounded in the distance and before long a flurry of red and blue lights flashed down the road ahead of them. Grandma kept it cool, easing the truck onto the shoulder to allow the string of police cruisers to howl by. She gave no reason for any passing car to notice them, to sense anything off or anxious about another beater truck on its way home from the job site or town or beers at Uncle Ed's. To the other travelers out that night, there was something else far more fascinating about this night. Something much brighter. Brighter and far more fascinating.

Savannah watched the orange glow of the blaze shrink in the rearview mirror. She had nothing to say, nothing left to think or feel. She'd blown an emotional fuse, gone numb, and for the rest of the drive she looked for sense in nothing, lest her mind crack open completely.

She barely noticed where they headed, even when the pickup veered off the highway and onto a dirt road. Only when it slowed before a familiar barbwire gate did Savannah's senses come flooding back over her. Like a bucket of ice water.

"What are we doing here?" she asked, gasping, inhaling her words. Teddy hopped out, ran to the gate and unhooked it.

"The horses," Grandma said.

As if in reply, a long whinny called out into the night. Savannah had forgotten all about the two scrawny horses, still tied to the fenceposts with their saddles on—no doubt feeling as trapped as she did. Teddy climbed back in, and Grandma rolled forward until the headlights struck the animals, their eyes bulging and shiny. Aside from the horses Savannah made out the pile of tarps on the ground where the water truck used to be, as well as the black flatbed with the camper on the back.

Grandma shifted into park and cut the motor. The horses' eyes seemed to glow and quickly fade with the headlights. Darkness now, quiet save for the tinkling of the engine and the crying of the horses.

Teddy let out a long breath. Savannah saw that he was hurting, as well as delaying whatever came next.

Grandma turned to face him. "Now who's going to get rid of my truck?"

"I will," Teddy said.

"What about *his*?" Grandma asked, nodding to the black pickup with the camper in the back.

Teddy snorted. "Shiloh was never exactly the type to stay current with the DMV. They're not going to connect it to him. More importantly, they're not going to connect him to us. If I have to I'll roll the truck into a ditch or something. You realize how many abandoned trucks there are scattered around this desert? Just worry about getting the girls out of here, Mom. I'll meet you all as soon as I'm done."

"I can't take them up there all by myself. We'll get lost."

"No you won't. All you have to do is follow my trail."

"In the dark? Besides, take a look at yourself. How will *you* even make it up there?"

"I got a little singed, so what? I'm fine."

Grandma sighed and squeezed the steering wheel. Savannah thought that after being in control of that wheel all day, it was hard for her grandmother to now have to let go.

"You weren't thinking, Ted. We needed his help."

"It's better like this, better that no one else knows."

"Then you should've told me before."

"Shoulda woulda coulda. Things change. Only thing that's for sure we're wasting time we don't have sitting here arguing." He opened the door, the cab light flashing on. "Now c'mon, let's get the horses out. Mom, you grab Amelia. Savannah, come with me."

"No," Savannah said.

Teddy stopped, his legs halfway out the door. "What's that?"

"I'm not going. Neither is Mía. We want to go home."

Her voice trembled on the final word and the whole thing came out weak. She'd been working herself up to say it, but when the time came she hadn't fully committed. Her breath caught in her chest, choked by a sudden sense of vulnerability.

He pulled the door closed and it was dark again. "What home is that exactly, Savannah?"

"Don't, Teddy," Grandma said. "Not here."

"Be quiet, mom, I'm talking to my daughter. Answer me, Savannah. What *home* are you referring to?"

It was the wrong word for her to have used. She understood perfectly what he was trying to lead her into. Just as she understood there'd be no reasoning her way out of it.

"Mía needs to get to a doctor," Savannah said. "And I'm scared of what else you're going to do."

"All I'm going to do is take care of you girls. I'm going to make sure Amelia gets better. That's the only thing I have planned for the rest of the night. No, make that the rest of my *life*. We've got food and medicine and beds all waiting for us. We just have to get there. What did you say this morning about trusting me? You promised me you would, Savannah."

"Everyone's going to be looking for us. What you did... What you did was—"

"What *we* did, Savannah. What *we* did. And it was nothing wrong, you understand me? We're not the bad guys tonight, kiddo. We're the heroes."

"But you... You killed people."

"No I didn't."

"I saw them… In the building…"

"No, the building was empty."

"I saw —"

"And okay, say it wasn't empty. Are you saying you want to turn me in? To turn us all in? Because guess what, Savannah, you're not so innocent yourself. Just by being there they can charge you as an accomplice. And then, instead of growing up comfortable and together like I've got planned, we'll grow up apart, locked away. You and Amelia can go to juvie and probably not see each other again for years. Is that what you want? You've already sent me to prison once. Are you telling me you're going to do it again?"

Silence in the truck. Savannah felt her father's eyes boring into her as her grandmother's gaze shifted downward in embarrassment. In that moment Savannah wanted nothing more than to become a part of the darkness, to dissolve into it and no longer be. To never have been.

She felt a hand find her own. A small hand, her sister's. Savannah squeezed it, sniffed and wiped her eyes on her sleeve.

"We don't have time for this," Teddy said, opening the door, the cab light turning back on. Mía's hand pulled out of Savannah's as Teddy reached over and hauled Mía against his chest. "Do what you want, Savannah, but Amelia's coming with us."

He carried her outside and disappeared around the side of the truck. Grandma gave Savannah a sympathetic look and patted her on the top of her head. Then she opened the driver's door and stepped out.

Savannah sat in the middle of the big seat, just like that, alone.

7

When Savannah was little she had a mare she called Beeswax. Beeswax had also once been a rez horse, ownerless and leading a life on the brink of starvation on the Navajo reservation. While many rez horses were born feral, many more were abandoned to the desert after years of being cared for — usually after growing too old to ride or else having simply been given up on. Beeswax was one such horse, although a lucky one to have eventually been rescued by a local sanctuary devoted to saving animals like her. Teddy adopted Beeswax from the sanctuary shortly after his release from Leavenworth — anxious it seemed for a project. As it would turn out however, Beeswax became Savannah's project.

When they first brought Beeswax home the mare's carmine fur had been peppered with nicks and whip marks, and one eye oozed infection. Her hooves had been cut down to the quick — a botched attempt to sore her and make her step more daintily. She could hardly stand. Savannah spent months applying ointment to the mare's cuts, swabbing her eye, force-feeding her medication. She remembered the first time riding Beeswax, how the horse had bucked and spun the moment Savannah got on top. Savannah hadn't even bothered to put a saddle on; the impulse to swing her legs over had just struck her, and before she knew it she was holding on to the mane for dear life. And yet, Savannah had done more than simply hold on that day; she gained control. After proving to the animal that she couldn't be thrown, Savannah had eased Beeswax into a smooth gallop around the corral.

Savannah remembered feeling powerful in that moment, beautiful even with her long hair flowing behind her.

Now, standing under a black sky at the edge of a vague future, Savannah brushed her hand along the scarred coat of another once-abandoned creature and recognized in it a familiar spirit. The horse before her was also a mare, tall and dapple gray with protruding ribs and a short tail that had clearly once been cut. The second horse, a brown gelding with a hitch in his right foreleg, stood a few feet over — nickering as Grandma tightened its cinch. The two animals had tried to rear and throw their heads when Savannah first approached them. But then Grandma poured water into the bucket hanging on the tree between them, lifted it for each one to drink, and finally loosened their tethers so they could graze on the few clumps of dry grass on the ground. With that the horses instantly settled and it occurred to Savannah it was not captivity these horses feared, but hunger. Indeed, as Teddy had suggested, neither animal was a stranger to a saddle or bridle. If anything, Savannah thought, the leather and steel might even feel like a relief to the two wayward horses, a sign that perhaps they had not been forsaken after all.

Mía sat slumped atop one of the backpacks on the ground, watching Savannah through half-closed eyelids. Teddy stood behind the gelding, tying one of the backpacks behind its saddle with a coil of twine. Savannah stroked the haunches of the mare and tried to ground herself. Beeswax had finally died of old age more than a year ago, but truth was Savannah had given up horses well before that. When Teddy was rearrested and sent to the state penitentiary — this being only a few months after he was released from Fort Leavenworth — Savannah had officially entered her black period. Her depression. The shame was too much for her, the idea that she might have been responsible for her father once more being locked away. It was as if her center had imploded, sucking with it all the lesser things orbiting around. After that, normal things like riding horses felt to her like betrayals. As if picking back her life back up as normal demonstrated she didn't care.

Savannah slipped her hands into the pockets of her new camo pants and rubbed them against her thighs to get the blood flowing.

Grandma climbed onto her own horse, and Teddy handed her Mía to hold in front of her, followed by another backpack which Grandma put on her shoulders. Teddy yanked the drawstrings dangling from Mía's camouflage hood, sliding the two plastic spring-stoppers high so that only her runny nose was visible.

"Hurry and go," he said. "No stopping, and when you get there start a fire right away. Amelia's not looking good."

"Neither are you," Grandma said. "You shouldn't be doing this by yourself."

"I'll be a few hours behind, don't worry. Get up there and sit tight."

"What if something happens and you don't make it?"

"Nothing will happen."

"But what if?"

"Then you do what we talked about," he said, lowering his voice. "Same place I told you, in the film canister."

Teddy walked over to Savannah and, without warning, hoisted her up onto the mare. The horse sighed under her weight, snorted, but otherwise offered no resistance. Teddy held Savannah's backpack up to her, guiding her arms through the straps. The pack stuck against the cantle and Savannah squirmed. He next handed her the reins, followed by a steel MagLite about the size of a magic marker that was attached to a leather thong. Savannah looped the thong over her neck.

"Try not to use it," Teddy said. "Stay close to your grandma and you shouldn't have to. Believe me, you don't want to get separated. Every single year people go missing in this wilderness. All it takes is one wrong step and you're falling off a cliff. Plus there's lions, and lions don't hibernate. They're most active this time of year. But I wouldn't worry about lions as much as other things I've seen around here at night. I'm not telling you all this to scare you. No wait, I take that back. You *should* be scared, just a little bit, because if you're not scared, then you're not alert. So be smart up there, Savannah. Until I come back, listen to what your grandma says."

He smacked the horse on the rump,

"Ted..." Grandma said, one hand on the reins, the other around Mía. "Ted, I'm not sure about this anymore. "Maybe it would—"

"Remember when you get to the reservation boundary not to cut the fence," Teddy said. "I've already loosened one of the posts and put a marker on it so you can spot it. You should be able to pull the post free. Make sure you put it back, though."

"Ted, you're not listening," Grandma said. "I'm thinking it might be better if you came with us now. Forget the truck. We can come back for it—"

"Nope, got to take care of it now. As long as it stays here this truck is the only thing linking us to this spot. A few hours, Mom, that's it. Then I'm right behind you. Now get out of here!"

Without another word he jogged over to the pickup, hopped in and started the engine. The three of them watched the truck swing around, the headlights sweeping across the sage.

Grandma sighed. "All right, let's go then." She turned her horse and nudged it in the direction opposite to Teddy.

But Savannah stayed where she was, watching the taillights on the pickup fade away like two big red eyes receding. A window was closing; she could feel it. She turned and saw her grandma's figure shrink, fade and dissolve into the greater shadows of the night. What awaited Savannah in that darkness? What would happen should she try and run away? She didn't have Mía with her, that was true. But if she made a break for it now and was fast enough, maybe she could find help and they'd come back for Mía, getting her before Grandma got them to wherever it was they were going now.

Savannah looked to the other vehicle parked a few dozen feet away, the black flatbed with the camper. Was the key in it? Could she even bring herself to get in that vehicle, knowing who it belonged to and what they'd done to him? She looked behind her and spotted what appeared to be a light in the far horizon. Could it be a house, or was it only an illusion? A minuscule spark sliding down her vision? If Savannah reined her horse and kicked off after it, right now....

A flashlight beam sliced through the night. It darted across the ground, strobing behind brush and branches, until finally locating Savannah. It leveled on her, patient. Savannah took one last look in the direction they had come. She let out a long exhale, then nudged her horse after her grandmother. Into the shadows of mountains and mesas.

For the first mile or so the way before them was level and mostly featureless except for a few junipers and empty arroyos. But gradually the earth began to rise and turn steep. The trees thickened, the junipers giving way to piñon and the occasional ponderosa pine. They crossed a streambed and ice crunched beneath the horses' hooves. Every so often her grandmother flicked on her flashlight to check some indistinct landmark, only to turn it off again and continue ahead in the darkness on whatever vague path she led them.

Once, Grandma turned on her flashlight and Savannah was surprised to see a barbwire fence with a brown metal sign attached between the strands. The sign read:

WARNING! RESTRICTED AREA
NO TRESPASSING
VIOLATORS WILL BE PROSECUTED
PUEBLO OF TONOLA

They turned and proceeded along the fence line. Secured intermittently between the strands were more of the same metal brown warning signs. After a few minutes Grandma pulled her horse to a stop and shined her light on a fencepost. A black feather stuck between the wire and wood. Grandma got off her horse, set Mía's hands on the saddlehorn and told her to hold tight. Mía's eyes fluttered open as she began to slide, and she came to just in time to avoid falling. Grandma grabbed the top of the fencepost in both her hands and rocked it back and forth. The post groaned, loosening in its soil before popping free, wires twanging. The strands had been slack to begin with, and letting go of the post Grandma was able to flatten a passable crossing with her boot. She led Mía and the gelding across. Savannah followed, the mare picking its way gingerly over the wires. When they were all across Grandma reinserted the post in its hole, left the feather in place, and the three of them resumed their ascent.

The clouds thinned in the sky and a bright half-moon emerged. The trees cast tall shadows that seemed to lengthen and bow as

Savannah passed. Except for a few thin patches of snow the soil was dry and firm in the deep cold. They reached a shallow creek crusted in ice. Both horses broke through without hesitation and drank greedily. Savannah held the reins slack and let the mare drink. Having been conquered by exhaustion long ago, Savannah was in awe of the two rez horses. Their skeletons protruded beneath the long winter hair of their coats. At the beginning of the ride Savannah had felt sure neither animal would have the strength for such a journey. The idea scared her when she recalled what her father had said about the backpacks, that some hiking might be required. She'd been especially worried about the gelding, whose bum front leg created a hitched stride that heaved Grandma and Mía up and down. But the gelding's hitch actually seemed to lessen the longer the night wore on until Savannah hardly noticed it. She wondered how long it had been since the horses were surrendered to the wild, whether becoming feral had unleashed an invigorating survival instinct. Savannah tried to picture her father catching them. She wondered if they'd been up here before, if they recognized their destination.

Halfway through a tall patch of brush, Grandma stopped and dismounted. When Mía once more began to slide off the saddle Grandma picked her up and plopped her in Savannah's lap.

"Where are we?" Savannah asked.

"Nowhere yet," Grandma said, "but hang tight a moment. I need to look for something. I'm getting mixed around out here in the dark." She turned on her flashlight and inspected the branches. She reached into a slight parting between the bushes and stepped through. The flashlight's beam danced within the thicket, dimming as it moved farther away.

Savannah's horse rubbed its face up and down against the second horse's rump.

"Everything is bendy," Mía said.

"What do you mean?" Savannah said.

"Bendy. Bending. When I look at it."

Savannah felt her sister's forehead. "You're hallucinating. It happens sometimes with fevers."

"I want to lie down."

"We're almost there. We have to be."

"The fire... What was that fire?"

The light brightened behind the brush as the beam swiveled around and Grandma burst through. "I figured this was it. Just had to really make sure. Your dad never took the same route more than a couple times so he wouldn't make a trail. Smart, except I don't know this forest like him. So last he took me, he marked the way with these...." She held up a black feather, the vanes radiating before the flashlight. "Crow feathers. She rolled the feather between her thumb and forefinger before putting it in her pocket. "They make for good trail markers as long as you tie them in place with a thin thread of some sort. No one thinks twice about a stray crow feather. This is the first I've ever come up here without him. I think I recognize things good enough, but just in case be on the lookout for any feathers."

"Are we close?" Savannah said.

"As the crow flies?" Grandma chuckled. "Yes. But as the horse plods, a ways to go."

After that the trek grew arduous, inscrutable, slow. Every few minutes they waited as Grandma hopped off her horse and shined her light around, sweeping aside pine needles or sifting through branches before finding a feather. Savannah kept hold of Mía in the saddle, feeling her sister's breaths grow deeper, wetter. The air turned thinner and Savannah's own lungs began to ache. And still they climbed higher, the junipers well below them now and replaced by the taller pines and even a few swaths of aspens standing ghostly without their leaves.

"Wait till you see it, girls," Grandma said. "You won't believe your eyes. It's so... so *perfect*, even down to where it's located and how they have it in the land office. If you zoom in with Google Maps, it's smack dab on the border of the Tonola and Zara reservations. Navajo's not that far either. The Indians have reasons for keeping folks out of this wilderness. Hardly anyone comes up here."

They came to a sharp gully where the horses' hooves struck through to a new, shallower streambed. When they reached the other side, Grandma dismounted and turned on her flashlight.

"We're here," Grandma said. "I recognize these trees."

Savannah looked around, expecting some sort of shelter but seeing nothing but forest. "We're where?"

Grandma tied the gelding, took the reins from Savannah and tied the mare beside it. She still had one backpack strapped over her shoulders but left the other tied behind the gelding. "Come over here," Grandma said. "I'll show you."

Savannah got off, cradled Mía into her arms and carried her over to where Grandma stood between two immense bristlecone pines. The gnarled trunks leaned toward one another so that the mostly dead and tentacle-like limbs entangled into what seemed an ancient archway.

"Well?" Grandma said.

"What?" Savannah said.

"Right there."

Grandma jiggled the flashlight beam. Savannah still didn't understand what she was supposed to be looking at. The light hovered over a featureless spot on the ground, only a bunch of sharp rocks sprinkled with pine needles.

And then she saw it. At first she thought it was the dark eye of the flashlight beam's center. Only it wasn't moving. The dark spot was on the ground, and it was dark because there was nothing to it—just a rocky hole, a portal leading down into the earth.

8

What else had she expected? After everything that had happened today — after riding hours through a nighttime forest — where did she think they'd end up? Had she really expected some "new house," as her father had said? A cabin perhaps, or possibly another trailer — either way something cheap that would blend in, so they could hide inside it without the prying eyes of social workers or parole officers. That might have been what she pictured at one time, but the truth was Savannah hadn't expected anything. After the events of the past twenty-four hours, expecting felt pointless.

Looking at that gaping maw in the earth — it really did look like a mouth, an unhappy one with toothless gums and down-curled lips — Savannah felt sick. "I'm not going down there."

"It's not how it looks," Grandma said. "Watch, it's tight only here at the entrance."

Grandma went to the opening, knelt next to it and took off her backpack. She shined a light down the cavern's throat, coated with jagged rocks. Not exactly toothless after all, Savannah thought.

"It's a squeeze for just a few feet, that's it," Grandma said. "But once you get through, you're in." She lowered herself inside, squirming in feet-first so that only her head stuck out. She grabbed the backpack and shined her flashlight on Savannah. "Here, hand me Amelia."

Savannah hugged Mía closer and took a step back. Grandma frowned, her lips tightening. They looked at one another for a moment, a cold breeze moaning through the trees. The grim hues of approaching dawn colored the horizon.

Grandma's face softened. "Look, Savannah, okay. I get it. I wouldn't want to crawl in either if I didn't know what else was down here. But you've already come all the way up here, and we're all tired. Come in and take one look. *Then* tell me what you think."

Annoyed, angry or sympathetic, Grandma was hard to take seriously with only her head poking from the hole. Her shiny glasses and spikey hair made her look like a burrowing owl. Savannah would have laughed if she wasn't so weak and cold and scared and utterly over it.

"What about the horses?" Savannah asked.

"They're fine for the moment. Let them rest."

Savannah glanced at the two horses, both animals already fighting sleep, eyes drooping.

"I'm not sure about you," Grandma said, "but I'm starving. I'm ready to eat something, fire up the stove and get in bed."

"There's a stove?"

"A good one. Big and hot. Plus, it's warmer down there even without the stove."

Manipulation, Savannah knew it when she heard it. But what was the alternative? Flee back through the forest and hope they didn't run into Teddy along the way? That they didn't freeze to death, starve or collapse from exhaustion? Mía could barely stand, and the fumes Savannah ran on were fast depleting. She didn't trust her grandmother, but she had to believe there were provisions inside. Otherwise the night ended in death, and if that had been the plan all along, why come way up here to carry it out? If following her grandmother into some dark pit in the middle of the woods meant surviving, so be it. What was one more act of manipulation at this point anyway?

She set Mía down and then handed her to Grandma. Grandma scooted down the tunnel with her, dragging the backpack behind. Savannah poked her head in after them but saw only a rocky tube, the top of her grandmother's head and her sister's face staring up at her. Mia's eyes were bloodshot and confused. Savannah slipped off her pack and took one last look over her shoulder—seeking, perhaps, some form of witness. She dropped her feet into the hole and plunged inside.

The first thing she noticed was the humidity, a stale wetness permeating the air, thickening it and making it feel warmer. The smell reminded her of being little, of crawling underneath the deck of their old house, the moist soil and dewy rocks. The decline was slight, and Savannah had to push herself along, her stomach and back and shoulders scraping across the jagged stones. Her body snuffed out all light but the occasional flicker of her grandmother's flashlight below her. Overhead, as if through a receding window, she still glimpsed the gray light of dawn. Then the darkness engulfed her.

Squeezed her.

Savannah's heart pounded, her breath pumping in short gasps. She kept pushing until her feet swung out over nothing. She shrieked, clawing with her hands for purchase on the stones. She tried to pull herself back up before dropping into the forever-blackness. Then something grabbed her feet.

"Whoa," Grandma said, "relax, Savannah, stop kicking. You've got about five more feet to go. Don't worry, I got you."

Beads of sweat burst from Savannah's forehead. She squeezed her eyes shut and concentrated on her breathing, straining to get it under control. Allowing her grandmother to guide her by the ankles, she pushed herself downward and then dropped. There came a brief moment of free fall, followed by the surprise of solid ground. Savannah fell backward into her grandmother's arms.

"There, not so bad, huh?"

Grandma lifted her up. The flashlight lay on the ground, its light spilling over loose rocks. With everything else concealed in darkness Savannah had the overwhelming sensation of standing on a vast precipice. She flailed her hands behind her, grasping for something and finding only air. She lowered herself to a crouch and set her palms across the sharp stones beneath her. She felt light, her entire body quivering.

Then she remembered her flashlight. Savannah patted along her front until locating the small MagLite. She removed the short leather loop from around her neck, held the light out and clicked it on. The beam fluttered across an immense round ceiling before coming to rest on Mía, who was seated on the ground. Grandma helped Savannah up.They were in a large, tube-like cavern of the same charcoal-colored stone that littered the forest above. The walls and ceiling were amazingly smooth, with dark wavy lines running along them, swirling in some parts, adding a woozy effect. It was as if the place had been dug by a giant, cindering earthworm. The air still smelled of stale water and water dripped somewhere in the darkness. Savannah thought she detected a faint trace of smoke, not to mention a trace of something foul, sewery. They were on top of an enormous pile of rocks, some of the rocks small boulders. From where she stood, Savannah could shine her light in both directions without seeing the tunnel's end in either direction.

"Don't shine the light too far down there," Grandma said, picking up her own light from the rocks.

"Why?"

"Just don't. And keep your voices low."

Savannah looked at the dark lines along the walls again. There was something fluid about them, similar to the water marks she'd seen on canyon walls.

"Where's the stove and everything else you said?"

Grandma held up a finger and grinned. "Ah, but we haven't even gotten to the good part yet. Follow me and watch your step."

Savannah went to Mía, picked her up and kept hold of her hand. They followed their grandmother down the rock pile and along a stony floor. The cave opened into a large, cathedral-like hall. Savannah was amazed to find her grandmother had been right: it *was* warmer down here. She couldn't help wondering if it was only her renewed anxiety at being underground, but compared to the freezing temperature up top Savannah felt downright hot the lower they marched.

She unzipped her jacket. Grandma came to a stop and aimed her flashlight at the ground. Something shiny glistened between the stones. It took Savannah a moment to realize it, but she was looking at about six inches of steel pipe jutting upward from the cavern's floor.

"The chimney," Grandma said. "It's about the only thing anyone might ever stumble upon from this level, not that anyone ever stumbles around here to begin with."

Grandma crouched, grunted and slide aside a flat, heavy-looking rock. A thick square of plywood lay beneath it. Grandma lifted the plywood and propped it on its side to reveal yet another dark hole. Savannah leaned forward and shined her flashlight through the opening. She saw a yellow ladder of shaved aspen, descending more than ten feet to a dirt floor enclosed by shadows.

"Okay, you go ahead this time, Savannah. I'll hand you Amelia."

Savannah's chest tightened at the thought of tunneling even deeper, confining herself in more stone and a darkness that seemed to build upon itself like water pressure.

Grandma must have sensed her anxiety. "This is it, girls. Down this ladder and we're done."

Mía swayed on her feet. Her face was crusty with dried sweat. Savannah took a few breaths and, before she could think about it anymore, swung her feet onto one of the rungs. The ladder wobbled beneath her, its posts tottering against the rim of stone on which they rest. She concentrated on the rungs, but in her periphery she noticed the walls on either side were lined with shelves. Halfway down she stopped and looked up. Grandma lowered Mía to her. Savannah reached for her but as she did the MagLite slipped from her hand. It clattered onto the ground and went dark. The room was suddenly black, save for the slight gleam from where Grandma had set her own light down. Savannah scrambled back up and looped an arm around Mía's waist.

"Got her?" Grandma said.

"Yeah."

"All right, I'm letting go." Grandma released Mía and Savannah climbed down, one arm squeezed around her sister, the other hooked around the rungs.

Her boots hit the ground and she backed away, keeping hold of Mía. She found the MagLite on the floor, shook it, and the light came back on.

Grandma climbed down after them, breathing hard as she reached the bottom. She draped a forearm over a rung and rest her head against it. "Jesus, I'm tired," she said, her shoulders heaving up and down. She turned around and swept the flashlight across the walls, illuminating more dark stone and a small landfill of colorful debris heaped around the floor. Within the rubble Grandma's light came to a rest upon an LED lantern. She grabbed it and switched it on. Savannah winced, shielding her eyes as the place flooded with light.

They stood within yet another chamber, this one much smaller than the one above, and also warmer. It stretched about thirty feet end to end and was shaped like a giant capsule. Vacuum-sealed plastic bags spilled along the floor in a ring around the room. The bags appeared to contain adult and kid-sized clothing, judging by the small sleeves and occasional pink fabrics pressed inside them. Hundreds of cans of soups were stacked in head-high pyramids next to still more glass jars of pickled meats and vegetables. Heaped against one wall were a few unopened cardboard boxes with labels reading *Mountain House Foods* or *SOS Food Lab Inc.* There were blue jugs of varying sizes, 'WATER' written across their fronts in black marker. A crude wooden shelf held books and board games.

Savannah noted first aid kits, batteries, hand tools, boxes of ammunition, sealed logs of chewing tobacco cans, bottles of bleach, cuts of rope and rubber hosing, tiny solar panels, and many more items scattered about to make her feel dizzy. After having climbed for hours through what felt like untouched wilderness, the room and its contents seemed otherworldly — an alien ship chanced upon in deep space.

Between all the supplies piled around the floor, not to mention the four cots arranged side-by-side, there was hardly any room to move around. A curtain hung behind the ladder, concealing a section of wall at one end. On the opposite end, near the beds, stood an oil drum, one section of its front cut out, slit with holes and reattached on hinges to create a grate. A chimney jutted from the top — the metal pipe they'd seen poking through the floor on the level above. Savannah looked along the ceiling and noticed a few more fist-sized apertures —

ventilation, she assumed. A small pile of wood lay stacked near the stove.

"C'mon," Grandma said, "let's get Amelia taken care of. I'll start a fire."

Each cot had a pillow, a down sleeping bag and a wool blanket. Savannah set Mía on the edge of the cot nearest the stove and removed the girl's boots.

"How is she?" Grandma asked, her back to them as she slid the wood into the stove.

Savannah set her hand against her sister's forehead. "Not very good. She's hot to the touch and can barely keep her eyes open."

Grandma pointed to a spot against the wall. "See those med kits? Grab the big orange one. There's Tylenol in there, and somewhere around here is some powdered sports drink, too. Check by the water."

Savannah helped Mía out of her coat and pants and eased her onto the cot. She retrieved the med kit and fished out a packet of Tylenol. She mixed the sports powder with some water, lifted her sister and had her swallow two of the pills. Mía drank heavily from the canteen and then began to hack. Grandma watched while chewing her bottom lip, flames licking through the grate behind her. Savannah rubbed her sister's back as Mía continued to cough. She pleaded with Mía to keep the drink down, knowing it was not her sister's conscious self she spoke to.

"I was the one who first said we should take her to the doctor," Grandma said. "This was your dad's call, and I just had to listen."

Savannah didn't reply. She held Mía and rocked her, feeling her sister's chest rise and fall with each wet breath. The fire crackled. Tinny snaps sounded from the stove as it expanded.

"But she'll be fine," Grandma said. "I know it." She checked the digital watch on her wrist and clapped her hands together. "Okay, follow me, Savannah. Time you get a crash course on this place."

"Not right now, Grandma. Please, I'm so tired. Let me rest."

"Yes right now. Pretty soon you're going to have nothing else to do but rest." She put her hands on Savannah's shoulders and shook her gently. "Now c'mon, this stuff's important. Your dad's trusting me here, and so far we're doing good. Let me tell you about the stove first."

Savannah started to huff, her eyes welling. She considered letting go and breaking down in front of her grandmother, perhaps even giving in to rage. She'd felt it building throughout the day and night, and if ever she had reason to….

She lowered Mía back down onto the pillow and pulled the blanket up to her chin. Savannah was too tired to fight. She had the reason but not the strength. And besides, what good would it do? To throw a tantrum now would only make her weaker, both physically and in her grandmother's eyes. And so she got up for the next few minutes and allowed her Grandma to tour her around the room. She only half-listened as Grandma every so often gleefully demonstrated some device, grinning either at its function or her own knowledge of it, Savannah couldn't tell. She got the sense that after weeks of having these things explained to her, Grandma enjoyed the chance to finally do the explaining herself.

She led Savannah over to the end of the room and swept aside the curtain hanging there. A smell of sewage and chemicals wafted out. Behind the curtain stood three five-gallon buckets. One of them had a plunger handle sticking out of its lid and was labeled 'LAUNDRY' in marker. A second bucket was labeled, 'BLEACH.' And the third, the one with a specially designed toilet seat and lid snapped onto the top, had written across it, 'MOUNTAIN WEST REFINING'. In front of this bucket was a milk crate containing a mound of old t-shirts cut into rags, as well as a stack of white tubs labeled Poo Powder.

Savannah noticed a plastic bin on the floor filled with dirt. No, not dirt, she realized, but sand. Sand and what appeared to be a meteor field of….

"Is that a catbox?"

Grandma rolled her eyes. "Oh yeah, I forgot to tell you about the demon cat. He's around here somewhere, but you'll only see him when he wants you to, and that's either when your dad's here or if he decides to eat your face."

"You mean…Tailypo? He's still alive?"

"I'm not kidding about him being a demon, or about eating your face. The very first time I slept here he pounced on me in the night, clawing my lips, chewing up my ear. When I threw him off he reared around in the dark and pounced again. Your dad finally had to grab him."

Savannah was flabbergasted. She'd given up on ever seeing the family's old black Bombay again, the little panther called Tailypo, believing him lost more than half a year ago during the move.

"You may see him, you may not. Just always make sure there's water in his bowl. He's pretty self-sufficient when it comes to food." Grandma brushed her hands together. "I guess that's about it. We got the creek for water and washing, and later, when things quiet down some, we can start hunting. Oh, and one last thing…." She reached beneath one of the cots and pulled out a long gray duffel bag. She unzipped the bag and removed a black plastic film canister. "You almost certainly won't have to worry about this, but just in case…." She pried off the lid of the canister and poured out a handful of pills. She held one of the half-blue, half-pink capsules between her thumb and forefinger for Savannah to inspect. "This little guy here is *not* to be played around with, understand? Don't go confusing this for an aspirin or something, or let your sister mistake it for candy. Two or three of these is all it'd take to put someone of her size into a sleep she'd never wake up from. You get what I'm saying?"

"What are they?"

"They're for emergencies only. Or *an* emergency. Otherwise, don't touch them." She poured the pills back into the canister, snapped the lid closed and stuffed it back inside the duffel bag.

"How long are we staying here?"

Grandma looked hurt. "We only got here."

"But… Grandma…."

What could she say? That she didn't want to live in a cave? That Mía was sick and needed help? That the two girls were just that, girls, and didn't want to spend the rest of their lives underground with the whole world looking for them until it finally looked no more?

Savannah never had a close, mother-daughter sort of relationship with her grandmother, but she nevertheless assumed her invested enough by this point to understand what Savannah wanted. Or rather what she didn't.

Grandma gave a sympathetic smile, eyes glistening behind her glasses, and in that brief look Savannah thought she saw a glimpse of who her grandma might have been when she was younger. She pulled Savannah in and hugged her.

"It's not forever, Savannah. Be tough. There are better things ahead."

Savannah stood there lamely, letting herself be hugged without hugging back.

Better things ahead.

Grandma let her go. "Where's your backpack?"

Savannah looked around. She didn't see it. Then it dawned on her. "I... I left it up there in the tunnel, when I...."

Started to freak out, she nearly said. She tensed with the memory of that dark, crushing passageway and the thought of going back through it.

"It's okay," Grandma said. "I'll go get it. You take care of your sister."

She started up the ladder while Savannah took a seat beside Mía. The girl's breaths had grown wetter, almost gurgling. Savannah put a hand on her sister's chest. A bad feeling crept over her. Something wasn't right, and not just with Mía. She looked to where her grandma's legs disappeared up the ladder. The plywood board clattering over the hole....

"Wait, Grandma—" Savannah said, scrambling for the ladder. She got halfway up it when something thudded against the board, dirt raining down the back of Savannah's neck. She pushed up but the board didn't budge. Her Grandma had pushed the rock in place, sealing them in.

"Twenty-four hours, Savannah," Grandma called down "Anything much longer than that and I already showed you what's in the film canister. You do what you think is best for you and your sister."

Savannah screamed and banged on the wood, the ladder shuddering under her feet. She begged for her grandmother to come back, to not leave them. She made as much noise as she could, so much she almost didn't hear the choking sounds behind her. Then it dawned on her. She looked over her shoulder to where Mía lay on her cot, convulsing.

9

The girl's chest arched toward the ceiling, her tiny body lurching with each desperate gasp for air. Savannah dropped down the ladder, an electric pain bolting from her ankles as she hit the floor, and rushed for her sister.

She pulled Mía to her seat, bile and saliva hanging from the girl's mouth as she gagged, straining to breathe. Her eyes rolled back to only their whites, her arms and legs flailing. Savannah slapped her palm against her sister's back, straining to keep her upright until Mía spasmed and her head snapped hard into Savannah's nose. White light exploded across Savannah's vision. She dropped her.

Hand across her nose, blood instantly spreading across her palm and down her wrist, Savannah tried to remember what to do with seizure victims. What was it teachers at school had told them to do after that boy had one in the hallway? *Find an adult* was all she remembered.

She flipped Mía onto her side, the girl's back and shoulder muscles rippling with electric currents, her face turning purple. What was it about the clenched teeth? Separate them? Avoid them? Either way, something was obstructing Mía's breathing, and so with one hand on the girl's forehead and the other on her chin, Savannah pried the jaws apart and opened them half an inch before they snapped shut. She pried again, wedged her forefinger in between. The teeth clamped down, biting through the skin and sending a stream of blood from the finger down the side of Mía's cheek. Savannah squeezed her middle finger in beside it, then, underneath those two, her thumb. She slid her hand down into the mouth, her skin all but scraping off against the teeth and, with her middle finger, fished down deep toward the back of the throat, searching, feeling for....

There, the tongue—folded entirely backward into the throat, half-swallowed. Savannah hooked her finger around it and drew it back, the air whooshing immediately past her fingers into the windpipe. Mía sucked in and exhaled. She began to cough, the seizure still racking her body. But she was breathing. Savannah could feel it. She saw the color returning to her sister's face.

She kept her fingers where they were, blood pooling onto the pillow under Mía's head as yet more drops of fell from Savannah's nose onto the blanket. Yet all this barely registered. Same with the ache in her fingers and her throbbing nose. She didn't even hear the words coming from her mouth, the chant of, "*Help her, help her, help her*"—a prayer, she supposed, although to whom she couldn't say.

The spasms gradually lightened in their intensity, growing sporadic. The bite loosened and Savannah retrieved her fingers. Mía's eyes darted around the room. They settled on Savannah and Mía frowned, confused. Savannah squeezed her sister's hands, lowered her face into the bedding and started to cry.

·   ·   ·

Savannah sat with a hand on Mía's chest for what seemed like hours, feeling her twitch and cough every so often but otherwise breathe steady. Her skin was hot and clammy, and Savannah told herself that all this was good, that it meant the fever was breaking.

Everything in Savannah's vision wobbled. Fatigue became a thick blanket wrapped about her, growing heavier by the minute, and before sleep sucked her under completely she made herself stand up. She took a breath and shivered. Although it was far from freezing, Savannah realized the cavern was still on the chilly side, especially since she'd neglected to feed the fire.

Savannah carried the lantern over to the stove and opened the grate. The steel was still warm, and inside a few red embers pulsed in the ash at the bottom. An axe lay propped next to the woodpile and Savannah used its edge to slice a stick into thinner strips, piling them on the coals until, after some blowing, the flames caught. She stared at them as they spread, breathing in the smoke, allowing it to sting her eyes.

Flames.

It all came back to her.

What had they done?

What role had she played?

She tossed a few logs in and closed the grate. She wouldn't think about it, couldn't bear to in her state. Wishing to occupy herself, Savannah climbed back up the ladder and spent a few minutes pushing up on the piece of plywood. At one point as she pressed, she felt the rung of the ladder she was standing on crack. She eased off. The rock on top must have weighed almost as much as she did. She realized there was no way she was going to push it off from her position.

Savannah climbed down the ladder. She didn't wear a watch and so didn't know the time, but remembering the dawn sky when they first entered the caverns she figured it to be at least midday by now—hard to imagine in this darkness. She raised the lantern closer to the ceiling, scanning in vain for any other method of escape. The chimney pipe was loose in a wider aperture of the rock ceiling and looked like it could easily be removed—not that it mattered, Savannah thought, as there was no way any of them would fit through the little chimney hole anyway. No, there was only one way in or out of this chamber. And for the moment at least, that way was sealed.

Her stomach growled. It had been more than twenty-four hours since she'd eaten. Grandma had shown her how to lower a piece of circular grating into the stove to boil water, and Savannah considered preparing one of the freeze-dried dinner packets. Instead, she tore open one of the energy bars. It looked like a large brownie but was hard as a brick. Gnawing at the corners, the back of her mouth smarting with the sudden rush of coconut-flavored sugar, Savannah stood debating whether or not to wake Mía so she could eat one. She decided to let her rest. If Mía was still having trouble keeping things down, Savannah didn't suspect a coconut brick would do much to change that.

Her gaze floated around the chamber, the eerily smooth walls, the ceiling that seemed to drip with thousands of perfect black spikes like shark teeth. They made Savannah think of melted plastic, solidified, as if the entire roof had at one time been ablaze before cooling abruptly. They'd studied caves before in her earth science class, but she didn't remember the stalactites pictured in the textbooks resembling anything like what she saw here. This didn't seem a place formed by wind or water or gases, but something altogether more powerful and immediate.

A white plastic thermometer hung tacked on the side of one of the shelves. The temperature read sixty-two degrees. Savannah observed a tin camping pot on the ground near the woodpile, half-filled with water. *The cat.* She'd nearly forgotten about him, and now wondered where he could be. She started looking through the things on the floor, inspecting them and pushing them aside. The bookshelf was waist-high and made of snap-together Rubbermaid plastic. It contained at least thirty books, almost all of them creased and dog-eared paperbacks. Louis L'Amour and Tony Hillerman Westerns, along with a string of James Wesley Rawles titles like *Patriots*, *Liberators*, and *Survivors*. There were some kids' books, including a Supergirl comic, an illustrated collection of scary stories, and two Calvin & Hobbes treasuries. Savannah assumed the treasuries were intended for Mía, who not only was a fan but liked to pretend Mauricio, her stuffed lion, was a sort of Hobbes. The rest were non-fiction titles: a history of the Mexican-American War, gunfighter biographies, a fat encyclopedia of firearms, texts on space and physics, and multiple studies of the Navajo and Pueblo Indians. The only two hardcovers stood as literal bookends for the small library, the spine of one reading, *US Army Special Forces Medical Handbook*, the other *How to Survive the End of the World As We Know It*, also by Rawles.

Wedged between two of the books on the shelf was a fat manila folder. Savannah pulled it out and opened it, finding it full of what must have been close to a hundred print-outs of internet maps and articles. There were mini topo maps of the Tonola Reservation, layouts of BLM roads, and screen shots from Google Earth. Savannah studied each of these, but without any visible points of reference around her could only guess at their location. Her father had taught her how to use a compass, as well as a little about navigating by star constellations, but he'd never showed her much in the way of maps. She figured a part of him disdained maps. Or, rather, those who relied on them.

She moved on to the internet articles. The black-and-white headers on the pages spanned a variety of websites, a large portion of them Wikipedia. The subjects of the articles extended across water filtration techniques, sewing tips, squirrel meat recipes, annual weather averages, edible plants of the southwest, and many more write-ups whose texts Teddy had peppered with underlines, asterisks, and annotations. Savannah shuffled through the papers, her stomach turning queasy as the articles grew more abstract and dire: minimum core body temperature, stages of starvation, insomnia, depression, suffocation, muscle atrophy, PTSD, nyctophobia, Diogenes Syndrome, Prisoner's Cinema....

Savanna closed the folder and inserted it back between the books on the shelf. She rummaged through the board games, the boxes of crayons and colored pencils, drawing pads and coloring books. There was a miniature basketball hoop and ball, as well as two unopened Barbies. Neither girl had ever been particularly into Barbies, and discovering them now Savannah wondered how much Teddy actually remembered about her and Mía, and how much he assumed.

A rusty tangle of chains lay heaped on the floor. Savannah lifted one to discover a heavy steel jaw dangling from its end. A bear trap. She counted four of them in the pile, each one big and sharp enough to chomp through the foot of a grizzly. Savannah remembered what her grandmother had said about hunting for food, and she wondered if that included trapping. Considering their size, however, Savannah thought her father had another purpose in mind for the traps—one Savannah didn't care to think about long.

She noticed a set of camouflage army fatigues, the shirt folded neatly to display the 'UNSER' name bar. It was a sloppy stitch job on the bar, and Savannah figured he'd probably sewn it himself and attached it to some basic fatigues from General Cody's Military Surplus.

Savannah never liked the name 'Unser,' and had more than once considered adopting a different last name. Her mother, Camilla, told Savannah that when she was being born, Teddy carried a boombox into the delivery room and, despite the protests of everyone in the room, blasted the song "Rooster" by Alice in Chains. Savannah's mother never forgave him for that. Whenever she told the story, she always said it had been "such an *Unser* thing for him to do," — saying the name like it was another word for asshole. As if they didn't all go by that name.

Savannah's gaze fell to the partially unzipped duffel bag below the cot. She felt around inside it. The bag was bulky with things, the surface level being mostly prepper gear Savannah had seen many times before: MREs, waterproof matches, water filtration pens, bunched spools of multicolored paracord.... She dug deeper until her fingers found the film canister. *Suicide pills.* Savannah shook one into her hand and examined it. She found she could twist the ends of the blue and pink capsule and open it, revealing tiny yellow beadlets. Savannah closed the capsule and dropped it back into the canister. She thought about tossing the canister into the stove, watching the black plastic melt, the deathly little capsules liquifying into a blob. She wondered if destroying them would really eliminate death as an option. Savannah then wondered if death was even the worst scenario.

She sensed the answer to the last question to be somehow no. As Savannah turned the little canister in her hands, something gold and shiny caught her eye inside the bag. She dropped the canister and picked up a small, gold-framed picture. It was a photo of her many years younger, wearing a blue dress and holding their cat Tailypo — little more than a kitten at the time. Her parents stood behind her, a collage of autumn leaves and an old woodshed in the background. The woodshed sagged, its red paint flaking. In another setting it would have looked trashy, but here it had the rustic effect they were no doubt going for. Savannah recognized the shed from the old property. She remembered her grandma taking the picture. It was supposed to be a day of family photos, except Camila had been in a bitter mood. It had been windy, and every photo contained at least one grimace, one scrunched up, funny-looking face, including the one they finally chose to copy and frame. In that one, Savannah and her father were both smiling, their eyes squinting. Savannah's mother, however, made no such attempt. Her dark hair fanned out in the wind. One hand interlaced with her husband's, she looked distraught—brow furrowed as she seemed to peer at something more distant than the camera. Something receding perhaps: the life she wanted as seen from the one she had?

The picture and its frame sat in the old house for many years, propped on the windowsill above the kitchen sink. When had it disappeared and come up here? How long had Teddy been filling this underground lair with its things, getting ready for what happened last night, and whatever was still to come? It was almost two years since he'd been released from state prison and gone missing. Had Grandma known where her son was the whole time, telling police otherwise?

Putting the picture back in the bag, Savannah recalled that it had a twin—another tiny portrait once positioned next to it on the windowsill. The second picture had shown Mía all by herself atop a bale of hay, wearing a pink cowboy hat and matching pink boots. Savannah dragged the bag out from under the cot to look for it. The bag was heavy and clinked with something metal at the bottom. Savannah zipped it all the way open. She peered inside and turned cold.

Fitted along the bottom of the bag lay three rifles, their trigger guards clamped with tiny combination trigger locks. One of the guns was a sawed-off shotgun, another a banana-clipped automatic of some caliber, and the third a scoped 30.06. She hadn't seen a gun in years until her father returned a few days ago with his Wrathful Judge. But she recognized the 30.06, stretched out there at the bottom of the bag like a real-life prop from a long-ago nightmare. Her chest tightened, the familiar anxious sensations coursing through her veins like poisons.

It happened not long after they met him at the airport, fresh out of Leavenworth. He wasn't supposed to have unsupervised contact with Savannah, not yet anyway. He also wasn't supposed to be in possession of a firearm. Nonetheless, he'd taken her out to the desert, driving for miles down dirt roads far from any highway, a picnic cooler and a fold-up picnic table bouncing in the bed of the truck. He talked a mile a minute as they drove. Savannah had said little, merely stole glances at him, searching for the man she remembered. They stopped at the foot of a mesa where they lined up rows of cans, bottles, and cereal boxes filled with sand. They then arranged the table a short distance away as a shooting bench. He gave her foam earplugs, helping her twist them into her ears until she could hear her own heartbeat. Teddy lowered onto his knees behind the table and lay the rifle across it. He showed Savannah how to open the bolt action and load it. When he took the first shot, Savannah felt its blare resonate in her bones and gut, the echo sweeping across desert and sky. One of the bottles shattered and dust billowed at the base of the mesa. Without lifting his head from the stock Teddy reloaded, ejecting the shell casing, aimed at the next target in line and fired. He did this three times, emptying the chamber. He then stood up and handed the smoking rifle to Savannah.

She'd shaken her head and tried to give the gun back to him, but he only pushed it back at her. He told her it was only the first shot that was scary. After that, he said, she'd be addicted. *Addicted.*

And so Savannah had lowered herself to her knees and, trembling, loaded the gun as he'd shown her. She felt him get behind her, smelled his musk, let him pull the rifle's stock tight against her. She peered through the scope, the sight wavering around one of the empty cans. She must have looked through it a long time because all of a sudden her father was pinching her right index finger and placing it around the trigger. He might have said something then — something like *do it* or *go ahead*, she didn't remember. Before she could think anymore about it, she squeezed the trigger.

The stock slammed into her, a burst of pain in her shoulder as she toppled backwards. She was dimly aware of her father cursing, leaping forward to catch the rifle before it fell to the ground. She lay there in the dirt, dazed and clutching her collarbone, gazing up at an unbroken blue sky. Then a black curtain lowered across her vision.

She didn't remember much about what happened next, only that it had been a long, dark ride jostling in the truck. She recalled screaming and crying while her father demanded that she relax, get a grip. She was completely blind, and yet her father kept trying to convince her she only *thought* she was, that she must've gotten dirt in her eyes. But Savannah, in her hysteria, recognized the panic in his voice and realized he was as afraid as she was. And then the truck stopped and it was her grandmother's voice she heard, angry at first and then scared. She argued with Teddy outside the truck while Savannah writhed and moaned inside. Grandma got behind the wheel and said she was taking Savannah to the hospital. Her father didn't even say goodbye.

They called it rhegmatogenous. Retinal detachment. Savannah underwent emergency laser surgery to weld her retinas back in place. When she woke, she found herself in a hospital room with a broken collarbone and her arm in a sling. A doctor stood outside the doorway, talking to a couple of police officers. The procedure had been largely successful, except that when she closed her right eye the world appeared as if seen through a murky glass of pond water. The doctor said the damage in the left eye was likely permanent, that she was lucky it wasn't completely blind. When he finished explaining things, he stepped aside and the police officers came forward. Savannah told them everything. She felt woozy from the drugs, and the idea of lying never once crossed her mind.

Her father went back to prison after that—state prison this time. Only Grandma visited him there. She told Savannah the court wasn't allowing the girls to visit, but at the time Savannah suspected otherwise. She assumed he didn't want to see her and, despite everything, the thought hurt her deeply. It kept hurting her too, especially when, after his eventual release, he disappeared. And so, more than three years after the incident in the desert when Teddy did finally come back to them, Savannah couldn't look at him without a sense of shame, a desire to somehow make it all up to him. When Mía confided in Savannah the night before Miss Jill's visit that she was afraid of Teddy and that she thought they should tell someone he'd come back, Savannah had refused. She wouldn't be the one responsible this time.

She'd never expected to see that rifle again, the 30.06 that had been the cause of so much trouble. And yet here it was. She recalled the police officers asking about it in the hospital. Looking at it now, at the bottom of the duffel bag, she guessed her father must have stashed it somewhere while Grandma drove her to the hospital. Savannah ran her fingers along the gun's mahogany stock and its freezing cold barrel, feeling a new kind of regret.

There were other things in the duffel bag, including a few magazines — *Penthouse, Hustler*, a few others with more graphic titles — as well as a couple of knives, a tin box, a legal pad, and a small nylon case. She picked up the tin box, flipped the tiny latch and opened the lid to find a plastic grocery sack folded over something rectangular and flimsy. Letting the sack unfurl, she reached in and pulled out a sandwich baggie containing a thin stack of cash.

She opened the baggie. The bills were mostly twenties, along with a few hundreds. Savannah fanned the bills out and counted. Eighteen-hundred dollars. Not much. It had probably been more at one time; something had to account for the mass accumulation of supplies in the cave. While Savannah never knew her father to have held a job, her grandmother once made a living breaking horses. But after one threw her and she fractured her hip, she'd since relied on disability and the small welfare checks the state sent to support the girls.

Savannah figured there was only one possible explanation for the cash. Three years ago Grandma took out a mortgage on her house. This was the old property in the country that Grandma had up to then owned free and clear ever since inheriting it from her own parents. As far as Savannah could ever tell, the mortgage went to a splurge. She spoiled the girls with shopping sprees at Wal-Mart while also buying a new truck and a number of horses. Savannah didn't understand much about what was going on at the time, but she'd come to understand a lot since then. Truth was, Grandma couldn't afford the loan, and when the foreclosure process inevitably began she'd turned desperate and sold a large portion of the mortgage itself to yet another lender. That lender in turn sold the loan to another company, and before anyone knew it the repossession trucks arrived and Savannah didn't even know if she'd get to keep her iPod.

The whole process had been a long string of one shady intention tied to another. Granted, everyone in the county was fighting to save their properties from MWR and the recent gas boom in the region. Certain folks, including Ray and Linda at the Mustard Seed, eventually lost their lots under something called imminent domain — or, as Grandma always described it, using finger quotations and a sneer, "the good of the public." Thing was, Grandma owned her mineral rights, and in all likelihood could have kept the house. Yet for reasons Savannah never understood she'd taken out the mortgage, and in one incredible irony to close the whole awful drama, the final buyer of said mortgage had been none other than Mountain West Refining.

Savannah studied the bills splayed out between her fingers. She looked up, struck with an epiphany. Grandma had visited Teddy a lot while he was in state prison, especially during his last year there. That was now right about three years ago. When had he first hatched this plan, to flee with the three of them into this underground lair? How much of his idea did he share with Grandma before she took the loan out? And, most disturbingly, what part had MWR played in his motivations?

Savannah closed her eyes and rode a sudden wave of nausea. She pressed the bills back into a stack and was about to return the cash to its baggie when she paused. She thought about the Velcro wallet in her back pocket that had never held more than a few dollars. Savannah wondered how it might feel to know a hundred-dollar bill lived inside. There was even a secret pouch where she could stash it. She wondered whether her father would notice if one was missing. Considering her present situation, she may not even get the opportunity to spend it. Then again, there might come a time when she—and Mía—really needed it.

Savannah slipped a hundred from the stack and secreted it away inside her wallet. She put the rest back as she found it, opened the duffel bag wider and pulled out the legal pad. An illustration on the front page caught her eye. Etched in ink, the picture featured a number of vertical squiggly lines and rough shapes. Only when Savanna noticed the compass and turned the pad sideways did she realize what she was looking at. She recognized the winding tube, the entryway to this place and the tumble of rocks beneath it. She recognized the cathedral-like dome and the ladder leading deeper into yet another chamber, this one capsule-shaped and drawn in dashes.

It appeared to be a map of sorts, except scrutinizing it revealed little more than what Savannah had already perceived while traversing the tunnels herself. She saw the word "Skylight" etched above the hole through which they'd entered, and under that the pile of stones labeled, "Breakdown". On the left side of the page the word "Dump" was written with an arrow pointing to a slight drop-off. Beyond that a dense mass of what looked to be a pile of rocks was labeled, "Collapse." The opposite end of the tunnel appeared to narrow slightly, with "Partial Collapse" written next to another rock spill. After that, a question mark had been scribbled where the tunnel disappeared off the edge of the paper.

Savannah flipped to the next page, expecting to see a continuation of the map, and found a simple drawing of a cat. She recognized Tailypo in the picture, complete with dark fur and nubby tail. The rest of the pages featured more random sketches from their life as a family: the old house before it was bulldozed, horses in a corral, a turtle that may or may not be stuffed, a decent portrait of Savannah herself. But as she kept flipping the pages—looking less now out of curiosity than compulsion—the images began to take on shapes more sinister and schizophrenic. Savannah's breath grew shorter.

She saw doodles of guns, of knives, of fire. One page in particular showed a stick-figure man surrounded by a dozen different weapons, all of them pointed at him. Another depicted a snake coiling up inside what looked like a human rib cage, while yet another presented a man leaning back in a chair, holding a fork in one hand and a knife in the other while feasting on his own sawed-open stomach. There were drawings of monsters: a squid gripping swords in its tentacles, round-headed aliens with almond eyes, a canine creature with two legs and giant antlers. And everywhere—scribbled in the margins or else repeated over and over to fill entire pages — were the words, "Ahmad of the White Mountains".

Savannah let the pages flip closed and shoved the pad back inside the duffel bag. She put a hand on her stomach and tried not to think about the tart energy bar churning inside. She felt like she'd peeked in on something not only private but vile. Something dangerous. The pages were a record of madness, and here she was in the madman's cell.

Her gaze fell to the nylon case inside the duffel bag. She picked it up, unzipped it and pulled out a camcorder — shiny and barely used by the looks of it. In the case's side pouch Savannah found three mini-dv tapes still in their packaging, some spare batteries, and a thin remote control the size of a business card. She examined the remote, found the power button and pushed. The camera beeped to life. She opened the side screen and was greeted by a blue screen with a videotape icon revolving in the center. In the top left corner were the words, 'VCR MODE', and below that '34 MIN'.

She looked at Mía, the girl's chest rising steadily up and down in the sleeping bag. She found the volume control on the remote and turned it to its lowest setting. She pressed 'PLAY'.

On screen, her father sat on the floor of the chamber, a flashlight set along a cot angling down to spotlight him, his bald head shining. He wore a white tank top. Arranged on a small blanket in front of his lap was a line of sewing needles, a rag, and two cups of liquid — one of them clear and the other black.

Teddy spoke into the camera: "I don't want to waste the battery showing the whole thing, but thought I'd give a peek at what I have so far." He twisted his torso and lifted a shoulder. There, the unfilled letters polka-dotted in black ink across his left bicep, was the tattoo Savannah had glimpsed in her bedroom.

It read, 'ONE LIFE, ONE CHANCE'.

Teddy lifted the rag, submerged it in the cup of clear liquid and smeared away the blood seeping up at the lettering's edges. "I can't remember if I saw this somewhere, or if I just made it up. But whatever, because it's something I've come to really believe in. I've had so much of my life taken from me. And not just years either, but people. Things and people. It's like no matter what I do, everyone wants to take from me and confine me. Despite what they say, the world doesn't like men of action. Everyone talks about taking action when real action scares them. So they chain up people like me, make sure I don't move too far ahead of them."

Dropping the rag, he picked up one of the needles and dipped its point into the ink. He was silent a long time as he worked on filling the letters, poking the needle tip in and out of his skin.

He set the needle down, looked around the chamber and smiled. "Everyone knows one day the shit's going to hit the fan. The event is coming. We all sense it, and yet we just wait around. Well I'm sick of waiting. I've gotten used to being confined. It's easy to change the world when the world is small."

With that he raised his bleeding shoulder to the camera one more time before reaching up to switch it off.

The image scrambled and jumped to a new one. This time Teddy's entire face filled the screen, his brown eyes boring deep into Savannah's. Again he was in the chamber with a flashlight beam shining on him. The image tilted and shook before sharpening back into focus. His gaze drifted to the side, and Savannah realized he was watching himself in the same swivel-screen she now peered into.

Something black and metallic rose into frame.

The Wrathful Judge.

He put the barrel of the gun into his mouth, his breath steaming along the steel and fogging the picture. He wiped the lens with a shirt sleeve, never once taking the gun out of his mouth. His breathing remained calm and steady all the while, his eyes expressionless as deep in their pupils shined the tiny red reflection of the recording light. He stared at himself, finger on the trigger.

Savannah stared back.

After a long moment, Teddy sighed. The screen shook and went blue.

Savannah sat there, the camcorder shaking in her hands. She rewound the tape until it read 34MIN, turned the camcorder off and put it back in the case. She took out her wallet, unfolded the hundred-dollar bill and ran it back and forth over her knee, trying to remove the crease marks. Then she reopened the tin box and put the bill back where she found it.

Savannah pushed the duffel bag under the cot, went to the bed next to Mía's and set the lantern on the ground beneath her. Afraid it would run out of batteries yet even more afraid of complete darkness, she turned the lantern off and clicked on her MagLite instead. Savannah gripped the little flashlight in one hand and lowered herself next to Mía. She lay holding her sister, incapable of anything else.

10

She slept hard, and would have kept sleeping too, despite the cold refilling the room, if it hadn't been for Mía pinching her arm. The pain stabbed into the thick swirl of Savannah's dreams.

"Savannah."

"Ow! What?"

"There's someone in here."

Savannah kicked her legs over the cot, surging awake, her senses keen as they reached out into the most impenetrable dark she had ever known. The MagLite was missing from her hand and dead anyway, apparently, wherever it was. A crunching noise sounded from somewhere in the darkness. Savannah padded her fingers along the icy earth, fumbling onto the lantern. She grabbed it and turned it on.

An explosion of light, and in the split second before she winced Savannah saw the eyes: two big pupils that visibly shrank in their green irises. The eyes locked themselves on Savannah from low on the floor. The lantern rocked by its handle in her hand, reeling shadows. Mía gasped and drew harder into her sister. The thing on the ground spat, arched its back, coal-black fur bristling, nubby tail poofed out like a chimney brush.

Savannah smiled. "Hello, Tailypo."

The cat stood near the woodpile with what looked like a patch of cotton clinging to his mouth. His fangs were red with blood. Something twitched on the floor in front of him. A mouse, chewed half-open but not quite dead.

The mouse dragged itself along the floor and the cat—his eyes never once leaving Savannah—swatted it still with a paw.

Savannah peeled Mía off of her. "Look, see? It's Tailypo. He recognizes us. He's been up here this whole time."

She doubted whether the cat really recognized them, but he did appear to at least accept their presence. His hairs slowly flattened, and his spine relaxed. Keeping his eyes locked on Savannah, he lowered his head and resumed his meal.

"You said he ran away," Mía said.

"I thought he did."

Which wasn't completely true. The cat had disappeared a few days before the move into town. The girls looked up and down for him, inside and outside, calling for him, placing pieces of lunch meat and bowls of milk in the hope he'd emerge from whatever hiding place he'd crawled into. The whole time they did this, however, Grandma grew strangely impatient. She kept telling the girls he'd run away, like she not only understood it for a fact but was okay with it. As if she knew something the girls didn't. This had bothered Savannah for a number of reasons, not least of all for her history of lost pets.

Yet here he was, chewing and ripping apart the mouse in strips. The family cat.

"He's fatter." Mía said.

"But it's him all right. Look at the tail." She pointed to the bristly nub, "Remember the whole reason for his name. The story? *'Tailypoooo. Give me back my Tailypoooo?'*"

"No."

"Mom used to tell it to us. I guess you'd be too young to remember. It's about a hunter who goes out one night and shoots the tail off a strange furry creature. The man's hungry so he takes what he's got, the long black tail, back to his cabin and cooks it up in a stew. Then, later that night, he wakes up to a scratching on the door. It creaks open, and he hears the thing scratch its way along the floor until it's at the foot of his bed and is climbing up his quilt. Two long black ears poke above the bed, followed by claws, followed by...."

She blew into her Mía's ear, making her sister jump, flush and giggle. It was more or less exactly how their mother used to end the story.

But now, watching the story's namesake chew on his mouse, Savannah felt a tug on her heartstrings. If there was anything she understood for sure about her father, it was that he loved his cat. He had found the cat crying in a gas station parking lot, his tail mysteriously lopped. Although it was the girls' mother who bestowed the name, Tailypo was Teddy's pet one-hundred percent, and after Teddy left the cat turned reclusive and mean, always scratching them whenever they caught it. But when Teddy was still around the cat was different. Around him Savannah remembered the cat being bold, jealous even—emerging from wherever he'd been all day to slink around Teddy's shins. He used to meow until Teddy picked him up and stroked him, the cat's eyes turning languid with pleasure yet at the same time alert of any nearby threat to his master's affection.

Tailypo picked up what was left of the mouse between his jaws and darted behind the woodpile. Savannah thought how not long ago she'd been kneeling there, slicing away strips of kindling for the fire, oblivious to another presence mere inches away. Had Tailpo been watching her the whole time, ready to explode out of the woodpile should she reach inside one more time or move just an inch closer? Savannah didn't think she could have handled such a thing at the time, so much shock.

Mía's hair was a rat's nest. Savannah tried in vain to comb her fingers through it. "How are you feeling?"

"Tired."

"Want something to eat?"

Mía thought about it. "Yes."

Savannah refilled the canteen with water, watched Mía drink most of it down without stopping, then handed her one of the energy bars. "It tastes like a cookie with too much sugar, so not bad."

Mía bit a corner off the bar, made a face.

"I know," Savannah said. "But eat it."

Savannah moved to the stove and got to work rebuilding the fire. Back at their old house it had been her chore to keep the stove going. She was good at fires and found building them soothing.

"I'm sore," Mía said. "Everything on me hurts, my legs, my arms, my neck. Everything."

"I believe it. Every single muscle in your body was straining to the max. Do you remember anything at all?"

Mía shook her head. "Only parts. Everything's hazy. Where are we? Where's Grandma?"

"We're in the woods, in a cave underground. This is his 'new house' for us, I guess. We're stuck." She wanted to know how much her sister remembered of the water truck, the explosion, the burning building. She would have liked for Mía to remember nothing, to perhaps imagine she'd dreamed it, but deep down Savannah knew that wasn't so.

The fire, Mía had mumbled on the ride up. *What was that fire?*

The flames caught in the stove and she closed the grate. She asked Mía if she needed to go to the bathroom. Mía looked around the rocky chamber. "How?"

Savannah walked her to the potty bucket behind the curtain. She helped Mía go, then went herself, grimacing at the sound of her urine stream in the bucket and the smell wafting up. When they were done they returned to the cots.

"Your hair is driving me crazy," Savannah said, and grabbed the one backpack that had made it into the chamber, hoping it was the one containing the hairbrush she'd packed — what, two mornings ago? She opened the bag and a tiny golden face peeked out at her from inside, the two beady eyes and button nose of Mauricio the Lion. Savannah took the stuffed animal and found the brush. She lay Mauricio down next to her sister, took a seat behind Mía and started brushing her hair.

Mía ignored the lion. Instead she pointed to a mustard-colored t-shirt hanging in a corner, the chamber's lone piece of decor. "I remember that, when we got those."

Savannah recognized it, too. When Teddy returned from Leavenworth, he'd brought a presents for the girls: t-shirts featuring a coiled snake and the words, "Don't Tread On Me." He wore an identical shirt himself, and said he'd bought them with all the money he'd saved up with his fifty-cents-an-hour prison job making braille books. The shirts were ridiculously large on the girls, dangling below their knees. Savannah could still picture the frowns they got in school the next day, from classmates and teachers alike, and how with no word between them the sisters decided never to wear the shirts again.

Savannah gazed at her father's old shirt hanging on the wall, another article of the *revolution* he always seemed to be preparing for. Of the soldier he always considered himself to be. "You'd think he'd want nothing else to do with the army," Savannah said.

"He was in the army?" Mía said. "I don't remember that."

This didn't surprise Savannah; her sister had never really known Teddy as anything except a prisoner, if even that. To Mía, who hadn't met him until she was five and then only briefly, he must have seemed an abstract. Someone whose name was mentioned and whose picture she saw on the walls of Grandma's house.

"You wouldn't," Savannah said. "You weren't even born yet. And hardly anyone ever talked about it. He wasn't in the army long."

"Why?"

"Because he deserted."

"Deserted?"

"Left without getting permission. Before his time was up."

"How come?"

"I'm not really sure, but I imagine he did something that was going to get him in trouble."

"Oh." Mía chewed on a nail and Savannah braced for what came next. "What did he do?"

Savannah felt a lot of things in the wakes of her father's imprisonments and her mother's death: devastated, betrayed, clueless. But rarely did she feel more *abandoned* than when answering questions like these.

"I don't know. Only that he was barely out of boot camp. I remember all this buildup for him before he left, Grandma throwing this big going-away party. And then it was like right after that the army was calling to say he'd gone missing. But then they found him, and there was this trial way on the other side of the country that only Grandma went to. Then he went to Kansas."

The rest Savannah had needled out of her grandmother over the years. Grandma didn't like to talk about her son's military experience, but, as Savannah got older, eventually conceded that her granddaughter had a right to know. Of course, when Grandma did talk about it she did so defensively, framing the story to underscore its injustice before making Savannah promise not to say a word about it to her sister. Savannah never did, but mainly to spare Mía rather than keep any promise made.

When Savannah said "barely out of boot camp," what she really meant was barely into Afghanistan. He'd been there less than a month when he had his first confirmed kill—an eleven-year-old boy, it turned out, who'd been harvesting wheat with a sickle. Grandma said the sickle was planted near the body by villagers after the fact, and that the boy had really been holding a pistol with which he was about to shoot Teddy. But whatever the case, Teddy hadn't stuck around to plead his side of things. Instead he fled right then and there, disappearing into the mountains where he survived off rabbits, birds and mice before crawling back to base a few weeks later with a bad case of giardia. He was detained and treated, then shipped to Maryland for trial. Savannah was six years old, but she remembered bits and pieces from this time well, including peeking in her grandmother's bedroom and seeing Grandma sitting at the edge of her bed, a suitcase open, crying. She remembered how her mother seemed to have a whole different attitude toward the situation: satisfaction. She'd even shown Savannah the local newspaper when it carried the story. And a little after that, while Grandma was still away in Maryland and the two had the entire house to themselves, her mother had conspiratorially lifted her shirt to show Savannah the slight bulge in her belly.

In the end, Teddy was never even charged for killing Afghan boy—something Savannah never really understood, especially when Grandma explained it to her by saying things like it happened all the time over there. Thus, his biggest mistake turned out to be panicking and taking flight. There was no escaping the desertion verdict, and for it the court came down hard: five years, the maximum sentence.

"Where is he?" Mía asked. "And where's Grandma?"

"I told you, I don't know."

"No you didn't. You didn't tell me."

"Well I'm telling you now."

"Are they coming back?"

"Yes."

"When?"

"Soon."

"How soon?"

"Any minute now. Turn your head around."

"But what if they don't? What if no one knows where we are?"

Savannah put her hands on each side of her sister's head and turned it. She resumed brushing, her gaze going to the floor and the duffel bag resting there.

"You've tried to get out?" Mía said.

"Yes. There's a rock on top of the board." She didn't want to scare her sister. Right now she wanted Mía complacent, resigned to where she was, to recuperate. Savannah picked up Mia's unfinished energy bar and handed it back to her. "Here, keep eating."

Mía nibbled at it, her head pulling back with the brush, hair crackling with electricity.

"Do you remember those two pictures on the kitchen window when we were little?" Savannah said. "One of them had you in it."

Mía nodded. "I had on pink boots."

"Yeah. What happened to that? Did it make it during the move? Did you take it?"

Mía shook her head, took one more bite from the energy bar before dropping it in surrender. "I don't remember and I don't care. Savannah can we just get out of here, please?"

"I told you, we're stuck. But Grandma said they'd be right back."

"I don't want them to come back. I want to leave. *Now*."

Mía whirled, knocking the brush out of Savannah's hand and jumped to her feet. Savannah could practically see the blood rushing to her sister's head—her eyes growing wide, spacey. She steadied her, eased her back to a seat.

"You see? You need to keep resting. Even if we were able to get out we're who-knows-how deep in the forest and I have no idea how to find our way out. I don't even know if the horses are still up there. So relax. Let the food digest, keep drinking water. We can't start freaking out."

She was afraid of this, of panic driving one of them into hysteria. She saw it building up in her sister—puffing and scared as if the reality of the situation was only now settling in, constricting around her like a python. Savannah felt it herself, a claustrophobia raring to take hold, angling for even the slightest crack in her already fragile defenses. Up until now she'd managed to keep the fear at bay, if only for her sister's sake. Because she sensed the girls would feed off one another, their terror contagious. And once terror got its foothold it would consume them. After that, chances were good one of them would do something crazy.

Which meant one of them would have to keep it together, and for now that looked to be Savannah. "There are books in here," she said. "Kids' books. How about I read you one?"

"*Pleeease*, Savannah. I can't be in here with him. You can, but not me."

"What does that mean?"

"He hates me."

"That's not true," Savannah said, picking up the hairbrush and bringing it back to her sister's hair.

Mía swatted the brush from her hand. "Stop doing that!"

"Your hair. I just want to—"

"Stop treating me like a *baby*, like I don't understand anything! You're doing exactly what he did, trying to trick me."

"I'm not trying to trick you. I'm…" Savannah stiffened, the rest of her sister's words sinking in. "Wait, what do you mean, 'exactly what he did?' What did he do?"

Mía's eyes fell to her lap. She seemed to retreat into herself.

"Talk to me, Mía. What do you mean he tricked you?"

Mía picked at the food wrapper, peeling the foil into slivers.

"What do you mean, Mía?"

"That night in our room… He heard us."

"Heard us what?"

"Arguing. He heard me say that we should tell on him. Tell someone he was back."

Savannah's blood ran cold. "But how? We were quiet. The door was shut."

"He just said he heard me. Knew what I wanted to do."

Savannah felt queasy, the words of that last night replaying in her head, who had said what. She remembered how they had ended it, or, rather, how they *hadn't* ended it—merely letting silence fill the bedroom, the gap between them. Resolving nothing. She recalled waking up to the sound of Miss Jill arriving the next morning and turning around to find her sister's bed empty.

"How did you end up in the other bedroom?"

Tears slid down Mía's cheeks and she turned her face away so that Savannah couldn't see.

"Mía…."

"He told me not to tell you. That I'd be in trouble. And Savannah I'm scared. I'm scared he'll find out and—"

Savannah took her sister's head in her hands and turned it so they faced one another. "Why did you leave your bed that night?"

Mía sniffed and wiped at her face. "He came and got me. When I was asleep. When we were both asleep."

"Why?"

"To talk to me. To say he had been listening to us argue."

"Was Grandma there?"

Mía shook her head. "I don't know where she was."

"But he said he was listening to what we were saying? He… He knew you wanted to tell somebody?"

Savannah saw her shiver. Mía nodded.

"Then what?"

"He said he was getting rid of me."

Savannah frowned. Granted her knowledge of her father was filled with gaps, but this didn't sound like him. Teddy wasn't usually so forthright when speaking to the girls, especially since his return a few days ago. Lately he seemed to act intentionally jolly, though the dodgy-ness never left him. He acted, Savannah had to admit, manipulative.

"He told you it just like that, 'I'm getting rid of you?'" Savannah asked.

Mía nodded. "He said I'd get my way and wouldn't have to worry about him ever again. He said that I shouldn't be his problem."

"What else?"

Mía shook her head, her gaze still fixed on the ground. "I can't really remember. I fell asleep."

"You fell asleep? How? Why didn't you come back to bed? You should have woken me up."

"I couldn't. I was too tired. I remember feeling…it. He gave me something."

"Gave you what?"

"A pill."

"A pill? What kind of pill?"

"He didn't say, just made me take it."

"Was it blue and pink?"

"I…." Mía shook her head. "I don't know. I can't remember."

Mia's eyes filled with tears and Savannah hugged her. Mía broke into sobs. Savannah held her, the tears warm at the base of her neck.

Savannah pulled away and jumped to her feet. She needed to find a way out. Mía sat on the cot watching as Savannah inspected the walls, the ceiling, the floor. Except for the boarded entranceway, the two small ventilation pipes and the chimney in the ceiling, the place was solid rock.

But there were tools, including the axe she'd used earlier for shaving kindling. She didn't think she'd be able to chop her way out of here — the rock on top of the board was bigger than the hole itself —

but if she managed to wedge the axe's edge below the board and pry....

Savannah grabbed the axe and climbed up the ladder. The rocky mouth of the entrance was anything but smooth, and as she ran her hands along the edges she felt cool air wafting in from the other side.

Then she heard it: voices. Words and the sound of rocks crunching under approaching footsteps. Something scraped against the plywood. The board began to move.

11

Savannah dropped the axe and jumped down the ladder. She ran over to Mía and huddled next to her on the cot as the plywood flexed and lifted open, a beam of yellow light lasering down.

Teddy popped his head in, affecting a British accent. "Pardon me, would you have any Grey Poupon?"

He lowered his boots onto the ladder and Savannah noticed the axe on the floor directly below him. She almost made a grab for it, anxiously calculating her chances of getting there and back before he climbed down. She was still making up her mind when Teddy hopped to the ground, his back to them, arms up while Grandma handed down three packs, including the one Savannah had left up above in the first crawlway. Grandma climbed down the ladder, sliding the plywood board back in place above her.

Teddy's gaze fell to the axe straddled between his feet. "Hmm, now what did I tell you two about picking up around your room?" He whirled around, his eyes bloodshot. His skin was ashy and a red and purple burn wound ran from his right jawbone down behind his neck. A grin spread across his face.

And suddenly he was leaping toward the girls, long legs kicking through the cots. He snatched Savannah by her shirt collar. "What were you trying to do, run away from me?"

Savannah grasped at his hands, trying to pry them off her. "No, I...I was just—"

"Because I just don't think I could *handle* that right now!"

He shook her, teeth clenched, a capillary visibly bursting in one of his eyes.

"Teddy!" Grandma shouted. "Ted, you're hurting her."

He flinched, the words like a splash of cold water, and the grip loosened. He appeared momentarily bewildered, turning his head back toward his mother, then to Mía who'd scooted far away from him on the cot, her hands tightened into tiny balls in front of her face.

"Whoa, hey," he said to her. "Don't do that. It's okay. We're okay. No one's mad, not really. See?" He removed his hands from Savannah's shirt and pulled her against him, stroking her hair. Savannah smelled fuel and singed flesh. "See? Everything's fine. I'm exhausted is all. I'm sorry. Come here, Amelia." He let go of Savannah and reached for Mía. "You're looking better."

But Mía only squeezed further into herself, peering at him from over her fists.

He sighed, stood up and moved to the drinking water on the shelves. He unscrewed one of the red jugs and tipped it back. Mía sidled over to Savannah and sat down behind her. Teddy watched this out of the corner of his eye and lowered the jug with an, "*Ahhh*," then rolled his shoulder and winced, touching his burnt face. "I'm going to need your help with something, Savannah."

He slipped out of the duster and then his turtleneck, groaning as he did. Savannah's eyes went from the revolver on his waist to the bare flesh along his back. And bare flesh it was, a lesion the shape of South America seared through his skin, exposing the angry red muscles below.

Grandma reached her hands out for him. "Here, let me help you with—"

"No. I want Savannah to. She needs to learn how to do these things."

Grandma pulled back her hands as if they'd been slapped. She eyed Savannah and hovered a couple steps behind Teddy, unsure of what to do. Teddy rummaged through the supplies on the ground until locating a large white medical kit. He set it down next to an empty cot along with a water jug, then pulled a bandana from his pocket and flopped down on his belly.

"I'm dying here, Savannah. Give me a hand."

She realized he said it only as a figure of speech, but wondered if he really was dying. To have let a burn that bad go untreated for so long....

"What do you want me to do?" she asked.

"The med kit. There's some things in it. First though...." Grimacing, he propped himself on his right elbow. "We need to rinse."

Savannah picked up the water jug and Teddy slid further so that half his body angled out over the edge of the cot.

"That's it. Pour a little on there, let it run to the floor. Christ, did I underestimate the size of that blast. Didn't even feel the heat at first, just a hard wallop, like a train plowing into me."

Savannah poured a thin stream of water over the wound. It drizzled down the seared flesh onto the ground, pooling on the rocks.

"Okay, that's good." He dangled the bandana. "Now wipe at it, but for the love of God gently."

Savannah stopped pouring, set the jug down and picked up the bandana. She inspected the wound, a sour odor drifting up from it, and thought of pink hamburger saran-wrapped in styrofoam trays.

Grandma shifted her weight from one foot to the other, brow furrowed, wanting—*needing*—to help. She reached for the bandana in Savannah's hand. "Here let me—"

"No, Mom," Teddy said. "Back off a sec will ya? Go get some water boiling if you can't sit still. Savannah, it's meat and bones just like you got. You're going to need to learn how to do things like this. It's part of growing up."

Somehow Savannah doubted cleaning severe burns in an underground cave was part of coming into one's own, but she folded the bandana until it was three layers thick and wiped it along his flesh. Teddy buried his face in the pillow, scrunched a handful of bedding and gave a pathetic-sounding whine as a wad of soggy flesh bunched at the edge of the bandana, exposing more stringy muscles and a white swath that Savannah realized was a section of shoulder blade. The peeled-away flesh fell to the ground with a splat.

"*Jesus. Jesus.*" Teddy cried into the pillow.

"Sorry," Savannah said, looking to her grandmother who held in her hands a pot that she appeared to have forgotten all about.

"Okay. Okay." Teddy flopped back on his belly, turned his head to the side and let out a few deep breaths. "Open up the kit. There's going to be a few packets of burn gel, gauze, and some bandages."

She opened the med kit, took a seat beside him and began applying the gel. Grandma filled a steel kettle with water and, over by the stove, found what looked to be an old metal refrigerator tray. The tray had been snipped to size and Grandma fit it into the stove before setting the pot on top of it. She fed a couple more small logs into the bottom and closed the grate.

"It's your own fault, Ted," she said, her hands on her hips. "None of us were supposed to be that close when it went off. No one was supposed to get hurt."

"There was only so much I could predict, Mom. Man plans and God laughs, that's how it goes. But what does it matter? We got it done, and here we are, just like we said. Nothing's changed."

"People died," Grandma said. "Everything changes with that."

"The building was empty."

"I'm not just talking about the building. I'm talking about...your *friend*."

"Not my friend, never was. Trust me, whatever happened to him he had coming and then some. You don't even know. And I say 'whatever' because for all we can tell he may be still be alive."

"Still alive? No one could've survived that."

"We saw someone running through that parking lot. Savannah, you saw him too, didn't you?"

If he was referring to the shadowy form darting through the lot into the trees, an inferno at its back as Teddy squeezed off one exploding bullet after another, then yes, Savannah had. Not that she was going to admit it. Even if that man Shiloh had survived both a splash of acid to the face and the exploding water truck, what kind of life would that be?

And, more important still: what would he do to get even?

Grandma was thinking the same thing. "So what are you saying, Ted? That he's still alive? That'd be even worse. Does he know where we are?"

"What I'm saying is all's well that ends well. I feel like we've gone through this already. Here we've finally gotten to this point and Mom you can't seem to do the only thing left to do, which is *relax*. Jesus, just be grateful. So many worse things could have gone wrong, yet here we are—all four of us safe and sound. Take a look around. We've got everything we need and nothing we don't. Let's all just...*appreciate* that for a while."

Grandma opened her mouth and then closed it. Teddy was doing as he preached, gazing about the room with a contented smile on his face, and apparently Grandma didn't have it in her to argue further. A happy person can't always improve your bad mood, Savannah thought, but they can at least make you feel guilty about having one. Savannah continued cleaning her father's wounds. She observed his satisfaction and remembered what he'd said in the video recording she'd watched, about how he'd gotten used to being confined. Maybe this really was comforting to him, to once more feel imprisoned.

Then again, there was still the black revolver attached to his belt, the same one she'd seen devastate an office building six stories tall. The same one she'd seen on videotape, stuck inside his mouth.

Mía yelped and Savannah turned to see her tucked in a ball, staring at the cat sauntering over beneath the beds, his black nub of a tail pointing straight up. Teddy swung his head over the side of the cot and slapped the ground "*There* he is! Terror of the kingdom of mice and spiders! Come here big killer, tell me all about it."

And indeed the cat told him in a whole lecture of short meows that were more like squawks. He ducked his head under Teddy's palm and walked under it, letting the hand caress his spine before spinning back for more.

"Bet you two girls were surprised to see him, huh?" he said. "Has he remembered you yet?"

Savannah looked at her grandmother. "You said he ran away."

"He did run away," Teddy said. "Same as all of us. He's part of the family too, you know."

Savannah kept her gaze set on her grandmother. "You knew about this the whole time. Where...." She cocked her head towards her father. "Where *he* was. And those nights you left us alone.... All this time we were lying to the police and Miss Jill."

Grandma pushed her glasses farther up the bridge of her nose. She raised a finger, but before she could get a word out Teddy jumped in.

"Now don't go blaming your grandmother who's done nothing but love and support you girls. And *you* never had to lie to anyone, Savannah. Your grandma kept you in the dark so when the cops or the social worker or *whoever* asked about me, you could always tell them the truth, which was that you didn't know a thing."

The cat flopped on his side and luxuriated under Teddy's hand. Grandma smirked and looked at Savannah as if expecting her do just that, thank her.

"Come on now, let's get this finished," Teddy said. "There's some gauze and tape in that kit."

The wound glistening with the ointment, Savannah found the gauze and a tiny pair of sewing scissors. She cut the gauze into strips, laid them across his back, picked up a roll of athletic tape and taped the gauze in place.

Teddy shooed Tailypo aside abruptly and dragged out the duffel bag below his cot. "Hey, did you check out the rifle?"

Savannah tensed, pressing into his back, causing him to gasp. She'd forgotten he was lying directly over the bag, and, by the looks of it, she'd forgotten to zip it back up. She had indeed checked out the rifle, and if he knew that then he must also know what else she'd checked out.

"You remember Old Long Tom here?" He reached in and slid the rifle partway out of the bag—for her to see, she realized with some relief, rather than to accuse her. "Yeah, I suppose there's no such thing as forgetting this guy, not for you. Guess I should've started you off with something a little smaller that day, a twenty-two or something. I never did get to tell you that I felt bad about what happened, about your eyes and all. I was too busy getting this thing hidden away because they'd be wanting it. It's an antique and no way was I about to lose it, so instead I buried it. When they came for me I showed them an old piece-of-shit deer gun I had and said it'd been that that did it. They confiscated it of course and sent me away, and this ought-six made it two winters under the dirt before I was able to dig it back up. Still works like a champ, though. Now that you're a little bigger and your eyes are welded in place right, we'll have to try again sometime."

Savannah felt queasy.

Grandma scratched at her neck. "I don't know if that's such a good — "

"Because I'll teach you again, Savannah. It's good you keep getting experience with it while you're young. The brain absorbs the most important stuff in its early years, the things that stick. It's when you build all your foundations — your skills, knowledge, beliefs. Too many people grow up with shoddy foundations and are funny for it. You can always spot these people. They're like wobbly tables." He turned to Mía and winked at her. "How's little sister doing?"

Savannah looked at Mía, still curled up at the edge of her bed. "Okay. Better, I guess. She was really bad though."

"Yeah, but she's a warrior. Huh, Amelia? You're invincible. I got some Calvin & Hobbes books. You like those, right?"

"She had a seizure. I thought she was going to die."

The smile that had begun to form on Teddy' lips dropped.

Savannah told him about the trek through the forest, how cold it was, the fever. She told him of the long hours spent over her sister, exhausted yet too terrified to fall sleep, a hand on Mía's chest feeling her heartbeat.

"She looks okay now," he said. "You feeling all better, Amelia? You are, huh?"

"It'd still be good to take her to a doctor." Savannah said, then added: "Be good for you, too."

Teddy laughed. "We're a long way from the closest ER."

"Or even go take a bath. She's cold. We're both cold and really want — "

"Listen Savannah, doctors and baths might as well be on the moon, understand? We make do with what we have. If you only open your eyes to it, you'll see it's enough."

She'd finished the bandaging. Teddy pushed himself up and inspected it with Tailypo rubbing at his ankles. "And hey girls. I'm sorry I snapped, that I grabbed you, Savannah. I don't want either of you to be afraid of me. Starting now is when we start making up for all this time we've been apart. I'm going to make things right, for all of us, I promise."

Teddy took off his belt with the revolver still attached and put it in the duffel bag. He snapped his fingers. "Oh, I almost forgot. Look what I got us."

He rummaged through an arrangement of food along the floor. He stood up holding a six-pack of root beer and a silvery packet with an astronaut on the cover.

"Root beer floats. I've been saving them for this exact moment." He took a seat on the edge of a cot, motioning Grandma over to join them. He handed them each a can. At first Mía hesitated but Teddy teased, "You're saying I can have yours?" She took it. He cracked his own can to demonstrate, took a deep gulp, jammed his thumb into the mouth and — just like he'd done his impromptu tobacco spitter — peeled the aluminum wider. He set the can between his knees, opened the ice cream packaging and dropped a pink, white, and brown tablet into the can. A surge of multicolored suds foamed up and he sucked it down.

"This was a real nice surprise, Teddy," Grandma said as the others prepped their cans. "What do you say, girls?"

The girls mumbled their thank yous. They looked at each other. Since when did Grandma care about manners?

"*De nada*," he said. "And I see you got into the calorie bars. Not bad, huh? Wait till you try the Mountain Houses though. I got all kinds — lasagna, teriyaki, gumbo, scrambled eggs, the whole menu. Enough to last us half a year if we ration right."

"But that's not how long we're staying, right?" Savannah asked. "Half a year?"

He didn't answer. He scratched at the bandaging, grabbed a few more pieces of ice cream and plunked them into the girls' cans. Mía drank her can down in seconds and Savannah did the same. She felt the carbonation swell in her stomach, spark as it trickled down her throat. She burped soft and long. Teddy held his own up in a weak toast, sipped and gazed at Tailypo between his knees. His shirt was off, but he still wore the camo pants he'd started this whole adventure in, the cuffs of which were wet and ruddy. Savannah looked at the cuffs of her grandmother's pants — also soiled.

"Where are the horses?" Savannah asked.

"You mean ol' Ma and Pa mustang? Released from whence they came." He offered his hands up to all that encompassed them. "The mercy of the wild."

"They weren't wild." Savannah said. "They were still good horses. Can you get them again?"

"We won't need them again. Not if it all goes right. But technically, sure, we could still get them. There's plenty of rez horses around here, and half of them are so starved they run to you the moment they see you. Probably hoping you're its old master. Sad." Something registered in his expression and he clapped his hands. "Presents! I've got presents for everyone! Oh, and I want to film you all opening them."

12

If Teddy had presents, they were to make up for something. Savannah knew this from experience. The 'Don't Tread on Me' t-shirts were the best he could do to apologize for the time away in Leavenworth, perhaps even the things he'd done to get sentenced in the first place. But the stuffed turtle was the one that crossed her mind that moment as Teddy had all three of them turn their backs and cover their eyes. She saw his old present in her mind's eye as she listened to him unzip the camcorder case. Savannah had lied to him while packing before they left: She remembered the stuffed turtle just like she remembered throwing it away soon after. For although she was six years old when she received the gift, even then she felt it concealing something else.

When she was nine she had a pet box turtle named Flash. Savannah used to set Flash down in the driveway and let him roam, following him in and out of the sage. The turtle earned his name. One day Savannah turned her back for only a moment, and like that he was gone. She looked up and down for him, and two days later found him crushed near the end of the drive. Her father was the only one who'd gone anywhere recently in the truck. Savannah told no one about it. She buried her pet in secret. But her parents sensed her discovery. Teddy got her a stuffed turtle to make her feel better, but it didn't help. If anything it caused Savannah to wonder if her father knew he'd run Flash over. And if he did, did he know she knew?

The camcorder beeped. Teddy told them to turn around. Savannah turned to see her father cradling three small bundles of blankets, the camcorder strapped around one hand.

"I guess wrapping paper is one thing we don't have," he said. "But like I said, we're self-sufficient around here." He handed the top bundle to Grandma, the other two to each of the girls. He was careful not to shake the camcorder. Teddy stepped back and flipped open the LCD screen. "Go ahead."

Savannah felt her face flush, aware of the red recording light on the camera. She put her hand up to her face and turned to the side. "Why do you have to film this?"

"Why not? A lot of parents record their children when they're younger. I've missed the last seven Christmases with you. Maybe if I watch this seven times it'll kind've make up for all that."

"It's not Christmas."

"It is if we want it to be. It's not like anyone's going to stop us. In here we make our own calendar. So from this day forth let it be known, November sixteenth is Christmas time in Unserton!"

November sixteenth, Savannah thought. She remembered her grandmother making a movie of her own, shoving the cameraphone into Miss Jill's face and declaring the date the fourteenth. Was that how long they'd been gone, two days? She wasn't even sure whether it had gone by fast or slow. Already time had taken a new form, weakening as they retreated underground, like light penetrating water.

Off screen Grandma unfolded her own bundle, revealing a gold locket and chain. Savannah watched her grandmother open the locket, a smile at the corner of her mouth.

"Thank you, son," Grandma said.

"Welcome," Teddy said, keeping the camera focused on Savannah and Mía.

"You going to open your dad's presents or not?" Grandma asked.

The girls peeled open the blankets. Savannah pulled out a black leather case a little bigger than a candy bar. She ripped open its Velcro top and shook out a utility knife. The black gray steel unfolded into a pair of plyers—a menagerie of small blades, files, saws, and openers on the handles.

"That's going to be your best friend in here, Savannah," Teddy said. "After me."

Savannah looked into the lens of the camera, then beyond it into her father's face. His eyes met hers for a only second, then jumped free. He swiveled the lens closer onto Mía. "Okay, you now. What do we have, Amelia?"

Mía turned an olive-colored piece of felt over in her hands, and only when Teddy told her to put it on did Savannah realize it was a neck gator. The gator was long on Mía and bunched up along her neck, making her chin jut up.

Teddy laughed. "Keep you warm *and* make you taller."

"What do you say, girls?" Grandma asked.

The girls mumbled some gratitudes. Savannah wondered again about Grandma's sudden attempt at whatever-this-was.... *Motherliness*?

The camera beeped. Teddy closed the screen and put the device in its bag. "Things like neck warmers are good things to wear around the clock, girls. Savannah I got a scarf around here somewhere for you. It's easy to pay so much attention keeping your head warm you forget about your throat and chest, equally important. But I make it sound like it's going to get colder in here than it is. Even without a fire, on the coldest day in January, our little casa here will never drop below fifty-nine degrees. That's the constant temperature of earth at this level, give or take. The stove can turn this place into a sauna if you don't watch it."

"This place is perfect," Grandma said. She looked tired.

Teddy looked down at himself, his burned and bandaged torso, the wet grimy trousers. "What a fucking day," he said, tottering a step, looking woozy. "I could go for a wash."

He went to work collecting supplies: soap, rags, a gallon jug of water. Grandma opened the grate on the stove and pulled out the kettle, steaming now. Teddy told her to start dinner as he set his supplies somewhere behind the black curtain at the end of the chamber. He reappeared and gathered a change of clothes, stepped back behind the curtain and drew it all the way closed.

"Play a game, girls," Grandma said. "Occupy yourselves."

Dutifully—if only to try and distract themselves from the sloshing, drips and sharp inhalations taking place behind the curtain—the girls ripped the packaging off a dusty checkers box. Grandma opened a carton of dehydrated food and selected one of the mylar bags inside. She tore the bag open, carefully poured the hot water inside, and resealed it. She stood with her back to the girls, massaging the bag, warming her hands against the softening meal inside. Tailypo lay curled atop Teddy's duster, which was heaped on the floor by the stove.

Mía reached her hand over the board to make the first move. Savannah grabbed it and mouthed the words, "I'll get you out."

Mía eyed the curtain and Grandma, then nodded.

As softly as she could, keeping her eyes on the board, Savannah whispered, "First we have to pretend—"

"Hey," Grandma said. "Don't do that."

Savannah and Mía looked at her.

"No whispering. We watch one another's backs, not conspire behind them."

"I was only asking how she was feeling," Savannah said.

"So why whisper it?"

The sloshing noises behind the curtain had stopped, and Savannah saw a finger nudge the cloth aside. Teddy's eye peeked through the gap. Savannah and Mía concentrated on the rest of their game in silence.

Teddy reemerged in a fresh pair of camouflage trousers and a black sweatshirt. Grandma opened the food pouch, poured soupy scrambled eggs into four cups and passed them around. There was a slightly sweet scent to the eggs that reminded Savannah of her school cafeteria breakfast. She wondered if it was indeed breakfast time there, and if so what her classmates were doing. Did they know about her yet, about what she'd been involved in? Had a big assembly been called, like the time those twin brothers in the grade ahead of her— what were their names, *Something* and *Something* Bukowski—died in a freak avalanche during a weekend ski trip? Savannah recalled the principal leading the school in a moment of silence, and afterward all the kids gathering in cliques to swear to one another they were actually really close to the twins. She remembered a few girls sobbing at their desks so that their friends could stand around them, similarly teary-eyed, the teachers handing out Kleenexes before gently announcing it was time to get on with the day's lesson.

Was all that kind of attention now on Savannah and Mía? She doubted it. For one thing, the girls weren't dead—or at least no one out there could believe that yet for sure, not without bodies. And for another, it wasn't a tragic accident the girls had been involved in. It was an act of terrorism.

Rather than summoning tears for Savannah, her classmates were most likely comparing rumors, spreading them until they mutated like sinus infections. Some students might even be questioned by the police. Savannah could practically hear Sarah Atkinson insisting the two weren't friends, not since she'd realized what a whacko Savannah was.

The four of them ate. The meal hadn't completely rehydrated, and Savannah chewed through crispy bits of egg. Still, her appetite resurrected the moment she closed her mouth around the hot fluffy morsel. She downed the rest of her half-cup's worth in a single gulp.

Teddy scraped the inside of his cup with a finger, tilted it back and tapped the last few remnants into his mouth. He lowered the cup and hiccupped. "It's not about keeping your mind occupied, that's not what's key to getting by in here. It's about distracting yourself. And learning to swap your sleep patterns. Not just your schedules, but how long you do it. I can seriously sleep sixteen hours and be awake only eight, the exact opposite of how you're used to doing it. And it's beautiful, girls. I promise, you will come to *love* sleep. It feels weird now, I know, not seeing the sun. But your body adjusts, and you'll find you function just as well without it. Actually, your senses grow stronger. It's fine we have the lantern on now as we get used to things, but pretty soon we're going to have to start saving power. Once you get the feel of this place you'll know how to get around it for days without ever once turning a light on. There are plenty of living things, mammals included, that get along with no or little light. Oh, and that reminds me, no more feeding the fire for a while. During sunup we let it die. We should be asleep by then anyway."

As if to emphasize his point he yawned, stretched out his hands and cracked his knuckles. He poured a splash of water into a brown plastic tub, collected the four cups, dropped them in and squirted a jet of dishwashing soap into the water. As he cleaned, he discussed the chores that needed to be done, the responsibilities they would all have.

This included the regular assignment of scrutinizing every nook and crack along the walls to inspect for evidence of critters, lifting up and shaking out bags in search of mouse droppings and spider webs.

"Tailypo keeps a tight patrol, but still, you won't believe what gets in here. More than once I've had a pika, those squeaky little mountain squirrels. Another time I woke up one morning, put my foot in my boot and felt something like a staple go into my big toe. I pulled it out and a fucking wolf spider the size of a silver dollar fell out of the boot. I was lucky I had on thick hunting socks, but it still hurt like a son of a bitch. Does it bother you girls that I swear?"

Savannah and Mía shook their heads.

"That's good. You both can cuss, too, if you want. How many dads you figure say *that* to their kids?"

He grinned and fake-punched Savannah in the shoulder. "For now though, everything can wait." He yawned again, then carried the lantern over to his cot, where he set it on the floor and crawled into his sleeping bag. "We've got all the time in the world."

Grandma, taking the cue, sat on the cot next to his and began untying her boots. Savannah put the board game back in its box, watching her grandmother shimmy into her sleeping bag and kiss Teddy's bearded cheek. "We did good out there, Ted. Despite it all, we did good."

"I know," Teddy said. He looked at the girls. "You two ready for lights out?"

"When can we go outside next?" Savannah asked.

Teddy turned his head away and closed his eyes, his face serene. "You're both going to know everything you need to. But for right now...." He reached his hand down and turned off the lantern, darkness swooping in. "Rest. Let's all just close our eyes, not think about a thing."

13

Savannah lay awake for a long time. She listened to the rustling of the sleeping bags and watched the grated patch of firelight play along the ceiling. Eventually the tendrils of sleep wrapped around her and, despite a half-hearted fight against them, pulled her under.

When next she woke, the fire was dead and a new light bounced around the room. It was a dim, alien-looking green light. Savannah craned her head up and saw the light emitting from a headlamp. It was strapped around her father's head as he rooted through one of the backpacks, pulling out something boxy and mechanical-looking. He flipped a switch and the device made a loud clicking sound. She watched him open one side, unfold a crank which he turned slowly. After a few rotations, he tried the button again. This time static hissed through a tiny speaker, and a numbered interface lit up blue. He set the radio on the ground and spun the dial. The digital station numbers climbed higher, but there came only static.

The beam of the headlamp pitched up into Savannah's face.

"You awake?" Teddy whispered.

Savannah nodded, shielding her eyes.

"You still want to go up top?"

Savannah turned toward Mía, still asleep.

"Leave her, let them both sleep," Teddy said. "We'll just you and me go."

Leave Mía? Her heart constricted at the idea. And yet, the very thought of fresh air — of the outside world — was irresistible. The more she considered it, the more she needed it. Besides, it wasn't like she'd be leaving her sister alone. Mia would be with her grandmother, and judging by Grandma's light snoring and Mía's half-open, drooling mouth, the two wouldn't even notice.

Savannah realized she'd already made up her mind. She slipped out of her bag and got dressed, making as little noise as possible. Teddy picked up the bear traps, steel jaws dangling by his shins. He tucked the radio under an arm. He'd replaced the batteries in Savannah's MagLite, and she clicked it on before following him up the ladder—peeking over her shoulder one more time at the sleeping forms of her sister and grandmother. Teddy pushed the board aside and climbed out. He reached a hand down for Savannah. She accepted it, letting her father pull her straight up and out of the chamber in one effortless curl. The bandage ruffled inside his sweater. But if there was any pain his face didn't betray it. He moved like a man wholly unburdened of pain.

Savannah found her footing and looked around, breathing in. The air in the upper tunnel felt cool, refreshingly absent of the smoke and smells of the one below—scents, Savannah realized, she'd ceased to notice until now that they were gone. Compared to the tomb-like capsule they'd just exited, this upper tunnel with its high ceilings could have been the open sky itself.

Teddy replaced the piece of plywood and lifted his head to shine his lamp around the cavern. He clicked a button and the headlamp went from green to unfiltered. This newer light was brighter, although it still rendered weakly against the vast darkness at the ends of the tunnel.

"It's really something, isn't it?" he said. "To think all this was created in just a matter of days, if not less."

Savannah thought about that, and something about it didn't sound right. She seemed to recall learning caves took something like thousands of years to form, millions perhaps for one this size. She wondered if her father was all of a sudden talking religious—that or else trying to distract her from something else.

"I'm not sure if that's true," she said.

"Oh it's true all right. I've read about places in Hawaii where you can actually stand right at the edge of a lava flow and see these things solidifying before your very eyes."

"Lava?"

"Well, yes. This is all one great big lava tube, Savannah."

She studied the walls, which were formed of the same charcoal-like stone she'd seen scattered about the forest on the way up here. *Lava rock*, of course. It swirled in places along the walls, flowing in neat cuts and gutters on either side of the floor. She thought of the roof of the chamber below and how it looked melted, like it had dripped.

"They're all over this part of New Mexico," he said. "A lot are still covered and haven't even been discovered. At least so they say."

He dropped the bear traps in a heap, picked one out and placed it near the lower chamber's entrance, just a couple paces beyond the plywood square. He pried the jaws apart, the veins in his forearms bulging in the light of his headlamp. When the jaws were all the way open, he lifted the circular plate at the center until the trap clicked, then carefully moved his hands away and stood up.

"Our own tube is pretty big," he continued, picking up the other three traps and moving farther down the cavern. "Complex, too. I've explored it from end to end and would say it's at least a quarter mile, and that's just counting the parts we can fit into. There's a collapse at the north end that I just couldn't squeeze through, but shining my light between those rocks I could tell it keeps going. I also suspect there's more to the second level. Our little room down there is just the only part with access. When the lava surged, it burst into new channels and sometimes multiple stories. If we were to somehow slice this whole section of earth in half and pull it apart, it'd probably look like a giant ant farm with all these different tunnels and levels."

He bent down and set a second trap, this one about twenty feet from the first. Savannah thought about the illustrated map she'd happened upon in the duffel bag, the question mark at the end of one tunnel....

She caught up to him. "So this upper level, it just runs straight before closing off? You said there has to be a, what, an outflow, right?"

"See that's what I thought. I've walked all around up top for miles looking for it and never found a thing. My guess is it collapsed in on itself and is overgrown now. The roofs to these tubes are super thin and it's amazing how, with time, Mother Nature will take back just about any soil. Thirty-foot pines grow above this rock. If you go farther down that end," he shined his headlamp and pointed, "you'll actually see roots dangling from the ceiling right before the tunnel becomes a dead end. But trust me, don't go *too* far down that way."

"Why not?"

He lifted his nose. "Smell that?"

Savannah stepped a little closer, sniffed. It was that stench of sewer she'd caught a whiff of when first entering the cavern.

Teddy smiled. "Our toilet bucket isn't bottomless, you know. And when it needs to be emptied, there's a nice little cliff down along there, very convenient. It's where I toss our trash, too—our own little dump."

He chuckled, moved farther along and set another trap. "The other end does go nicely for a while, but you don't want to go too deep there either. Not unless you want to wake up a whole mega-colony of screeching bats."

"Bats?"

"Hundreds of them. Here, we can go down just a little bit. I'll show you."

"No, that's okay. I believe you."

He laughed. "It's not like they're all going to wake up at once, start flying around in your hair, try and suck your blood. That's just a myth. These are just little guys in hibernation. Probably won't even know we were ever around."

He started off in that direction. Savannah, not knowing what else to do, followed. She didn't think it possible, but suddenly the cavern was feeling too big, and in the enveloping darkness she couldn't help sensing a thousand blind eyes and tiny pink ears following her every move.

She jumped as her father stopped and hissed, "There. Right there, look."

She darted her gaze in every direction, cowering without realizing it. As if the bats were about to swarm in on her all at once.

"Do you see them?"

She looked in the direction her father pointed, scanning the area along the roof where his headlamp shined, but saw only rock. She shook her head.

"Two brown dots, right in the center," he said, keeping his light steady.

She could have looked at that spot a hundred times without noticing anything funny. But sure enough there they were: two round and tiny spots like moles on the cave's ceiling. They were upside down but not exactly hanging like she'd been expecting. Instead they seemed to *suction* to the rock, their little bodies bunched beneath furry wings.

"Those guys are pretty far out from the rest of the colony," he said. "Usually they're all much farther down. Wait 'till it gets warmer. In July you can sit outside the cave right at sunset and see them all stream out like infinity. The sky will turn black with them, these giant screeching clouds that swirl and pulse before they all fly away. It's really beautiful."

Teddy lowered his light from the ceiling and looked at Savannah. He put a hand on her shoulder, gave it a gentle squeeze, then continued back the way they'd come. Savannah didn't follow him right away. Instead she stood there, watching him, feeling nostalgic as well as a little sad. This was how she remembered her father—or rather what she had forgotten about him. He was an interested man who had once enjoyed sharing with Savannah all the things he knew, read, or in some cases experienced. She remembered him telling stories and pointing out certain small miracles in nature. He enjoyed doing this for her, and Savannah enjoyed it in turn—attracted to the curiosity her father showed life. It wasn't a life that had treated him well, nor one he had always made the best of. But despite all that he could still recall something like an outflight of bats at sunset and remark with sincerity upon its beauty.

They moved farther down the cave, stopping below the tumble of rocks and the small portal above it through which a pale beam of starlight shone through. The natural light seemed so rare and precious

Savannah was almost reluctant to disturb it. The wind rushed overhead, the entryway whistling like breath over the mouth of a glass bottle.

He climbed up the rocks without setting the trap. A few icicles hung from around the skylight and Teddy broke one off and bit off the end, crunching it between his teeth. The radio under his arm, he formed an upside-down cradle with his hands and signaled for Savannah to step in. She put a hand on his shoulder, lifted her foot into his hands and let him boost her up. Once more she found herself squeezing through the narrow crawlway, the jagged rocks cold as she scraped along them, wriggling as fast as she could to the surface in a race against her own terror of getting stuck. Her head popped above ground and she ripped her arms free, pulling herself the rest of the way out.

Climbing to her feet, she was instantly struck by the wind that rocked her sideways. The air up here was bitter cold, shocking in its crispness. The back of her throat ached breathing it in. She stared up at all the light of the stars exploding between the clouds, the treetops immense, trembling shadows. The whole forest around her was a chorus of cracks and groans with the swaying trunks. Savannah felt tiny, vulnerable. After being trapped underground, the earth seemed to have grown bigger in her absence, all but overwhelming.

She turned to see her father shimmying upward out of the hole with his hands above him, resembling some perversely functional take on the dance move called The Worm. Being more than twice as large as her, she was amazed he could not only fit through the entrance, but in fact make it look easy. He stood up, brushing off his trousers at the knees. He put his hands on his lower back, bent and cracked it. "Feels good doesn't it, the fresh air? Perfect example of not appreciating what you got until it's gone. It's why I believe every single person should spend at least some part of their life locked up, just to learn the things they take for granted. Folks waste thousands of dollars on therapy because they get these depressions and midlife crises and emotional breakdowns they can't explain. Well fuck therapy I say, go to prison. Just a few months is all it takes. You'll come out and colors will seem brighter, the sun warmer, the stars…" he held his hands out in display "…multiplied. Everything you need, you all of a sudden have."

"Is that why you're keeping us down there?" Savannah asked, allowing some cynicism into her tone. "To make us more *grateful*?"

"First of all, I'm not *keeping* you down there. This is just a place we're staying in at the moment. Is it different than what you're used to? Sure. But what's wrong with that? Take a look around, Savannah. Not a city light or telephone pole or strip of asphalt to be seen. No car horns or annoying neighbors. Families come up better in nature, away from everything that only pulls them apart. And so if our time here makes you better appreciate not just your things but your family, then yes, I suppose that is my intent."

He clicked off his headlamp and told her to do the same with her flashlight. She did, her body becoming another invisible form on the dark earth. It would be so easy to slip away right now, tip-toeing over the rocks and through the trees. He wouldn't even know she was gone until it was too late. But where would that get her except stranded and alone? And where would that leave Mía except abandoned?

No, this wasn't the time for escape. If anything, Savannah suddenly wanted to stick close to her father. To actually prolong this moment with him. She didn't know whether it was because she'd left the chamber and was now in the emboldening freedom of the outside world, but she no longer felt so afraid. Her father was talking honestly, and she sensed it was because he spoke only to her. Was he so mysterious and imposing a man that she felt just a little bit privileged to have all his attention to herself?

"Mía is afraid of you," she said. "She thinks you want to get rid of her."

He had the radio in his hands, holding it skyward so he could see its buttons. "She said this to you?"

"Yes." The wind howled through the trees, fanning Savannah's hair around her face.

"I don't know what you're talking about."

But his voice lacked conviction, and any sense of contentment Savannah may have been entertaining was abruptly checked. She wasn't going to mention the story her sister told her about the night before they left, about how she was drugged. Something about bringing that out into the open seemed…dangerous.

"I seriously can't even imagine why she'd think that," Teddy said. "Maybe I was never as close to her as I was you. But hell you've got to remember I didn't meet your sister until she was already five years old, and even then just for a couple weeks. Sure, I'll admit that when I first heard she was born I couldn't help resenting her some. How could I not? It wasn't her personally I was resenting, just the *idea* of her. I understood your mother wasn't going to wait around for me once I got sent away. Shoot, she was running around with someone else when we first got together. But for her to all of a sudden be *pregnant* again, and so soon…. Don't take this the wrong way Savannah, but you're lucky things turned out the way they did with your mother. We all are."

Savannah's teeth began to chatter. She wasn't cold, at least not from the wind. She'd never heard him talk about her mother directly like this. Not since what had happened.

"Why?" she asked.

"Well, not to burst whatever happy bubble you might have about us, but your mom didn't marry me out of love. She didn't even do it to stay in the country like everyone said behind our backs at the time. Camila married me because of *you*. I was ready to fight tooth and nail that you grow up here, as were my rights. Unfortunately, I lost a lot of those rights in Leavenworth. Lost a lot of my fight too, for that matter. Your mom knew this, and when Amelia was born the only call I got from your mom was to tell me she was filing for divorce, that once it went through she'd be taking you two with her back to Colombia. It wasn't going to be easy for her. Wasn't even going to be altogether legal. But Camila was ready to break the law if she had to, no doubt about it. Too bad that little boyfriend of hers had to get behind the wheel fully loaded, and too bad she didn't know any better than to get in the car beside him. She was a foolish woman, your mother. But in the end it was that foolishness that saved us."

In the darkness Savannah listened to him spit and wipe his beard, as if what he'd just said tasted as foul as it sounded. All this was news to Savannah. Her mother had never said anything about going back to

Colombia, and neither had her grandmother. She wondered if Grandma had ever even known, whether her daughter-in-law had ever told her she was preparing to leave with the girls. Savannah wondered if Teddy, and now she, were the only two people in the world who knew.

"I don't like talking about these things," her father said. "And I do it now just to say I decided a long time ago I'd care for Amelia as if she were my own. Being around her more now it'll get easier to do that. It's not blood that makes a family but what they do together to survive. Here we have the ultimate chance to learn everything there is to know about one another, no secrets or grudges or little alliances. Our biggest danger up here is us turning against one another. If we can avoid that we're going to do just fine. Who knows, we may even have a little fun."

He spat again, and stood for a moment in silence. Then: "I'm glad we're getting this all out now, Savannah. As long as you feel it settled I'd prefer we not bring it up again. But, if it'd make you feel better, I can have a word with your sister."

Savannah imagined him leading Mía up to the surface on a late-night stroll, telling her things.

"I'll talk to her," Savannah said.

"With me there, though. Remember, no secrets or teams among us."

This seemed hypocritical, considering where they were and what they were doing at the moment, just the two of them. Not that Savannah regretted it, knowing how it'd eat her up inside to be the one left below. Moreover, she wasn't sure she wanted her sister to know everything her father had just revealed anyway.

So they'd be hypocrites together. "I don't think we need to say anything to her," she said. "She's okay."

"Good. That's reassuring to hear." He swept the ground with his boot and took a seat. Setting the radio in his lap he flipped a switch. Once again the blue interface lit up and this time there was a scramble of music crackling in waves under the static. He opened the short antenna, held the radio a little closer to the sky and tilted it, aiming for a break in the clouds. He scrolled through the frequencies, fuzzy chatter and the occasional blurred song popping in and out of the radio's single speaker. It hung for a second on a country song, one Savannah recognized with lyrics about "chilling in the back of a four-wheel drive" and "tailgate dancing." She still had a magazine with the song's singer somewhere in her bedroom. Or did she? Was her room ransacked by now for evidence? Savannah didn't like that idea, of having literally nothing as she left it, and she was glad when he changed the radio's channel because she could feel the song and its feel-good lyrics being soiled.

A few more bumps of static, followed by a loud, angry beep. More like a squawk, one that fell silent, then squawked again, sustaining. The noise died and in its absence a fog of static rose that Savannah recognized even before the voice emerged — the robotic announcer who always sounded worlds away and alone. It was the emergency alert system. She'd heard it countless times on the tv and radio, usually to announce freak weather.

"New Mexico State Police have issued — "

He abruptly flipped the radio off. Reaching into one of the large cargo pockets along the side of his pants, he felt around until pulling out what looked like a coil of white string. He untangled it, and in the pale light she recognized her earbuds. He squeezed them into his ears, plugged the cord into the radio and turned it back on. For a long moment he sat listening, saying nothing, the sounds of his quickening breaths all that Savannah heard between gusts of wind.

Finally he sighed, switched off the radio, recoiled the earbuds and returned them to his pocket. Still seated with the radio in his lap, he put his hands on the ground behind him and reclined, looking skyward. Savannah followed his gaze to see the moon peeking between dark clouds.

"You know there are lava tubes up there," he said, "on the moon. Mars has them too, formed almost exactly like ours did here. Some say that's how we'll start to colonize Mars, by taking shelter in those tubes. Wild, huh? And here I thought I had all the good ideas."

He stood and said they'd better get back down. Savannah followed him. Directly below the skylight entrance, they set the final trap.

14

With no clock and only the irregular glimpse of the outside sky, the family gauged time by the dull routine of the chamber: the eating of meals, the drinking of water, and the use of the toilet. Between the four of them the toilet bucket filled up at a vulgar rate, and Savannah came to dread every tightness in her bladder and bowels, associating it with the unavoidable trip behind the curtain and the stench awaiting on the other side — a stench so thick and humid it seemed to coat the inside of her nostrils and the back of her throat like a glaze. The Poo Powder solidifying mix only seemed to add a starchy element to the smell. Teddy showed them how to use "the washing machine" — the bucket with a plunger sticking out of the lid. Half-filled with water and detergent, they dropped their dirty laundry inside and took turns plunging up and down. Yet no matter how fresh her clothes were or how rigorously she bathed herself with the cold wet rags, Savannah knew she reeked. And it disgusted rather than relieved her to find that she was gradually growing so accustomed to the stink of the chamber that she noticed it less and less. At least her father insisted upon being the one to empty the toilet bucket, hiking up the ladder with it swaying from one hand, the wire handle stretching dangerously with its weight before he disappeared up top to slosh the contents over that precipice in the upper cavern, the "Dump".

To minimize these trips as well as to conserve their water supply, each member of the family was relegated to three glasses of water a day. The first glass came in the morning when they woke from the longest of their numerous sleeps, and a breakfast of sorts was served, usually oatmeal or a calorie bar. A few hours later they drank a second glass of water, and this would be lunch. Finally, near the end of the day, the stuffy air of the bunker filled with anticipation for the preparation of supper. Here the meal options, while never complicated, were more diverse, and all four stood before the wall of dehydrated foods discussing it like a bookshelf. More than once they gathered spices, jars of stewed vegetables and cans of meat and, their stomachs groaning as the pot simmered, boiled a stew. They sipped with these dinners one final glass of water, then cleaned the dishes and brushed their teeth. With that, the day was over. The lantern would go out, the fire left to die, and each one of them fell silent in their sleeping bags. At this time it often occurred to Savannah how it might very well be a bright morning sky high above and, upon thinking about this, it would then take her hours to fall asleep.

It didn't help that, as her father had predicted, she slept so much otherwise. Both she and Mía took long naps while curled up on top of their sleeping bags, blankets pulled up over their faces. Despite being limited to moving no more than from one end of the bunker to the other, Savannah grew more and more tired. She dragged through chores, reanimating only for meals. She found herself using her utility knife often, just like her father had suggested, although less as a practical tool and more a source of whimsy — bizarre scenarios playing in her head as she fingered the knife's small blades. Most other times she sought distraction in books and board games, or simply lay on her back and stared at the ceiling — thinking of different ways to pose the questions she'd already asked, chief among them being *how much longer*.

She observed the same lethargy taking root in her sister and grandmother. Whole days passed without Mía saying a word, and Savannah couldn't tell whether her sister was giving up or trying to be invisible. After her trip to the surface with Teddy, Savannah had decided their best approach to gaining freedom was patience. Endurance. At least that's what she told herself. Whether it be due to weariness or uncertainty, truth was the escape Savannah had promised her sister had somehow lost its urgency. Mía must have sensed Savannah's resolution, or lack thereof, for she never brought the subject up. Not that the girls were ever afforded the chance to have such a conversation; if Teddy wasn't in earshot, Grandma invariably was. And so, unable to talk privately with Mía, Savannah made constant attempts to engage her in games—checkers, Connect Four, Yahtzee, dominoes, Go Fish, War—or else beautification, which was pretty much limited to creative hair-braiding. The games inevitably grew tedious, and the hairstyling—without anyone to show off to—pointless. Still, Savannah continued these pastimes, if only to keep intact some solidarity with Mía. To remind her sister that they were in this together.

Finally, one day while Teddy was behind the curtain and their grandmother napped, Savannah penciled the words, *Tell me what we should do* on the back of Mía's Yahtzee scoresheet. Mía read it, peeked at the closed curtain and wrote, *Get us out.* Below that, Savannah wrote, *How?* But just as she was turning the note around for her sister to see, Teddy's belt buckle jangled and Mía snatched the paper, crumpled it up and tossed it in the stove.

Grandma slept more than any of them, and rarely got off her cot unless it was to use the toilet or help with some chore. She sat up to take the meals and water cups Teddy handed her, like a child taking medicine in bed. She began to talk to herself, muttering under her breath as the other three glanced at one another, embarrassed.

Teddy on the other hand remained fidgety. His burn slowly scabbed over yet continued to seep red pus that turned the bandages soggy and required constant changing. The wound itched, and he kept looking for things to distract him: organizing and reorganizing shelves, taking things apart and putting them back together. He chewed tobacco non-stop, spitting into what was apparently the designated cup. He pinched the wet plug out from under his lips whenever he was done with it, putting it back in its can so he could get another couple chews out of it later. He brushed Tailypo daily, piling the clumps of black hair and then disposing of them in the toilet bucket. He even cleaned the cat's teeth, rubbing a small cotton pad dabbed with toothpaste across the animal's yellow fangs.

Once Savannah woke to feel something pressing against her back and was surprised to find Tailypo curled up with her. The instant her hand alighted on his fur however, Tailypo sprang from his sleep and sank his teeth into the soft spot between her thumb and forefinger. He disappeared into the darkness, and it was the last Savannah tried to pet him.

They burned all the trash they could, and what they couldn't burn Teddy disposed of with the sewage. He ventured to the surface alone, filtering water or collecting wood or placing the battery-charging solar boxes. He took his revolver with him every time and was never gone for long. When he climbed back down he'd talk of elk droppings or bear tracks or a rabbit scurrying by. He said soon they'd begin supplementing their diets with wild game. How soon he never specified, though Savannah could see the food supplies dwindling.

Teddy talked relentlessly, and Savannah got the feeling it wasn't because he had so much to say but because he didn't like silence. Usually it was long blather, rambling tangents made while inspecting some gizmo or picking at the scabs on his back. He held forth on how to make a whistle out of an acorn cap, different brands of hunting knives, or the under-appreciated presidency of James Polk. He reminisced about the family and insisted upon memories Savannah knew to be false.

Still, between the ramblings and fibs, Savannah preferred all this to the *stories* Teddy told, all of them aimed seemingly at scaring her. He went into great detail relating the predator attacks that had occurred in the area: the backpacker mauled by a black bear, the fisherman killed by a cougar, the cross-country runner whose foot had to be amputated after a rattlesnake bite. He described the lava tubes nearby in The Malpais National Monument where bodies from unsolved murders were stashed. He told of the vast, featureless plains of lava rock that swallowed backpackers and mummified their corpses.

One night, while the four of them stood brushing their teeth following a particularly talkative supper concerning this latter story, Savannah got to thinking about lava and caves, and she remembered something her grandmother had said the night she'd brought them up here.

"How come there aren't people exploring this place?" Savannah asked. "What's to stop, like, a regular hiker from coming in?"

"Nothing really," Teddy said, "except the fact we're on the Tonola reservation and it's illegal for anyone other than a Tonola to set foot anywhere around here without permission."

"But Grandma, you said the Indians have reasons for keeping people away from here. What reasons?"

"It's because the Indians believe —"

Teddy held his hand up. "I got this, mom. It's because the Indians believe this is a sacred place. The Tonola are well aware of these tunnels, but they won't come anywhere near if they can help it. And they don't talk about them either, especially to outsiders. They keep it a secret. We're one of the very few people in the world who know about this place."

"How'd you learn about it?" Savannah asked.

"Cellmate I had."

"What makes it sacred?"

"Some think this is the birthing place of all the Tonola people, their point of origin." He rubbed his hands together, getting into it. "In the story, the Tonola came into this world after the gods decided to destroy their old one. One of the gods took pity on some of the people there and, wishing to see them live on, opened a portal in the sky leading to a new dimension where the people could start over. The people climbed up through this sky portal and through the ground of the next plane. Tunneling...," he smiled, pointing along the length of the chamber's ceiling, "... until they broke the surface and spread across the earth, forming new clans and ways of living — some more in tune with nature than others. To the Tonola this is already the fourth world they've been given, and this one too will eventually end. Some of the other Pueblos around here have similar creation stories. To the Hopi their birthplace is called Sipapu and is hidden somewhere in the Grand Canyon. They keep the exact location hush-hush, just like the Tonola. Although unlike the Tonola the Hopi still take pilgrimages to their place while the Tonola won't come near. When the Tonola abandoned their old world, they left behind a dark dimension of angry gods. A place of monsters."

He put a hand against the rocky wall, as if feeling for a heartbeat. He looked at Savannah. "To the Tonola, this system of tubes is no Calvary to pray around. It's a Chernobyl, meant to be quarantined."

Savannah thought about this. She imagined the tunnels going even deeper and recalled the feeling of being watched she'd experienced in the upper tunnel. She shivered at the thought of other creatures living within these dark corridors of stone. "What are the bear traps for, if no one *dares* come in here?" She tried to sound incredulous, even though she wasn't.

"Just a precaution in case someone does," Teddy said. "Someone like me who might've heard about these tubes when he wasn't supposed to and wants to check them out. This whole area, even up top, is an archaeologist's wet dream. No matter which direction you walk you're bound to stumble into Anasazi ruins, most of them unexcavated. It's really something to see, these old ruins with pottery shards still scattered all over the place. I've explored a few, even spent some nights in them just for fun. I like old, undisturbed places. I can always feel the souls who were there before me: The Ancient Puebloans who built the ruins, the later tribes that ransacked them, the early cowboy who found those few remaining walls a nice place to rest along some journey. You start to wondering if all of them felt the same thing, the souls who came before. Or, for that matter, if the ancient civilizations that built the original structures sensed things in reverse. Like when they crawled into their covered kivas for their vision quests—when they sat before the fire meditating, breathing in all that smoke, on the edge of death. Do you think any of their visions showed them a big bald guy with a beard, his mom and two little girls making a home in one of their caves? What would they make of such a picture? It'd be alien."

"I think some things they'd understand," Savannah said.

"You may be right. The further you go back in history, the better humans understood the things that mattered. The Anasazi were all kinds of attuned. Some of them built elaborate cities aligned with the stars. At Chaco Canyon you can still see petroglyphs of a supernova from a thousand years ago, the one that gave birth to the crab nebula. Can you imagine that, this big weird light that suddenly appears in the sky, even in the daytime, and lingers there for two years before just as quickly winking out? Combine that with all the drought and enemy invasions happening around the same time and how could the Anasazi *not* think the exploding star was an omen, a sign to abandon everything they'd built?"

Savannah didn't answer him. Tailypo appeared out of nowhere, sat on the floor beside Teddy's cot and looked up at him. The cat's nub of a tail twitched like a dying fish.

"Think about this," Teddy said. "A race of aliens living a thousand light-years away. If they were looking at one of those ruins I'm talking about right now through a super high-power telescope, you know what they'd see?"

"What?" Savannah said.

"The people building them. That's how light speed works. They'd see the Anasazi going about their business, the rest of the earth's civilizations still unaware of this entire continent. And as the planet spun the aliens would watch the Crusades scroll by, followed by some Chinese emperor of a once-upon-a-time dynasty. Who knows, maybe at this exact moment the aliens are readying a message for the Anasazi and all the rest of the planet now long, long dead."

"I like that," Savannah said.

"What, the idea of a message from the past?"

"The idea of everything being watched."

Teddy chuckled. "You are wise beyond your years, child-o-mine." He reached down and picked Tailypo up into his lap. "And for that I am both proud and afraid."

Savannah became aware of a scraping sound. She turned to see her grandmother sitting fully upright on her cot, grinding her teeth.

Teddy noticed her too. "What is it, mom?"

"The person who told you about this place, this cellmate of yours. Who is he?"

Teddy stroked Tailypo, and the cat looked up at him in pleasure. "You all met him. 'Twas none other than our good friend Shiloh."

Savannah's heart quickened at the mention of his name, the ironic tone her father gave to the words "good friend."

"He was a Tonola?" Grandma said.

"Oh no, definitely not. Shiloh's Navajo, although technically he doesn't belong to any one particular tribe. Not anymore."

"Because he's dead?" Grandma said.

"Because he's persona non grata, a pariah."

"What do you mean?" Savannah asked, aware, like her grandmother, of Teddy's describing him in the present tense.

"I mean he's been cast out. He went down a path and his people turned their backs on him. Go down that road, and you don't have a people anywhere."

"What did he do?"

"It's not just what he did, it's what he *is*."

Teddy pet the cat in silence, drawing out the moment, the suspense, or else debating how much to say—Savannah couldn't tell. He shooed Tailypo off his lap and scooted around to better face them. "You hear the Indians out here talk a lot about preserving the old ways, the traditions, languages and the like. The Navajo language was close to dead in the forties when the Windtalkers used it to help us win World War Two. It's come back some since then, but still, more and more kids on the reservation are growing up speaking only English.

"On the other hand, there are some places deep in the deserts and canyons between here and Arizona where the old ways are alive and well. These families—or clans—are rare, but they do exist. They might put up steel fences for their livestock or start fires with matches or, I don't know, smoke a Marlboro from time to time, but you won't find televisions or radios inside their homes, or even electricity for that matter. They won't use paper money if they can help it, usually just trading instead. And they'll take a horse over a truck any day. In many ways they're like the Amish, except they're not much for farming and would probably prefer to roam if the whole goddamned country wasn't fenced in. I'll tell you what the real wild thing is about these last few stalwarts. There are some that to this day speak *only* the Navajo language."

"Shiloh was one of those…those Amish-type Indians?" Savannah asked. Her skin prickled saying the name out loud, as if doing so had just committed her to something. It felt wrong to be discussing him. Dangerous. Capable somehow of giving away their position. Of attracting attention.

"That's right," Teddy said. "Shiloh was brought up what you might call a *fundamental* Navajo, I suppose. When I first met him he still didn't speak a lick of English. Our first month together in that cell was spent mainly in silence. Just a hand gesture or grunt every so often. But unfortunately for Shiloh, prison isn't the desert where you can disappear and be who you want all by yourself. In prison you adapt or you die, and that's no exaggeration if you're in there with a charge like his. Even the small Diné Pride faction didn't want him. And the sad truth was Shiloh wasn't ready to rely on someone other than himself. It's a good thing then that he got me for a bunkmate."

Savannah studied her father, his broad chest, his shoulders — burnt as they were — built like a linebacker's. Even sitting down hunched he had the presence of a giant. Or better yet, since he now lived underground and only came out at night, a troll. Either way, she knew first-hand how powerful he was, the violence inside him, and had always pictured him being an intimidating figure in prison. She could only imagine the ways he might've protected Shiloh.

"He learned English then?" Grandma asked.

"And me some Navajo. Not a whole lot. Neither one of us ever got exactly fluent in the other's language, but when you're stuck with someone in a ten-by-twelve block of concrete for twenty hours a day, sooner or later you get to talking."

"And you guys became close?" Savannah asked.

Teddy shrugged. "As close as you can get to a guy like that. Shiloh isn't exactly what you look for in a pal."

"Why'd he go to prison?" Grandma asked. "You said before that what you did to him he had coming. What crime did he commit?"

Teddy looked down, began to fiddle with the zipper on his sleeping bag. Savannah thought it might be the first time she'd ever seen him at a loss for words.

He cleared his throat and gave a weak laugh. "I actually think it's worth admiring how he lived like that out in the desert, all in tune with the land. With his ancestors. It's terrible what he did, but it wasn't his fault. It was society's. The modern world. For almost twenty years Shiloh got by out there just fine. In a lot of ways Shiloh was real capable, skilled even. He could shoe a horse or build a shed or, after some practice, play a decent game of chess. He could understand the basic rules of the chess board, figuring out how all the different pieces moved and interacted with one another. Thing is, something about him never could seem to understand the basic rules of *people*. In prison I saw him take food off other guys' trays, cut in line, piss in the courtyard — none of it done out of bad intent exactly, but simply because the piece of food looked tasty, or because he figured one spot in line was as good as any other, or because, I don't know, he had to piss. At first I thought he had a death wish, or else that he didn't know any better given the way he was brought up, being isolated and all. But the more I learned about him the more I realized he'd always been that way — oblivious, even while tucked away out there on the desert. Actually, it was because he couldn't think ahead and didn't know what consequences were that he got into his mess.

"He lived with his folks, a grandpa, a little brother and a baby sister — all of them bunched together in one little house. Shiloh was the oldest of the kids, going on twenty when his baby sister was born. The family raised sheep and goats, most of which they traded off to a cousin. The cousin drove this old pickup, and whenever he came for sheep they loaded the animals straight into the back. As far as I could tell, these rides with his cousin were the only times Shiloh ever left the ranch. When you think about it, that old sheep truck probably represented everything Shiloh thought of the outside world: fast, powerful, loud.... It's easy to believe then he became fascinated with it, that truck.

"One day, when his cousin wasn't looking, Shiloh carried that baby sister of his — he never did tell me her name, probably never told anyone — out of the house and into the truck. He told me that at first he just wanted to show the vehicle to her, see if someone else found it as incredible as him. But when she only wriggled around on her back on the seat next to him, looking a little sleepy, he decided she needed the full effect. So he started the engine and put the truck into drive. He'd seen his cousin do it a hundred times over the years, and the moment the truck jolted forward he said it just felt natural. Before he knew it, Shiloh was cruising down the dirt road away from the house, his baby sister bouncing in the passenger seat beside him.

"He didn't admit this to me, but I'm sure that never once did it occur to him what he was doing, where he was going, what would happen. He probably never even glanced in the rearview mirror. He drove from one dirt road to another, connecting to the highway which he then took all the way to town. He said his sister was having fun— whatever that means I don't know, maybe just that she wasn't crying or anything. Whatever the case, here's this Navajo boy who's likely never seen more than fifty people together in one place all of a sudden surrounded by civilization. All the lights and the sounds and big buildings…. He wasn't scared though, or at least he didn't say so. If anything he was probably thrilled.

"And thirsty, apparently, because just as he got to the edge of town he decided to stop. He said it was the Coca-Cola logo beneath the grocery store sign that caught his attention, that he'd recognized it from the cans of pop his cousin would sometimes bring. He didn't have any money when he walked inside, so right off the bat he walked into trouble. And he had to have been on-edge already getting out of that truck, his little vessel in this strange town. It must've seemed the safest place to him, because when he entered the store he left little sister in the cab.

"This happened in mid-September, not exactly a hot time of year in northern New Mexico, but certainly not cold either. It doesn't take much to turn the cab of a two-passenger truck with a lot of windshield into an oven. On a seventy-degree day all you need is ten minutes for the inside of a car with the windows up to reach ninety degrees, another twenty minutes and it's at a hundred-five. The day Shiloh's baby sister died it was close to eighty out and she'd been in the cab more than an hour by the time they got to her. What's worse is that it wasn't even Shiloh's fault, not entirely. The second he walked through the doors of that store the manager was on him, following him around the aisles, figuring Shiloh drunk or a vagrant or whatever based on his clothes and the bewildered way he must've wandered the aisles. The fight came when Shiloh finally stopped before a wall of soda, tore open a case and started chugging a can right then and there. The manager tried telling him he had to pay for it first but of course all this was gibberish to Shiloh. All he understood was the blame in the man's face, the other folks all circling around. It was so much that when the manager tried putting a hand on Shiloh's shoulder, Shiloh cold-cocked him.

"He made for the exit, the entire store in a hubbub. And who knows, things might've ended right there with no more damage than an opened pop can and a cracked cheekbone if it weren't for the good samaritan customer who tackled Shiloh at the last second, holding him with a knee in the back until the squad cars arrived. Of course, not a single person in the grocery store that day spoke Navajo. And never did the police stop to consider whether this belligerent, dusty young soda thief had arrived in a vehicle, let alone if anyone else was still in it. Not until too late. By the time they finally got to her, the poor thing had pulled out most of her own hair."

The fire in the stove had almost died, leaving just a few dim embers. Savannah could see their breaths in the lantern light.

Teddy scratched a thumbnail down the zipper of his sleeping bag. "It was a tough, tough go for Shiloh after that. There's no worse charge to walk around prison with than child abuse. Guys don't care to hear your side of the story. It's not something you can laugh at or brag about like just about every other dickbrained crime that might've sent you there. In prison an abuser is an abuser. There's no degrees of offense. You got a target on your back everywhere you go. Still, I don't think that's what ultimately pushed Shiloh over the edge. Shiloh had a tolerance for pain that amazed me, just like it always amazed the guys dealing it out. So no, violence didn't do in Shiloh, and neither did being ostracized. Really, Shiloh held it together pretty good in prison. It wasn't until he got out that he finally cracked. When his family renounced him."

"I'd do the same," Grandma said. There was a lull after this that seemed to emphasize the heartlessness of the statement.

"Yeah, maybe," Teddy said. "Thing is, Shiloh really loved his family. They looked after him, and I don't think he quite realized just how much until it after it all happened. He was especially fond of that baby sister, probably because she was someone for *him* to look out for. When it turned out he couldn't though, that he didn't, he just as well died."

"So what'd he do after jail?" Savannah asked.

"He wandered," Teddy said. "His family shoved him off with nothing but the cousin's old sheep truck. No one had bothered trying to sell it, almost as if the truck was cursed and kept specially for him. He accepted it like a punishment, a penance, and disappeared into the desert for three-and-a-half years. When I finally managed to track him down he was almost unrecognizable. By then he'd finished his…*transformation*."

Teddy coughed. He got up and poured himself another glass of water—his fourth of the day, Savannah couldn't help but notice. He returned to his cot and gulped down the water. He looked straight at Savannah and said, "You ever hear the one about the man driving through Navajo Reservation late at night, that long, deserty road on the Arizona side of Four Corners? Man's driving along when he sees two gleaming eyes appear in his headlights. A coyote, just standing by the side of the road, watching him. But when the man pulls up, expecting to pass by, the coyote starts running beside him. Running *fast*, like sixty miles per hour, right there keeping even outside the passenger side window. The man's watching this flabbergasted, and when he takes his eyes away one second to glance at the road, next thing he sees running out there is a full-grown man. A man with the same bright coyote eyes. The thing starts banging on the side of the car. The guy driving is freaked, puts the pedal to the metal. For nearly a mile the thing stays right there with him, banging on the car, until finally it starts to fall behind. The last thing the man sees, looking at his rearview mirror, is the creature changed back into coyote form, its eyes fading in the taillights."

Teddy shot his hand out and grabbed Savannah. She jumped and he started to laugh. She didn't think it was funny though, and no one else appeared to either. Savannah thought there was something familiar in the story he told. It sounded like one she'd heard before, either at school or perhaps even from her father years earlier.

"The thing that changed from a coyote into a man," Savannah said, "it was a—"

"A *skinwalker*," Teddy said. "The Navajos have their own name for them, but they hardly ever utter it. The whole subject is taboo."

"What are they?" Savannah asked.

"Witches, bad ones. It's said they've been around for hundreds, if not thousands of years. I've heard that they started with a curse by the Anasazi, which just so happens to mean 'ancient enemy' in Navajo, and that to this day these skinwalkers sneak onto forbidden Pueblo land to conduct rituals in the old ruins."

"What else do they do?"

"Shapeshift, a lot like werewolves only they can turn into more than just one creature: wolves, coyotes, cougars, foxes, owls, crows. Most people won't even touch those kinds of pelts on the reservation. That's why some believe skinwalkers came about during the time of Kit Carson and the Navajo Long Walk, that a desperate, starving few began transforming themselves into animals in order to escape. I've heard that they can also mimic voices perfectly."

"Your friend does all this, changes into animals?" Mía said, surprising them all with her voice. Once more Savannah couldn't help hearing the use of the present tense, and for the first time asked herself what Mía must be thinking of all these stories. Of what she might remember about the man who'd reached into the cab on that gray, sick morning to feel her pulse.

Teddy looked up at the ceiling and chewed on a thumbnail. "I don't know about the shapeshifting part or what all they're really capable of. But I do believe in skinwalkers. I witnessed Shiloh become one."

"What do you mean?"

"I mean it's not just about the shapeshifting. It's a way of life. You choose it. That's another way skinwalkers and werewolves are different. Werewolves have the bad luck of getting bit. Becoming a skinwalker is intentional. You have to do something unforgivable for your people to cast you out. Only then can the transformation really start. Not physical transformation either, more of a spiritual one. It's a path that only takes you deeper as you vow more and more of yourself away to hatred or revenge or gloom or whatever other negative force drives you until all that's left inside is black energy. And black energy, if practiced and focused, is a powerful energy. It's a path there's no turning back on. After prison, after he lost everything, Shiloh retreated into the desert to walk that path. And he's walked it ever since."

"But can he really change into things?" Mía said. "Like… monsters?"

"That's not what's most important. What's important is that if a man *devotes* himself to an evil, he gives that evil existence."

It was quiet. The last flame in the stove shrank to nothing and died, a waft of smoke pouring out from the grate like the ghost of that flame. All four of them turned to look at it, watching the smoke spread out along the rock ceiling.

Grandma cleared her throat. "I can't decide if you really think he's still alive or not, Ted."

At this Teddy laughed, clapping his hands. "Ha! And here I thought it was the girls getting goosebumps with all these campfire stories. Turns out Grandma's the biggest chicken here!"

"I don't see what's so funny about it," Grandma said. "It doesn't bother you there might be someone out there who *knows* where we are?"

"I didn't say he knows where we are. I just said he was the one to tell me about this place. And he did it a long time ago too and has probably forgotten all about it by now. I never told him this was where we were going to hide out. And even if I had there's no safer place for us than these caves so far as Shiloh is concerned."

"Why?"

"Because he won't set foot inside them. He'll go on Pueblo land and desecrate their ruins, but this…." He held his hands out. "This *Sipapu* is farther than he's willing to go. It scares him, bad juju."

"So you're saying he *is* still alive?" Grandma said.

"I didn't say that either."

"You seemed pretty damn sure it was him you were shooting at before we drove away."

"And you seemed pretty damn sure it was a deer."

"Okay, so once and for all Ted, which one was it?"

Teddy strained to keep an expression of amazement as he looked at his mother, struggling to continue making a joke out of the whole argument. Savannah didn't know whether her father truly believed everything he'd just described. But, in the frustrated, childish, way he rolled his eyes, turned his back and then climbed into his sleeping bag, she realized he had finally talked his way into a corner.

"Teddy..." Grandma said.

He reached over and flipped off the lantern.

They all remained still in the darkness, not saying a word. After a while Savannah fumbled her way into her own bag. She lay awake for a long time, trying to decide which was more stupid: believing her father or not believing him.

She got her answer a few hours later when the noise of a zipper drawing open startled her and she looked over to see him lying on his side with the headlamp muted in one hand, the other rummaging through the duffel bag below his cot. Savannah didn't move a muscle as she watched him pull out the Wrathful Judge. He flopped back over, lay the gun on top his stomach, and turned off the light.

She didn't believe every story that came out of his mouth. The trick, she decided, was figuring out which ones *he* believed.

15

She spent most the night turning in her sleeping bag, trying and failing to redirect her spiraling thoughts. Finally Savannah fell into a restless half-sleep that seemed capable of only skimming the dream world. For while Savannah indeed dreamt, she dreamt that she was underground in the chamber. In the dark. In her sleeping bag. Except something was off. Someone, or something, new was inside with her. It was in her bag. Small and hairy and crawling along her bare calf. A tarantula, she realized. She tried to kick, except her legs wouldn't move and besides, the spider was stuck inside the leg of her sweat pants. It crawled up her, slow and confident, its countless eyes like black suds. She felt the creature elongate and flatten against her bare leg, and suddenly it was no longer crawling but slithering. The spider had become a snake, its forked tongue flicking against the inside of her thigh as it moved higher, absorbing her skin's heat into its own cold reptilian body. Again Savannah tried to squirm and scream herself awake, but all of it in vain. The snake ducked its head below her panty line, its dead scales scraping away on the elastic trim as its tongue continued flicking.

Savannah groaned and opened her eyes. She jolted up into a sitting position and batted at her lap. She reached inside the sleeping bag to feel her crotch. Wet.... Warm....

Blood.

She wanted to die.

When Grandma had told her to pack everything they needed, Savannah had never even considered the box of Tampax below the bathroom sink. And with everything that had happened since, she hadn't even thought about her period. When was her last one? Something like a week before they left the house? Had they really been here in this black pit for three whole weeks?

Either way, here she was, sitting up and bleeding inside her sleeping bag. In utter darkness.

Savannah squirmed out, felt around on the ground until locating a bottle of water. She grabbed the bottle and — stepping lightly, one hand out in front of her — made for the curtain. She slipped behind it and used the water and one of the strips of cloth to begin cleaning herself.

There came the rustling of bedding on the other side of the curtain and Savannah froze. A pair of socked feet hit the floor and a headlamp clicked on, flooding Savannah in a dull green light as it filtered through the curtain. Savannah pulled her sweatpants back on as her father tiptoed over.

"Everything okay?" Teddy whispered.

"Fine."

"Are you not feeling well?"

Savannah considered how to respond. She was revolted by the idea of discussing her period with him. But at the same time, what if he had something stored away for just such an occasion? Something she hadn't happened upon yet.

"Girl problems," she whispered.

A pause, then: "Shit."

"Get Grandma."

"I didn't realize you...that you — "

"Just go get her. And please will you start a fire? I'm freezing."

"It's about to get light up there. I don't want smoke to — "

"Pleeeease," Savannah groaned. She was on the verge of crying.

Teddy hesitated, lurking outside the curtain. Finally, he turned and plodded back to the cots. There were whispers and a shuffling of sleeping bags. Savanna heard the grate on the stove squeak open, twigs cracking. One of the plastic clothing bags crinkled, and after a moment Grandma came over and handed a change of clothes around the curtain. "Sorry we don't have anything for it, Savannah," she said. "Your father forgot."

"Forgot?" Teddy hissed a few feet behind, moving over from his place by the stove. "You never told me!"

"She's fourteen. What'd you expect?"

Savannah cramped, dense throbs in her abdomen and the discs of her back—already achy from the cot. The insides of the open toilet bucket clearly hadn't been treated with Poo Powder in a while. Savannah tucked her nose into her collar, wadded two cloth rags between her legs, and delicately hoisted up her underwear. She had the sensation of viewing herself from a distance—from outside her body, as if her mind was succeeding somehow in drifting into away oblivion.

"You were in charge of supplies for things like…that" Teddy hissed at his mother. "You weren't thinking!"

"You're never thinking!" Grandma fired back, and Savannah caught a brief silhouette of the woman's arm flailing. "You give them to me to raise their whole lives. And then when you're ready I'm to just…*debrief* you on their lives. You said you had everything covered. All this was your plan."

"It might be my plan but it's your mess."

"What does that mean?"

"Means you gave us no other choice than this when you lost the property, the only real thing to our names."

"No, Teddy, *you* lost that property. That was mine and you bankrupted me. I could've kept it. I had my own plan."

"Would that plan involve getting the lenders, all the goddamn gas company men, to get up on the roof and fix the tv antenna for you?"

There was a smack, thick like a piece of raw steak hitting a tile floor. Then it was quiet, save for the crackling fire in the stove. Through the curtain Savannah saw the still light of her father's headlamp, her grandmother's heaving silhouette. She heard something scraping on the ground and looked down to see Tailypo's two green eyes gleaming up at her. He was sitting on his sandbox.

Teddy cleared his throat. "Sorry. I didn't mean…. I'm just…flustered is all. Going a little bat crazy perhaps. You didn't force us into this and neither did I. MWR is why we're up here, not that we didn't leave them limping on our way out."

"This isn't even about the property for you," Grandma said. "It never was, admit it. Tell me the truth."

"The *truth*? But don't you already know it, Mom? Haven't you already found it out? All this is about *freedom*, what else? How else could we all four have had it — together in the same place, at the same time?"

"This isn't freedom," Grandma said. "Not for me."

Teddy scoffed, started to say something but then stopped. Savannah saw his headlight swivel onto her, hold a moment, fall away. Then: "I think we need to get some fresh air. All of us. We need to do a wash."

Savannah felt a tingle of anticipation move up her spine at the prospect. She pushed the curtain aside and looked at them both expectantly. Grandma didn't say anything, but Savannah knew she wasn't going to turn down an opportunity to get out of here, no matter the excuse. After being cooped up this long, who in their right mind would? And they were all still in their right minds, weren't they?

They bundled up, Savannah helping Mía into her camo suit and boots. Teddy put on his black duster, unbothered apparently by the burn hole along the coat's back. He removed the plunger from the laundry bucket, resealed it and beckoned Grandma who took the bucket from him without saying a word. He gave the bleach bucket to Savannah, buried his nose in the crook of his elbow and peered under the third bucket's lid. He quickly closed it.

Teddy set the bucket at the base of the ladder and collected the empty water jugs, some blue dishwashing gloves, and a black nylon pouch that he gave to Mía. He unzipped the duffel bag below his cot, pulling out the camcorder case and the 30.06 rifle. With both of these slung over his shoulder he climbed up the ladder. Grandma followed after him, stopping in the middle, and the girls worked together to lift the buckets one by one up to her so she could then pass them on to Teddy. The toilet bucket was last, and there was a brief but terrifying moment as Savannah held it over her head when she felt sure, by the law of calamity governing her life now, that it would spill. But her muscles held, her grandma grabbed the bucket, and Savannah climbed from the chamber feeling like she'd cheated fate.

Smoke rose from the chimney and swirled about the upper tunnel. At this point it almost didn't seem real, not just the fact they were about to step foot in the outside world, but that the outside world still existed. Anymore it was about as real as one of Teddy's stories. Sure the world beyond this chamber felt more vivid, what with Savannah's past memories of it providing color. But that didn't make it feel any less unattainable. In her confinement, the outside world had become abstract. And what was another abstraction, Savannah thought, amid so many more: memory, imprisonment, freedom, loss, fear...? What was one more made-up thing when her whole life no longer seemed real?

Teddy and Grandma wore headlamps, and every time they came upon a bear trap, one of them would hold the light on it so the girls could safely hike around. They followed Teddy into one of the dark ends of the tunnel where he stopped before a ledge and sloshed the contents of the toilet bucket over. He poured the sudsy water from the laundry bucket into the first bucket, swished the water around, then tossed that over as well. They moved onward to the skylight where Teddy delicately picked up the fourth bear trap, the one directly below the opening, and set it aside. By the time they wriggled to the surface only a few stars remained in the sky and the eastern horizon was a dull gray on its way to blue. The air was calm but brittle, and Savannah felt her boogers freeze.

There was a sense that nothing had changed in the world, that indeed the earth had stopped turning when Savannah left it in order to wait for her. She thought of the old tree falling in the forest paradox, and considered that perhaps life above ground didn't exist when she wasn't there to experience it. If she was the center of her own universe, what happens when that universe abruptly caves? Do all those outer layers go dark, almost like a refrigerator light?

Savannah pondered this as they hiked downward this time. She felt like she was moving about within a dream, as if she were watching herself from afar. She wondered if it was the fresh oxygen, giving her a buzz. The two bristlecones shrank in the distance behind them, and they dropped down an embankment to a creek bed. The inside of the ravine was a glimmering chute of ice. Teddy stomped on the ice. It cracked and he kept stomping until finally a chunk fractured and dropped into the trickling water underneath. He kicked the hole a little wider and then took the black pouch from Mía. Unzipping it, he pulled out an aquamarine water pump coiled within two long rubber tubes. He dangled one of the tubes into the creek and the other into a jug.

He looked up at the sky as he pumped. "It's hard to believe we're not the only ones in the world."

No one replied. It seemed to be what they were all had been thinking. The water squirted in rhythmic jets against the inside of the jug.

"Maybe we are," he continued. "For everything we know all of civilization has been wiped out by a freak solar flare or some terrible epidemic and we're mankind's last living family. I don't know about you three, but I for one would love that. First thing I'd do is move you all into a big mansion somewhere, probably on the beach...."

"One of us should think about going down and doing a supply run," Grandma said. "For Savannah, you know. Plus, there's other things we forgot. Nail clippers would be nice. Cigarettes, more bandages and ointment for your back. And I don't know if you noticed but we're running low on food."

"I got us enough food to last half a year." Teddy said.

"No way is that enough food for half a year," Grandma said. "Not for all four of us."

"Shh, keep your voice down. And don't shine your headlamp up like that."

"It's something we got to fix sooner or later, Ted. All I'm saying is one of us goes down with a backpack, fills up and comes right back. It wouldn't take forty-eight hours. And if you're worried about getting recognized or something, I don't mind being the one to go. They won't be on the lookout so much for an old woman. My hair's grown and I could even take off my glasses. I'd leave the girls with you and—"

"You'd like that wouldn't you?" Teddy said. "Unload them on me and then run off. Probably run to the closest police station and spill everything in exchange for a plea deal. Send me right back to a prison cell where I belong, right?"

"That's not what I'm saying at all! I got just as much guilt on my head as you. But that doesn't change the fact we're down to less than a dozen dehydrated dinner packs and a couple boxes of calorie bars. Even counting whatever few jars and cans might be around we got two weeks left *at best*. And you know it, Ted."

He stopped pumping and looked at her, then at the girls who were both shivering. He handed the pump to Mía, the girl's eyes poking from out of her hood, and said it was her turn, that it would warm her up. He turned back to Grandma. "No one's going anywhere," he said. "We stay together. If it really comes to it, I'll start hunting for food, but only after things calm down some."

"So you say," Grandma said. "Thing is you can't hunt these woods for tampons, Ted. We're not you. We're not used to living like you. These are little girls you got. There's a limit to what you can ask of them."

The water overflowed from the container Mía pumped into, and without instruction she pulled the tube out and inserted it into the next container and continued pumping. The act made her look capable, something Savannah regretted in that particular moment as it seemed to contradict her grandmother's point.

"No one's going anywhere," Teddy repeated. "We stay together." He waved his hands in front of him to show that the conversation was over, then turned his back to his mother. He kicked at the ice again, stomping down along the shoreline until a large swath had opened up. A hooting sounded overhead and all four of them jumped, looking up to see an owl gazing down from a tree.

Teddy chuckled and shook his head. "Getting a little late for you to be out, wouldn't you say?" He spoke quietly, as if to himself.

But the owl didn't answer. Teddy passed out dishwashing gloves, and they rinsed the buckets and the laundry. The water was painfully cold. Savannah had to look at her hands to know whether she was holding something. While cleaning the bucket of bleach and its soiled rags, she lost her grip on one of the cloths. It darted downstream below the ice.

Teddy glowered at her. "That's the sort of thing that gets us in trouble, Savannah. One little shitrag found floating downstream."

She felt her cheeks grow hot. Mía kept her head down, working steadfastly. Savannah supposed this should be reassuring, that her sister's sudden ability was a sign that she'd made a firm decision to survive. Nonetheless, the sight of Mía scrubbing beside Teddy — concentrated and seemingly unaffected by the aching cold or even the scolding her sister had just received — filled Savannah with a heavy sense of loneliness. And like many feelings of loneliness, lacing it was a thought Savannah didn't want to face: the idea that maybe she wasn't needed. Even by her little sister.

Teddy unshouldered the rifle and fiddled with the combination trigger lock. The lock popped open and Teddy stuffed it in a pocket. He leaned the rifle against a tree, kneeled and set the camcorder pouch before him. "You girls have grown up spoiled," he said. "You've always had clothes on your backs, a roof over your head. You don't know what it's like for food not to be just a few steps away in the kitchen. Neither of you has ever known hunger. Not *real* hunger. And with so many teachers and social workers and cops buzzarding around you there's never been a chance for you to feel unsafe, nothing that's forced you to protect yourselves. It's getting worse and worse, not just with you but with everyone, adults, too. You look back at how we evolved, how our ancestors always had to be alert and how they were constantly being forced to take risks. They had to, or else their clans would die. Famine, weather, invasions, you name it — there was always something keeping them sharp. Well all those instincts that put the human race at the top are now dulling. There's nothing keeping our senses sharp, no risks being taken. Comfy in our sofas and office chairs, we're losing touch. Losing touch with the things that make us strong."

He removed the camera from its pouch and slid his hand through the strap. He told the girls to take off their gloves.

"What are we doing?" Savannah asked.

With his free hand, Teddy picked up the rifle and held it out to her. "Take it."

Savannah put her hands behind her and stepped back. She shook her head.

"You can't be afraid of this just because of one bad experience. You do that and you surrender your power to it. It's just like getting right back on a horse that bucks you."

The expression evoked only a weak throb of *déjá vu*, a faint memory of someone in her distant past saying the same thing about something else entirely. But all that was obscured by the power of that rifle, forever imprinted in her brain and against her shoulder which tingled suddenly with the muscle memory of that stock kicking like a mule. The horrifying moment when the curtain had fallen over her eyes.

"There's no need for that, Ted" Grandma said.

"Put out your hands," Teddy said to Savannah, and the way his eyes went dead told her he wasn't going to say it again.

He held the rifle out and she accepted it with a grimace, as if it were something contagious. The gun was heavy and ice-cold. The trigger lock was gone.

Teddy stepped back and opened the side monitor on the camcorder. It beeped as he pressed record.

"This is unnecessary, son," Grandma said. "It's just…wrong. Let's go back inside."

"You were the one who said we needed more food," Teddy said. He looked up until his headlamp illuminated the tree branches. The owl swiveled its head at them. "Take the shot, Savannah."

Savannah shook her head and held the gun out for him to take. "I don't want to."

"Yes you do, you just don't know it." He made no attempt to take the gun or even push it away. Instead he moved behind her. At first Savannah thought it was to get both her and the owl in frame. She was surprised when his big arms came around her and guided the rifle into position.

And, just like that, everything was exactly like it had been that day in the desert more than three years ago. His scent thick and earthy in her nostrils. His chest warm and strong like a brick wall in the sun.

And of course, the rifle: heavy and solid. It scared her, yes, but at the same time it....

It *aroused* her.

After all that had happened, she'd forgotten the gun could have this effect. Recalling it now she wondered whether this was what it felt like to do drugs. The elation before the destruction.

Yet still she resisted. "My hands are too cold."

"You got to be able to adapt to every condition, including the cold."

"I don't want to shoot an owl."

"No, but you heard your Grandma. She's worried about whether we got enough to eat, so from here on we take all the food that presents itself. People have gotten by on much worse."

"This is just stupid," Grandma said. "Last thing we need is a busted collarbone or that girl to go blind again. Savannah, don't listen to him."

The beam of light disappeared from the branches. There was a scuffling of feet, a cry of surprise, and Savannah turned just as Teddy grabbed his mother by the front of her coat and threw her to the ground. She landed hard on her stomach.

"Tell my own daughter not to listen to me?! Whose side are you on?"

Grandma lifted her head, her glasses sideways on her face and smeared with dirt. Her eyes squinted and her mouth hung open with her lips sucked over her teeth in a sort of soundless wail.

Teddy whirled back around and raised the camera, its red light shining. "Take the shot, Savannah."

"I don't want to."

He reached over her, put his thumb on top of the safety and flipped it off. "Shoot that motherfucker."

His words came out in a cloud of breath that floated and dispersed in the beam of the headlamp. Grandma stood and wiped herself off, tears rolling down her cheeks. Mía waited far off to the side with her hands over her ears.

Savannah looked up at the owl, its eyes fixed on her, burning like twin planets in the light.

She pulled the stock tight against her shoulder and widened her stance. Peering through the scope, she saw a blur of branches and a murky blue sky before focusing on the owl. At this close distance, the bird was magnified to the point Savannah could make out individual feathers, the black spots within the hazel. She hooked her finger over the trigger, acknowledging somewhere in the back of her mind both the final second of the owl's life as well as hers as she knew it once this act commit her further to the man who ordered it.

Without thinking twice, Savannah squeezed the trigger.

The barrel jerked wildly upward. She felt something tick. No bang, no kick. Just the steely clack of the firing pin.

The gun was empty.

Teddy burst into laughter. "Jesus did you flinch! That bullet would be straight above us right now! Whooooweee, we've got some work to do, Savannah." He pressed the pause button on the camcorder and took back the rifle. "Shoot an owl, what an idea! Then again, for all we know that's Shiloh perched up in that tree." He laughed harder, opened the bolt and retrieved a handful of cartridges from his pocket. He slid them into the magazine and reinserted the trigger lock back in place, clacking it shut. Teddy slung the gun back over his shoulder and set a hand atop Savannah's head. "Seriously though, I just wanted to see if you were capable. I'm going to have to train you all over again, but it's good to see you've still got the foundation. 'Cause that's what matters." He turned to his mother who stood glaring at him from over the top of her glasses, her head down and her mouth pursed. "See, Mom? And here you were getting all upset over nothing."

They rounded up all their items, Teddy chuckling to himself every so often. He led them away from the creek, back to their hole in the ground, and as they marched, buckets in hand, Savannah could feel the satisfaction radiating off him. She trembled uncontrollably. There was nothing she could do to stop it, not with the deep cold and the lingering nerves of the rifle. Not with the hairs on the back of her neck standing under the gaze of the owl somewhere in the darkness behind.

They were a few steps in front of the entrance when Teddy abruptly stopped. They all did. Teddy turned around and looked up to the sky, his lips parting. And for one brief, unabashedly hopeful moment Savannah thought he might be experiencing some internal failure, like a heart attack.

But then she heard it. Slowly she turned, following his gaze heavenward. From out of the east, far below the treetops as if from the rising sun itself, came the thick *whup whup whup whup whup* of a helicopter.

16

The helicopter soared into sight above the trees, black with blinking red and white lights. Teddy ran up and tossed his bucket into the hole, sending it ka-thunking off the rocks all the way to the floor below. He waved for the others to follow.

"Get in, get in!"

Grandma jumped in first, followed by the girls. Teddy dropped in behind Savannah, his boot heel swinging out and smashing her in the forehead. She saw a burst of stars and fell, landing on Grandma.

Savannah gathered herself, dizzy, and stood up. The four of them grouped together around the collapse of rocks, the only light that of the bleak early morning pouring down the skylight. The helicopter was almost directly overhead now, its roar filling the cavern like some invisible physical force that drilled into Savannah's ears and shook her bones. She kept expecting the sound to fade, for the helicopter to move on, but the noise and the helicopter lingered, hovering.

"The hell they doing?" Teddy said.

"Looking for us?" Grandma asked.

Mía coughed and Teddy scowled at her. Then he sniffed it, too: "Jesus, the smoke!"

The light swirled with it, a white haze twisting upward in the skylight beam as if trapped in a bottle. Savannah hadn't even noticed it at first, but now that she did it seemed to be everywhere in the tunnel, floating up from the chimney in the lower chamber.

Teddy flipped his headlamp back on and hurried to the chimney. He ripped off his duster, folded it over on itself a few times and draped it over the chimney top. After that he grabbed a few rocks and placed them over the two ventilation holes.

"That's why we don't make fires during the day," he said, glaring at Savannah.

"The helicopter's still up there," Grandma said.

"What am I, deaf?" Teddy picked up the rifle, turned his headlamp off, and looked up at the skylight. "They're spotlighting, but I don't think they've seen the smoke yet. The sun hasn't risen so it may just be dark enough. This time of the morning there's a chance it's Game and Fish."

"Game and Fish?" Grandma said.

"Department of Game and Fish. They might be doing a game count — elk or deer, maybe even bighorn sheep."

"So they're not looking for us?" Grandma said.

"I didn't say that, just that it's a possibility. Either way, guaranteed every law enforcement agency in the Four Corners, including Game and Fish, have got an all-points bulletin on us. If they have even so much as an inkling that we're in this area then they're keeping an eye out for any sort of sign: trash, campfire rings, anything colorful or reflective or out of place...."

His voice trailed off, eyes drifting down. He turned his headlamp back on and scanned the floor, lips moving but no sound coming out. A supply inventory, Savannah thought, following the light along the floor as it came to a stop at her feet.

"Savannah, where's your bucket?"

Her stomach clenched. She turned around, letting the light cast upon her calves, and looked about for the bucket. Her mouth opened and she uttered a weak, "It's...." as she made a show of scouring the ground around her. The silence was painful, the eyes of the other three like knife tips pressing in as Savannah struggled in vain to produce what she knew was not there. She had left the bucket up top, above ground, when the helicopter roared into sight. While the rest of them bolted for the cave's entrance, Savannah had hesitated as she tried frantically to decide what to do — whether she should start screaming and waving her arms and jumping up and down. Only if she'd done that he would have had ahold of her in less than two seconds. So she'd opted for something more subtle. She'd dropped her bucket.

The thick drone of the propellers thundered overhead. Savannah braced herself. She didn't know what was coming, but in the blinding light of her father's headlamp she pictured the image of her grandmother's dirt-smeared face as she picked herself off the ground.

But Teddy only shook his head, let out a sad exhale, told them to get down below.

They followed him from the skylight over to the lower chamber. Grandma, carrying one of the water jugs, put a foot on the top rung and froze. She looked up. The sound of the helicopter began to fade. "It's leaving," she said.

They all looked at each other, listening.

"It's leaving," Grandma said again.

"Hurry up, get down there," Teddy said.

"Shouldn't we go get the bucket?"

"I'll take care of it. Just get in. We never should've left."

"Maybe if we weren't playshooting owls and—"

Something cracked underneath Grandma and suddenly, eyes shooting wide, she plunged out of sight. A bizarre thought flashed across Savannah's mind of some cartoon character like Daffy Duck standing on air, the split second he realizes nothing is under him. She heard her grandmother land with a sort of slap on the hard floor below.

Savannah, Mía and Teddy crowded around the entrance and peered down. The top rung of the ladder had snapped, the two pieces hanging from their sockets. Below that the room was a haze of clogged smoke. Grandma lay on her side at the base of the ladder. She began to moan, then scream—an escalating salvo of *unnnh, UUnnnh, AAAHHHHH!*

"*Of course,*" Teddy said.

She kept screaming, her palms flat on the ground as she strained to look at something low on her body: her legs or else her hips, Savannah couldn't tell which. The way her grandmother writhed made her think of Tailypo's half-eaten mouse, dragging itself across the floor.

"Go see what happened," Teddy said to the girls. "And for God's sake be careful."

Mía went in first, followed by Savannah. They had to hop off the bottom rung to avoid stepping on their grandmother, who had yet to pick herself up. A wall of smoke wrapped itself around Savannah, stinging her eyes and burning the back of her throat. She coughed as she found the lantern and turned it on. Waving the smoke away from her face, Savannah knelt over her grandmother who was writhing in agony and clutching her left leg below the knee.

"Is it broken?" Savannah asked.

Grandma sucked in and breathed out through her teeth, spittle flying.

"What's hurt?" Teddy called down.

"Her leg," Savannah said.

She heard him curse. Savannah gently removed her grandmother's hand from the spot on the side of her leg and felt something sharp bulging under the jeans. Grandma gasped at her touch. Blood seeped around the spot, and Savannah noticed a second liquid pooling on the ground. The woman had wet herself.

"I'm going to go get the bucket before the chopper comes back," Teddy said. "Do what you can."

Savannah lifted her head just as the plywood slid over the hole. She heard the rock flip on top of it with a thud.

Savannah screamed up at him, her breath cut short as she choked on the smoke. Tears ran down her cheeks, eyes burning as if looking through a chlorine pool.

"The bone..." Grandma said, "...it's snapped."

Mía emerged from the haze like a wraith, her head tucked up to her eyebrows in her coat. "What should we do?"

Sealing the chimney left the smoke nowhere to go but out through the grate. Savannah was tempted to completely douse the embers, but resisted for fear of creating a greater eruption of smoke. She thought about draping the stove with something, but the only things big enough were the cloth curtain and the nylon sleeping bags. All of which, she felt pretty sure, were highly flammable.

A wave of dizziness rocked her, and in it a strange thought crossed her mind of how many brain cells all this standing around thinking was costing her—how every lungful was another step toward unconscious, possibly even death if Teddy didn't hurry back. Her gaze fell to the water jug that had fallen in with Grandma. Savannah grabbed it and handed it to her sister.

"Get some socks and soak them in water."

Mía grabbed a wad of Teddy's thick hunting socks and poured water over them. The girls held the socks over their mouths and noses, the fumes harsh against Savannah's throat but not as bad, even with the sour tang of her father's feet mixed in. They put a third sock across Grandma's mouth. She moaned but was otherwise still. She looked to be on the verge of passing out—from smoke or pain or both.

Savannah unzipped one of the sleeping bags, opening it wide like a blanket, and pulled it over the three of them. There was nothing else they could do, she'd decided, except lie low, filtering their breaths as much as possible until Teddy got back.

Only where was he? If all he had to do was get the bucket, he should be back by now. Had something happened? Had the helicopter come back and spotted him? Savannah didn't hear a helicopter, or at least she didn't think so, but deprived of oxygen and overloaded with carbon dioxide, her brain and senses were failing her. Pink and blue fireworks exploded across Savannah's vision in the darkness of the bag. She saw an image of a catfish gasping on a pebbly shoreline, eyes bulging, mouth popping. She tried focusing on her grated throat, her stinging eyes, the hard floor digging into her bones. But her consciousness kept floating away, as if dropped into a current. She grew dimly aware of her sister saying something to her, but the voice sounded far away, echoey like when the girls used to talk to one another from either ends of the big steel culvert pipes that ran beneath their old driveway. The steel pipe Savannah used to light her grandmother's cigarettes up in—unknowingly preparing herself it seemed for the day she'd be sucking down smoke in a different kind of tube. Savannah mumbled something in reply that even she didn't understand. Something about smoke or trout or tubes, it didn't matter.

Because just then it occurred to Savannah how *relaxed* she felt. How for the first time in ages, she felt at peace. Mía was with her, as was her grandmother, and beneath the sleeping bag, sharing one another's heat, they were warm. Even the hard floor had become soft. Or maybe it was her bones. Either way, all was perfectly comfy as long as none of them moved.

And all of a sudden she understood: her father had been right. They *did* have everything they needed. It felt so good to finally get that. Her father was right. He'd been right this entire time. He'd done so much for them, and in return all she'd done was doubt him.

But she wouldn't beat herself up over it. Although it'd taken her this long to get it, she got it now. She wished he was here now so she could tell him. But at least he had left them with what was most important: his love. Savannah felt better for it. She felt full because of it. She loved him back. She loved her sister and her grandmother and everything. She even loved mean ol' Tailypo, who she could hear mewling either somewhere in the chamber or in the dreams that engulfed her.

If there was ever a difference.

17

At first she thought she was draped bareback on top a horse, the animal's pulse thudding against her own chest. But when Savannah opened her eyes it wasn't the flowing mane of a horse she saw but her father's bald head. The moonlight glistened in the oil of his scalp, his moles like meteoroids. They were in the forest, and he carried her.

She stirred and he slowed to a stop. "You awake? Good, then you can walk the rest of the way."

He set her on the ground, her legs numb yet supportive, as if they operated by will separate of her own. The black shapes of treetops wavered overhead, and the sky was thick with stars. When had night fallen? Wasn't it just morning out here?

"Where are we?" Savannah asked.

"We are on the go," her father said. "No more lounging about for the Unsers. Got things to do, people to see."

Something on the ground caught Savannah's attention: movement and what appeared to be two shiny green marbles. The marbles dimmed then reappeared, and Savannah realized Tailypo was looking up at her, blinking. Teddy led the cat by a long piece of twine.

"Where are we going?" Savannah asked.

"Just a little farther. I've already taken you most the way. So come on, unless you want to stay here and wait for the mountain lions to get you."

He turned and proceeded through the forest, walking Tailypo beside him. Savannah had never known Tailypo, or any cat for that matter, to walk on a leash. Teddy carried no light but Savannah could make out the way the by light of the moon and the stars. She watched her father's big form navigating the trees, interweaving with the shadows, the hem of his black duster scraping brush.

Savannah started after him, but took only a few steps before halting.

"Where's Mía? Where's Grandma?"

Her father stopped but didn't turn. Instead he held up a finger. "You smell that?"

She sniffed. It was faint in the forest air, but now that he mentioned it she did smell something. It was an intimate smell. She couldn't place it, even though something told her she shared a vital history with it.

Smoke.

"Got to be close," Teddy said, and resumed walking. Savannah stood where she was a moment longer, waiting for a better answer to her question. When it grew clear she wasn't going to get one she followed after him.

A few minutes later a light flickered through the trees. They followed it to a small campfire burning inside a ring of black lava rocks. Four dead trees had been dragged over and arranged into a square around the flames. The fire was unattended.

Teddy put a hand on Savannah's back and guided her over to one of the logs, where they took a seat. Tailypo turned around a few times and sat between Teddy's feet.

"Where are they?" Savannah asked.

"Coming." Teddy leaned forward, picked up a stick and prodded the fire. A burst of embers rose from the flames. Tailypo watched them, the twirling sparks reflected in his pupils. Savannah looked around the forest, her eyes darting to movements that were only licks of the dancing firelight.

A twig snapped in the darkness. Savannah jumped. Teddy straightened, dropped the stick he'd been playing with and wiped his hands along his front. Someone approached from within the trees— slowly, cautiously, it seemed. The person stopped a few steps short of the firelight's edge. Seconds passed in silence, as if the visitor awaited an invitation.

"*Yá'át'ééh*, Shiloh," Teddy said.

The figure stepped into the light.

Savannah's mouth shot open and immediately Teddy had his hand clamped over it. She tried to stand but he held her fast, and all she could do was scream muffled into her father's palm.

The visitor was dressed like she remembered him, in red flannel and jeans. Except this time he wore no coyote pelt over his head. This time his head *was* that of a coyote. And not a small coyote either but a big one with a long snout and chewed-up ears that aimed towards her.

Between those ears, spindly like tree limbs in the dead of winter, sprouted a rack of antlers two feet high.

"Shh," Teddy said, squeezing his hand over her mouth. "It's only a mask."

Tailypo spat as the creature stepped closer. Savannah noticed how the snout drooped and how the coyote's eyes were not eyes at all but empty slits. Deep behind those slits the real eyes shone: big and alive and yellow. Tailypo spat again, and Teddy thumped him on the head. Tailypo growled, ears flattened back, and kept his gaze fixed on the newcomer.

"*Jizdá, ak'is*," Teddy said, gesturing to the log across from them. Shiloh stepped over it and sat, his hands on his knees. The droopy eye slits aimed at Savannah.

"*Adeezhí*," the thing across the fire said, the voice scratchy and muffled behind the mask.

"Yes," Teddy said, nodding. "Her big sister." He eased his grip over Savannah's mouth, and when she'd settled let go of her completely. He put two fingers in his mouth and whistled. The whistle was loud, echoing across the night. Teddy took a breath and held it, listening. Savannah could still sense his readiness should she make a break for it. Not that she was going to, and not because it was her father she feared coming after her.

Suddenly, without so much as a sound to announce her arrival, Mía appeared. She had on the same pair of sweats she usually wore to bed, and below them a pair of untied boots. Her face was gaunt, and her hair had been pulled back in a ponytail. She approached the fire and stopped.

The thing in the mask, keeping its gaze fixed on Savannah, held a hand out to Mía.

"No!" Savannah jumped to her feet, but Teddy snatched the tail of her shirt and yanked her back down. Savannah reached for her sister. "*Please* Mía, come here."

But Mía regarded her without emotion. She looked at Shiloh's outstretched hand. She took it.

Savannah screamed, only no sound emerged. The forest was abruptly mute. Her head filled with a dull ringing, as if her eardrums had burst. Shiloh guided Mia to him, and Savannah could only notice, like the storybook wolf in grandmother's clothing, how big the creature's teeth were, how long and sallow they were as they jutted from a mouth that visibly elongated into the furry snout of a coyote.

The creature slid Mía's coat sleeve up, exposing the delicate skin of her tiny arm. The mouth opened, slowly, and fitted itself over the arm above the elbow. The jaws clenched, teeth sinking through bone, blood bursting from flesh....

. . .

Savannah burst awake gasping, her vision opening like the aperture of a camera lens. Teddy's face hovered above her.

"Hey, come to me, Savannah. Come up."

"Where is she? Where's—" Savannah pushed herself to a sitting position on the ground and was immediately overcome by a coughing fit. Her throat felt scarred, her nasal cavities thick with phlegm that burned as she coughed it out all over her hands.

"Easy, easy now," Teddy said, holding her. A lantern stood shining by his feet. "Just take some breaths."

"Where's Mía?"

Teddy looked at her a moment, confused, then turned toward the cots. Mía sat with her head between her knees, her nose runny and her eyes splotchy. Savannah reached for her with both hands, and as Mía lifted her head Savannah experienced a nightmarish wave of *deja vu*: the sudden certainty that Mía would refuse her.

But Savannah was wrong. Mia leapt from the bed and rushed into her arms. Savannah pressed her face into her sister's neck and began to cry.

"Yeah, that's it," Teddy said. "See, she's just fine. We're all fine."

A moaning rose from the ground beside Savannah. She pulled away to see her grandma still laid out next to her.

Savannah looked at her father. In that precise moment, coincidence or not, a headache slammed in with the force of a semi.

"You...*bastard*," Savannah said.

Teddy pulled his face back like he'd just been spat on. "Hey, whoa, c'mon. That's no way to talk to your—"

"You ran away. You left us."

"Excuse *me*, Little Miss Hostile, but I did no such thing. I'm right here, aren't I? And correct me if I'm wrong but wasn't it *you* that fucked all this up, leaving the bucket up there? It was your fault I had to run up and grab it. I'm sorry if I forgot about unblocking the chimney. I really didn't think there would be that much smoke. But again, remind me who it was that *insisted* on starting a fire in the first place."

All Savannah could see was red. Red so dark it veered into black. Her brain pounded against her skull, painful currents running all the way down to her jaw. Screws drove behind her eyes as she glared at her father.

"You let him eat her," she said.

Teddy frowned. "*Eat*? Eat who?"

"Mía. You just sat there and let him bite her."

Only when it came out of her mouth did it not sound right. But she was still woozy, and deep within her aching mind she saw the scene so clearly: the spurt of blood as the teeth pierced Mia's arm. The image and the horror so livid it must have been real.

"What coyote?" Teddy asked.

Fresh tears squeezed out of Savannah's eyes. She brushed them away. "Shiloh...I saw him."

"You *saw* him?"

She nodded.

Teddy studied her for a long moment, chewing on the insides of his cheeks. His gaze lifted to the ceiling where a thin fog of smoke still hovered. Their own personal overcast. Tailypo appeared from wherever he'd been lurking and sniffed at Grandma. She groaned.

"Sounds like you had a little vision quest, Savannah. You took in too many chemicals and you started to hallucinate. I bet you felt euphoric at one point, too. Like, really happy and warm?"

His smile was patronizing, but Savannah saw through it. Something she'd said bothered him, striking a chord she hadn't meant to pluck. And as the last of the wooziness cleared from her head, she understood that something in Teddy had changed; the severity of their situation had deepened.

Grandma breathed in sharp inhalations. Teddy glanced at her and sighed. "Your Grandma's broken her leg," he said softly, like it was a secret. "I think it's her fibula — must've jammed it just right so that it snapped in two. She should've known better than to have fallen the way she did. That's not how you land from a fall."

"We have to take her to a hospital."

"Forget it. Not with choppers buzzing around up top. If she was able to walk down by herself, then yeah, maybe. But there's no way I could take her and still get back up here without getting caught. Besides, after this fiasco I'm not leaving you two alone again. Don't worry though. I think I'll be able to fix her. Before it chewed me up and spit me out the Army did manage to teach me a thing or two, including first aid. Plus I got a book in here that's going to help us."

"It doesn't just have to be you that takes her," Savannah said. "Why can't we all go? Why can't we just…quit?"

Savannah dropped her head into her hands and began to weep all over again. Mía hugged her. Savannah felt small.

But after a long moment passed with no one speaking, it occurred to Savannah that Teddy had yet to shoot her idea down. Was he thinking it over? Was it possible that he too sensed what she had just moments ago, that from this point forward there was no way to go but down? Could it be that he too, finally, was ready to leave this place?

She lifted her face, not even realizing she was holding her breath.

He set a hand on her shoulder. "I don't think you understand. There's nothing to quit. We already did that when we came up here. We quit the world to build a new one for ourselves, a better one. This is our life, and unfortunately it's not always cozy naps and root beer floats. Sometimes we get hurt. But as long as we stay together down here, we mend. Because I promise you the hurt that's waiting for us up there is so, so much worse. Worse than I expected."

"How? What can *possibly* be worse than this?"

His eyes narrowed on her and she could tell he was deciding whether to tell her.

"What?" she said.

Teddy reached behind him, feeling for something tucked under his belt. He brought his hands back around. A blade lay flat in his palms, shiny in the lamplight. Savannah looked at it, confused at first. Then it dawned on her, and her heart seized in terrible recognition.

It wasn't just any blade her father held, but one she'd seen before. One whose edge was long and serrated with a tallow-colored antler handle

"I found it stuck in a tree up there," Teddy said, eyes darkening. "*He's* here."

18

They cut Grandma out of her pants, revealing a shard of bone poking through the skin just above the ankle. With his *US Army Special Forces Medical Handbook* open on the floor beside him and his mother biting down on a rolled-up t-shirt, Teddy poured disinfectant over the wound. Grandma passed out within seconds of the clear fluid splashing then sizzling over her flesh. Teddy took the opportunity to prod the fractured bone jutting out, pushing it down and letting it bounce back up as if it might just click back into place. He swabbed the area and wrapped it tight with gauze and athletic tape. They changed Grandma into fresh clothes. Teddy used a collapsible handsaw to cut the wooden handle from the axe which he then strapped alongside the leg as a splint.

"Nothing for us to do now but give it time," he said.

And so time was exactly what they gave it, the most excruciating stretch yet. For in the days that followed, Teddy succeeded in his apparent quest to introduce his family to true hardship.

First it got cold. The firewood had been low even before their brush with the helicopter, but once Teddy ceased all excursions to the surface, including his own, the small woodpile rapidly dwindled. They burnt the bottom layer of rotting logs, followed by the mess of splinters and bark until all that remained was a scattering of mice pellets. They burned all the books, all of Teddy's maps and papers. Then, once all those were gone, the stove grew cold. The chamber's thermometer from then on never rose above fifty-nine degrees. And though Teddy insisted fifty-nine degrees was warm and so no one should be complaining about the cold, a dense chill sunk into Savannah's bones, and she succumbed to a constant state of shivering. She grew feverish, and before long fifty-nine degrees felt subarctic. All their trapped breath gave birth to a stale humidity that seemed to cling to everything, tiny beadlets of condensation running down the rocky walls, dripping from the ceiling. Their sleeping bags became wet and heavy. Sometimes when a light turned on after a long period of darkness the whole room sparkled with moisture and for a brief moment Savannah didn't know which way was up. They dressed in nearly every article of clothing they had—Savannah herself wore six layers—and then burrowed into their bags, pulling the drawstrings taut over their heads. But even like this they trembled, their sleep troubled by the sound of the chattering teeth and cramped muscles, growling stomachs and tight bladders—the knowledge that sooner or later they'd have to crawl out of their bags into the cold of the chamber. Savannah fantasized about steaming baths, recalling with a gnawing sense of sorrow the times she'd grown too warm or else too bored in a bathtub and gotten out early. She invoked memories of hot summer days on the old property, how the sun cracked the dirt and baked their attic, and she lamented those days as if they were dead friends she never rightfully appreciated.

The rechargeable batteries drained, and the lantern was rendered useless. A couple headlamps and a few small flashlights still worked, including Savannah's. But Teddy was adamant about conserving them. During the fleeting moments when he did turn one on, the family was at first stunned and blinded, then transfixed by the light pouring from the flashlight like a precious fluid. They ate and drank in the dark. They used the toilet in the dark. They endured all their sufferings—little and big, public and private—in the dark. Savannah never did decide if her father's prediction came true—whether her senses actually sharpened in the darkness. It was true she could navigate the room from one end to the other without so much as bumping a toe, but this was due mainly to her memorizing the place. Her nose had long ago turned numb to the stench of the chamber and herself. There was an ever-present ringing in her ears that became the sound of the chamber, the sound of being buried alive. All the coughs, moans, sneezes, sniffles, farts, sighs, scratchings, whimpers, sobs, and rustlings of her family members became little more than muzak. As for touch, all Savannah felt was cold—her fingertips either icy or puffed-up and itchingly painful after warming them in her sleeping bag. She didn't taste much since she tended to gulp her water and wolf down her food.

As for her sight.... Her sight she just wasn't sure about anymore. Engulfed in impenetrable darkness, Savannah saw the same things with her lids closed that she did with them open, including the colorful bursts and blobs that appeared when she rubbed her eyes. And as more and more time passed, the length between flashlight uses extending, Savannah didn't even have to rub her eyes to see those colorful shapes. They were always there. She began to see objects in them. Faces. Entire scenes of betrayal, violence, and drawn-out rituals of debauchery.

When the last of the jugs ran out, Teddy turned to collecting water from whatever scarce amounts dripped into the tunnel above. He reduced each member of the family to two glasses of water a day. Savannah's scorched throat felt like it had scabbed over, and her voice carried a newfound raspiness. Whenever she finished a glass of water she immediately yearned for another, and in the hours until the next one came she'd vow to make it last, to sip and savor the precious fluid. Of course, when the time did come and the first drop passed her lips, Savannah gulped with abandon. The yearning then resumed, and the cycle continued.

And then there was the hunger. Hunger that ached like a disease. During the first couple days following the helicopter visit, Grandma's fall and their near-asphyxiation, Teddy allowed the family to binge on all the remaining food. It may have been his way of saying sorry, perhaps even an attempt at taking their minds off the other miseries settling in. Whatever his reasons, they finished the remaining supply at a ravenous pace, going through it faster than they had since first arriving in the chamber. They ate three dehydrated food packets a day. Each. Even when the firewood ran out, they mixed the water in cold and ate the contents of the packets soggy but still crunchy. And when it seemed the cold and lack of a woodpile refuge had driven all the mice away, Teddy even gave bits of food to Tailypo. No one complained. In fact, at the time Savannah hopefully considered their reckless consumption of food a sign her father was finally facing the music; that pretty soon they'd have to evacuate, no matter who or what might be waiting for them up top. Because it was do that or starve.

It shocked her then when one day Teddy gave the girls an MRE to share and said it was the last of their food.

"This is it?" Savannah said, her fingers squishing ravenously against the squishy MRE packet. She tore it open. Lasagna it smelled like.

"Yep. So better enjoy it."

"When are we getting more?"

"Eventually, maybe."

Maybe? Savannah thought, passing the MRE back and forth with Mía, sucking out its cool and salty paste. What did *maybe* mean? Was there an alternative to eating that she had yet to discover?

"We have to go get more," Mía said, speaking Savannah's mind for her. "If we don't we'll die."

"Geez la-*weez* girls, why is everything worst-case scenario with you two? Our bodies can go, like, three weeks without food, and here you are talking about dying when we haven't even started day one. Think of all the kids around the world that go days and days without eating, and yet you're griping when you've got a full meal right there in your hand. What's wrong with practicing a little self-restraint, getting better control over those base needs? What's wrong with losing a bit of weight?"

Savannah could sense her sister gaping beside her, at a loss for words. They both seemed to be waiting for the other to say something, to not give up on the argument. Savannah hoped in vain her grandmother would pipe up from where she lay on her bed. But Grandma offered only a slight moan, her breaths resuming their quick in-and-out cadence. It was about all Grandma did anymore, moan and breathe.

Savannah knew she'd already lost weight since arriving in the cave. She hadn't been plump to begin with, but never could she remember feeling the contours of her ribs so plainly beneath her skin. She recalled a PE teacher once showing the class how to use a set of plastic pincers on their bellies and triceps to measure something called their body mass index. After the first few weeks in the chamber, Savannah had tried pinching herself in those places, only to find there was hardly anything to pinch. Her belly had become a taut drum, her arms the drumsticks. Even so, this had barely concerned her at the time. As long as there was food to eat, she didn't care how she looked.

But after finishing the last MRE, the fact that there was nothing else left felt surreal. Following their binge, the intensity with which hunger swooped in took Savannah by surprise. It scared her, and at first she refused to believe they weren't overlooking something. She rummaged in the dark through backpacks and coat pockets, brushing her fingers along the floor where it met the wall. Days—or what she supposed were days but could have really been weeks or just hours for all she knew—passed and the hunger turned painful. When growling no longer worked her stomach started biting, and with teeth. She grew weak and found turning over or sitting up in her sleeping bag to be chores that left her exhausted, her heart pounding. She fell into an addiction to food fantasies, torturing herself with thoughts of fast-food cheeseburgers drippy with grease, of fresh-caught fish sizzling in a pan with a little bit of lemon and onion dashed in, of the Fiery Hot Cheetos that were so popular with her classmates but unpopular with the teachers because of the red fingerprints they left on homework assignments. She thought of pepperoni, green chili and artichoke pizza dipped in ranch dressing, her favorite dish in the world for which she'd cut off a finger—or two or three—right now for a single slice. On and on like this, awake and asleep so that her life twisted into one long sadistic dream.

A hot shower, a glimpse of sunlight, a peach Snapple, a scoop of mustard potato salad—Savannah would auction off pieces of her soul for any one of them. Might as well, considering her soul was being stolen from her anyway by cold, darkness, thirst and hunger: the four agonies a band of thieves, a collection of invasive species eating her from the inside out.

Once, when Grandma began a moaning fit that wouldn't stop, Teddy abruptly ripped open his sleeping bag, turned on a headlamp and jammed his feet into his boots. As her eyes adjusted the sudden light Savannah caught a glimpse of her sister and thought for a moment that she was looking at a tiny skeleton. Mía's cheeks were sunken, her eye sockets so dark they could have been painted. Her lips were cracked and her complexion had faded from a once-healthy chestnut to a light sepia that reminded Savannah of old Westerns.

"Where are you going?" Savannah asked.

Teddy finished lacing his boots, grabbed his revolver and a plastic grocery sack. "Away from your grandmother, before I lose my mind."

He left them, climbed up the ladder and sealed the hole behind him. His footfalls pounded overhead and faded away. Tailypo sat looking up at the hole, meowing. He cried incessantly as of late, his own ribs showing beneath his fur.

Grandma sniffed in the darkness. "It's all my fault, girls. We shouldn't be in here. I take it all back."

Her leg wasn't healing, at least not correctly. They changed her bandages and readjusted her splint often, but the leg looked like a rotting aspen burl. The spot where the bone had broken through the skin was swollen, sour-smelling and purple. Undoubtedly infected.

Mía tapped Savannah on the shoulder. "Do you think he's going all the way up? I mean to the *top* top outside?"

"I don't know," Savannah said.

"His gun...is he hunting? Will he get food?"

"I hope so. I'd eat anything right now."

"But his friend.... Savannah, is he really up there, waiting for us to come out?"

Grandma began to weep, but Savannah barely noticed her. She focused on how to answer her sister's question. Mía had endured so much—the same if not more than Savannah—that to sugarcoat the truth would be insulting. But the thing of it was, Savannah didn't have an answer for her sister. She didn't even know how to answer the question for herself. When Teddy first brought the knife with the antler handle down with him into the chamber, Savannah suspected he was lying to them about having found it up top stuck in a tree, that really he must have swiped it from Shiloh before abandoning him in the water truck. She figured he'd held onto it this whole time as a prop he intended to use to scare the girls into staying put. Staying under control. It wasn't exactly a reassuring scenario, but in this particular case she'd much rather believe her father lied than believe he told the truth. In fact, whenever her mind began to wander to thoughts of another presence lurking up top—man, owl, coyote, whatever…the images varied but the threat felt constant—Savannah shook the thoughts away like they were bugs in her hair, reverting each time back to fantasies of baths and hot Cheetos.

"Savannah." Mía said. "Is he up there?"

"I haven't decided," Savannah said. And that was the truth.

Just a few minutes after leaving, Teddy returned. The plastic sack now looked heavy with something weighing down the bottom. Tailypo romped over and sniffed the bag. Teddy reached inside and tossed what looked to be a wet scrap of leather into the corner. Tailypo darted after it, catching the floppy scrap in his claws. He licked it a couple of times before chomping in.

It was a dead bat.

"Like picking apples from a tree," Teddy said, moving over to the stove, opening the grate and plucking at least a dozen more of the furry creatures from the bag. He set each one gingerly on the makeshift grill inside the stove. "Got to cook them though. Real good. I've never seen any sign of rabies in that colony down the hall there, but you can never be too sure. Roasting them does the trick, makes 'em pretty safe. They're not bad tasting either."

"How are we going to cook without firewood?" Savannah asked. It never even crossed her mind to be repulsed. Looking at the tiny brown bodies draped out on the grill invoked thoughts of barbequed chicken wings. She salivated.

Teddy got up and rifled through the clothing bags. He pulled out everything they weren't already wearing and made a heap next to the stove. Below the grill he stuffed socks, underwear, jeans, a stocking cap. Next he opened the med kit and produced the last of the cotton gauze. He stuffed the gauze wadded into the stove. It took a long time and a lot of matches—his striking them one after the other, holding them till the flames licked his trembling fingers—but finally the flames caught. The chamber filled with the pungent tang of burning fabric. It mixed with the smell of burnt hair and finally the sweet aroma of sizzling meat. Savannah stared at the crisping bodies on the grill, salivating.

Teddy skewered the grilled bats out one by one with his knife and passed them around. The creature was hot in Savannah's freezing hands, appearing indeed like a chicken wing except black of course with two wings instead of one—not to mention the dark veins still visible through the thin wings. She could make out the pointy-eared head and the charred once-pink snout. Bristly tufts of fur sprouting from the back and belly....

Savannah stopped examining and bit in. She ate everything but the head. And after she was done with the first one, she ate a second. Then a third.

Grandma was the only one who didn't join in. When Teddy set one of the cooked bats in front of her, she pushed it to the floor. Tailypo, having finished the first bat, pounced on it and scampered out of sight with the body dangling from his jaws.

"Picky, picky," Teddy said to his mother. He warmed his hands by the opened fire grate, the clothes crackling and melting.

Grandma turned on her side, seething in pain. "Tell us the truth, Ted. Is he up there?"

He stared at the flames, getting lost in them.

"Teddy—"

"Flirs," he said absently.

"What?" Grandma said. "Please son, I just want to know—"

"Flirs, F-L-I-R-S. Infrared systems that detect body heat from 30,000 feet high. We got to look out for those. They flew them in the Gulf but they got them here, too. You know they tried to use them on me in Afghanistan, the sons of bitches, in the White Mountains? They kept asking me all these questions afterwards about where I went and how I stayed hidden all that time, like they couldn't believe one guy with a fifteen-minute head-start could outsmart their million-dollar machines. Embarrassed them, especially considering these were the same mountains bin Laden was supposedly hiding out in. Good thing I found a cave. I actually kept hoping I'd run into ol' Osama so I could personally punch his clock and then come back a hero. Rub it in everyone's faces. Too bad I didn't."

Eyes bloodshot in the firelight, he stuffed a whole bat into his mouth and crunched down. His face had shrunken considerably, and a stubbly ring of hair grew around the sides of his head. For the first time Savannah noticed long streaks of gray in his beard. He chewed, mesmerized by the flames. Almost under his breath, he said, "Although there was one man I ran into while up in those mountains...."

He swallowed in one hard gulp and rubbed his face. "Yep, they wanted to know all about my time in the Afghani wild, how I got by. Call me a kid-killer then ask for my secrets? I don't think so. You want to know how I did it, girls? Desperation, that's how. And if I hadn't fucked up and gotten sick I'd probably *still* be in those mountains, making Uncle Sam's best look like fools. All I need is a decent cave. Blistering heat or freezing cold, I don't care. Darkness? Shit, between sleeping and blinking we live half our lives in darkness. And as far as food goes, I'll tell you one thing: bats ain't nothing compared to what I ate in those White Mountains."

He produced a can of chewing tobacco and pinched out a pre-used cud. He inserted it below his lip and spat. It was the first they'd seen him spit on the floor he'd otherwise kept so immaculate. Savannah grew aware of a sick churning in her stomach, the charred meat having taken her otherwise empty stomach by surprise. It wasn't sitting well, despite her persistent craving for more.

"My leg is bad, son," Grandma said, her voice taking an affectionate tone. "Real bad. I'm ready to throw in. I know I said to you I wouldn't, but...I'm sorry. I'm just not strong enough. Never was. I'm too old. I...I didn't see it happening like this."

"Can't do it," Teddy said.

"No one is up there. That man is dead. I'm not saying you're lying, just that you might've mistook—"

ADAM JAMES JONES

"Can't do it because there's no place to take you. The closest town's thirty miles away, and without a vehicle or a horse I'd say you've got approximately a snowball's chance of making it. No, better off just sticking it out in here if you ask me, wait to get better."

"But I'm *not* getting better, can't you see? There has to be someplace closer than thirty miles."

He took a moment to think. "Well, there is *one* town, but I don't think you want to go there."

"What town?"

"Little off-the-beaten-path place ten-or-so miles from here. But again, Mom, you're not going to find what you're looking for in that place."

"Take me, Teddy. *Please*. Someone there will help."

"Hmm, well only if by someone you mean a ghost. Because only place around here is La Gloria, and La Gloria is a ghost town."

Teddy laughed. Grandma gaped at him and then began to cry. At this Teddy went in one fluid transition from laughing at her to mocking her, bellowing out long exaggerated sobs that made even Tailypo appear from wherever he'd been hiding and stare. Howling with his mother, holding the note, Teddy jumped to his feet and snatched Tailypo by his front paws. Bending over, Teddy began to dance with the cat, singing:

"What's new, pussycat? Whoooaaa, whoooaawhooaaa.... What's new new, pussycat? Whoooaaa, whoooaawhooaaa...."

Mía grasped Savannah's arm. Teddy let go of Tailypo and the cat darted back into the shadows. Teddy returned to the cot, laughing hysterically until his gaze fell to Savannah and abruptly he stopped. The grin disappeared from his face, and in the quick second before his gaze twitched away from her's Savannah realized he'd just viewed himself through her eyes.

It was silent for a long time after that, save for Grandma's soft whimpers. Teddy worked at peeling off the tip of a chipped fingernail, concentrating on it as if it were all of a sudden the most important thing in the world. He bit the nail tip and spit it out, then put his head between his knees.

The fire was almost out and he grabbed the last of the clothes and dropped them in. A pair of eyes stared out at Savannah from the rising flames, and she recognized Mía's stuffed lion. Old Mauricio. She looked at her sister, expecting anguish on her sister's face, but was surprised instead to see an expression of wonder. Mía's eyes visibly widened, the flames bright in their reflection. Savannah wondered if the lion even meant anything to her, whether the toy had been ruined the moment it entered this nightmare with her. The way the girl watched the blaze consume her cherished stuffed animal, resigned and fascinated, she may as well have been watching the sun consume the earth.

Teddy poked the flames with his knife "I wish you'd kept track of that stuffed turtle, Savannah. That you had it back at the house when we were looking for it."

Savannah felt her face flush with anger. This is what he did, talk to fill the noise. Drown out his thoughts. Be his own television.

"I thought for sure you'd still have it. You're going to think me more nuts than you already do, Savannah, but I envied that old turtle of yours. Still do."

"It was just a stuffed animal, nothing special. I didn't even —"

"No, not the stuffed animal. Flash, the *real* turtle. The one that ran away."

She experienced a pang of grief at the mention of the name, grief mixing like a blot of ink into the anger that filled her. *Ran away,* she thought. He still couldn't admit what really happened.

"I remember how precious he was to you," he continued, "how heartbroken you were when you lost him. I kept thinking about that after I got locked up, wondering if you felt the same way about me, heartbroken. I thought, here you knew nothing but good things about that turtle, and that's *all* you'll ever know of him. But as you grew up, what would *I* mean to you, your own dad? All those years cooped up and not seeing you, I could practically *hear* the things your mother was saying about me. Same with the lawyers, social workers, your teachers and friends probably, too — everyone else painting my picture but me."

"I could form opinions on my own," Savannah said.

"Any of them good?"

She'd been asked questions like this before. When she and Sarah Atkinson were closer, Sarah, whose own dad left when she was a baby, used to ask whether Savannah planned on forgiving her father once he was released. Savannah understood Sarah asked because she was testing the idea of her own father one day returning, and Savannah would always tell her friend the truth: that she had no idea. Protective services posed similar questions in the days leading up to his parole, asking what the girls thought about Teddy resuming a part in their lives. Every time Savannah answered on the side of neutral-positive. She refused to sound disloyal, if perhaps simply out of fear of her father somehow finding out. It was only now, scanning his face in the firelight for signs of set traps, that Savannah felt that same family loyalty come back to bite her.

"I said, any of them good, Savannah?"

"Not all of them," she said.

The remark stung him. He crossed his arms over his chest and looked down. "I know. But I've got good in me, and I want you to see that. I can't keep you with me forever, and I never planned on it. That whole business with MWR? Blowing up their offices, getting revenge? I couldn't have given two shits. That old house had it out for me since the beginning. It was cursed, not to mention cold and about to fall over by itself anyway. It *needed* to be condemned and bulldozed. Sorry, Mom, but it's true. All I wanted was for us to do something *big* together, to make the whole world go, 'The Unsers, now that's a family you don't want to fuck with.' I wanted us to *survive* something, you know? To come out of it stronger and closer than we've ever been. To reach a point where we'd eventually go different ways without regretting one another. That's what this whole thing's been about from the very start. I can't decide why you don't call me 'Dad,' Savannah. You refuse to call me anything. Is it because you don't want to give me the satisfaction, or is it because I'm still a stranger to you?"

"That's what all this is about?" Savannah asked. "You're saying all I have to do is call you 'Dad' and we can leave? That we can go get food — some *real* food — and end all this?"

"I don't...I don't want it like *that*. It wouldn't be real if you said it right now. You wouldn't mean it."

"But you're saying there's no reason for us to be trapped in here? This whole time we're starving and freezing and.... And Grandma's leg? You didn't really find that knife up there, did you? There's no one up there. Tell us!"

"Stop being so dramatic. No one's starving in here. Did you just eat or did you just eat? And how are you cold when we've got a fire going? That helicopter was real, and I wouldn't exactly call the cops, FBI, National Guard and whoever else wants us nobodies. They've all got at least an inkling of where we are if they're surveilling this area, so no way we're going up top and risk getting caught."

Teddy spat, took the plug out of his mouth and tucked it back in its can. "As far as our young Navajo friend goes, I saw *somebody* make it out of that explosion. And I think you did too, Savannah. Now I'm telling you if that somebody was Shiloh, then he's not going anywhere or doing anything except coming after us. This is a debt he's not going to forgive, believe me. You want to take Grandma to the hospital, turn ourselves in while we're at it? Okay, but just know that after they lock me up and place you two girls wherever, Shiloh is going to get you. It may take him a while, but he'll be patient. Could be a week later, could be a year. Could be five. But watch out, 'cause one night there's going to be a knock on your window, and when you hear that knock you're going to know who it is."

"Liar," Savannah said. "You don't think we know what you're trying to do? You're trying to scare us, make us afraid to run away."

"You *should* be scared, Savannah. If you weren't so thick you'd be terrified."

"Well we're not. All we are is sick. Sick of your bullshit. Mountain lions and werewolves and other dimensions.... Bullshit, bullshit, bullshit. And you're an idiot if you think we're believing any of it."

He flushed red and she felt herself do the same. She didn't know what she was doing talking to him like this, or where it was going to lead. But now that she'd started she couldn't stop. It seemed she — not her grandmother, not Mía, but Savannah — was the only one capable of hurting him. And that was *exactly* what she wanted to do. And if by calling out his bullshit she just so happened to cut through it, then even better.

"Idiot, huh? Call your own dad an idiot? A liar? I don't let anyone talk to me that way and I'm sure as hell not going to let my own daughter. Keep pushing and you may just get your way. You'll go to the surface all right, but not with me this time to protect you. Just you and your sister. *Then* we'll see how you fare against Shiloh."

"Being that he's not up there," Savannah said, "I think we'll do just fine. And besides, even if he was, it's not *us* he wants. It's you."

"Oh? And what makes you so sure?"

"Because it wasn't us that tried to kill him. You did."

"True, true," he said. "You're right on that front. I don't doubt Shiloh would skin me alive given the chance. But make no mistake about it, it's *you* he wants. No, no, wait, let me clarify. Not you, Savannah...." He swiveled, jabbed a finger at Mía. "*Her.*"

Savannah's back stiffened. Mía tightened her grip around Savannah's arm. "What do you mean by that?" Savannah said.

"Oh, so now you *don't* know everything?"

"Why does he want Mía?"

"Why you think? Why else would he agree to get involved in all this? The water truck, the offices? The gas company didn't confiscate any property of his. Shiloh was an ex-con camping on the backwaters of the rez. The only thing Shiloh ever lost that *meant* anything to him was a little sister."

It felt like a punch in the stomach. Nausea washed over Savannah at the memory of Shiloh reaching past her in the cab of the truck, setting his fingers against the side of Mía's neck.

Grandma pushed herself up to a sitting position without so much as a wince. She glared at him. "You.... You promised him Amelia?"

"*Now* can you see why I tried to kill him?"

Mía scooted closer behind Savannah. Savannah curled her fists into balls. Teddy noticed them and pointed. "You going to do something with those?"

And for one quick moment Savannah thought she would. There was the surge of adrenaline to her legs, her chest and her arms as she prepared to leap on him. Like any animal impulse, there was no thought for the future, no scenarios running through her head of what would happen should she attack her father. It was a need to hurt as fierce and thoughtless as the need to survive.

Teddy put his hands behind his back and stuck out his chin. "Go ahead, I'll give you a free one, just to get it started."

Mía put her arms around Savannah's waist, and just like that, whether it was her sister's embrace or her father's belittling challenge, the spell was broken. Savannah relaxed her muscles, slumped.

"Too bad," Teddy said. "If you and me need to do it, I'd rather it happen now than let it simmer. That's how fights work, you get it done with and move on. Not to kick you when you're down, Mom, but Dad was a mean bastard all the way until the day I finally swung back. That's a memory I'll never forget. I can still feel the squish and crack of his nose on my knuckles. He took on this crazy, surprised look, the blood just streaming down him. But he stopped hitting me, and I mean not just that time but for good."

Savannah shook her head, repulsed, the bat meat sour inside her and wanting to come up. It wasn't just Teddy devastating her with the things he had done and continued to do. It was knowing that none of this was over. That right now was no dream. That right now...was right now.

"Please," Grandma said, "just tell us the truth. Is he up there?"

The flames in the stove had begun to die, a burnt blob of stuffing the only thing remaining of Mauricio the lion. Teddy moved over to his mother and sat on his heels. He put a hand on her broken leg, inspecting it, then turned his face up to the ceiling.

"You really want to find out?"

19

He'd take Grandma and only Grandma. The girls begged to come with, but Teddy refused, insisting it was too dangerous. He said there was a sheep ranch eight miles west of them, and that he'd take Grandma to the doorstep. After that she'd be on her own.

"What do I tell them about you?" Grandma asked. "About the girls?"

"I'm still thinking on that one," Teddy said, glowering at her as if resenting having to concoct another story. "Just get yourself ready. Tighten up in that sleeping bag."

"You can't get her out of here by yourself." Savannah said. "We're coming too."

She took her sister's hand and pulled her towards the ladder. Teddy stepped in front of them, blocking their path. He turned around and grabbed the ladder by its posts and hoisted it away from the outlet. He laid it flat on the chamber's floor.

"What are you doing?" Savannah asked.

"Building a sled. It's the only way your grandmother's going anywhere."

Teddy snatched blankets from Grandma's bed and his own. He wound each blanket tight over the middle of the ladder, binding the wrappings in place with paracord. He dragged the stretcher over to where Grandma sat on her cot, bundled in her puffy green sleeping bag, looking like a caterpillar. Teddy rest his mother atop the stretcher and started work strapping her in place with all the ropes he could find. Her arms were left free, but the rest of her was securely wrapped in sleeping bag and rope. By the time he was done she looked like a caterpillar caught up in a multicolored cobweb.

Teddy poured water from one of the jugs into a steel canteen. He swished the remaining water around in the jug, gauging it. "There's about two liters left in here girls," he said, offering no further explanation. He handed the canteen to Grandma. "This is for you *and* me. Don't drink it all until we can get more."

Savannah eyed the outlet in the rocky ceiling above her. It was still boarded over for the moment, but he'd have to open it to get Grandma through. And he'd have to climb out somehow himself....

Teddy snapped his fingers in front of Savannah's face. "I know what you're thinking, and I'm telling you to stop. I can't protect all three of you up there. I don't even know if I can your grandmother. Before all this got started, Savannah, I asked you for one thing. I asked you to trust me. I said you can think of me however you like. Hate me if you have to, I won't deny you it. But I asked for your trust, and you gave it. Well if your word is worth anything, then prove it now. On this one thing. *Trust me*, Savannah, when I say I can't take you up there, that I cannot take the risk."

"And if something happens to you?" Savannah asked. "What then? Do Mía and I sit here in the dark, wait to starve?"

"You have flashlights, so it won't be dark. What I say about being dramatic? I'll be back within twenty-four hours. Promise. Drink the rest of the water, I'll bring more. And food."

"You'll bring food?" Savannah said. "Real food? Not bats?"

"Not bats, promise," he said. "I'll find something to hunt and bring it back. I swear. Now give me a hand hoisting your grandmother out of here."

Without warning Teddy crouched and lifted the top of the ladder. Grandma's eyes widened as she abruptly turned vertical. She seethed in pain as her weight settled in the sleeping bag. Savannah observed something pointy sticking out of the bottom of the bag, and she realized her grandmother was still wearing a cowboy boot on her one good foot. Savannah didn't know why she suddenly found this funny. Or what about it was also so sad.

Savannah helped Teddy drag Grandma and the ladder over to the exit. Grandma moaned as they pressed her higher on the stilts, resting the tops of the posts back against the rim of the hole. Savannah held the ladder in place as her father grabbed things from his duffel bag. The ladder trembled under Grandma's weight. Savannah wondered if it would support her if she were to try and somehow climb over her grandmother. She wondered if she and Mía could be fast enough. She looked at her sister whose anxious expression asked her the same question. Savannah glanced up the ladder, then back at her sister. She shook her head. Their chance was coming. She knew it like she knew the sun still rose in another world. But this wasn't it.

Besides, there remained the possibility Teddy told the truth about what lurked above, the blade he found stuck in a tree. Savannah hated that she couldn't disbelieve him on this, but there it was. The possibility.

Mía appeared to feel the same; her face relaxed when Savannah shook her head. She looked relieved.

Teddy stuffed items from the duffel bag into a smaller bag which he then strapped behind his back. Savannah noticed him wince only slightly as the backpack rubbed against the burn scar that had certainly not yet healed. He pulled out the 30.06 and slung it over his shoulder. He stood decked in full camo below his duster. The black revolver jutted out from his belt shortly above one front pocket, while the antler handle of Shiloh's protruded above the other pocket. His green headlamp shined on his forehead. He looked like some cowboy soldier about to embark on a covert mission in the night.

Taking a step on the bottom rung of the ladder, Teddy reached up and heaved the plywood off the hole. Next he placed his hands over the rocky lip and, breathing deep, pulled himself up, out of the chamber. His backpack scraped against Grandma on the way up, and one of his feet kicked into Savannah's shoulder. Otherwise his whole top half was out in one deft motion, and his legs immediately after. Once more Savannah was amazed by the strength her father continued to display.

He poked his head over the hole, the green light of his headlamp pouring down like the beam of a flying saucer. "Okay, girls. Say goodbye to your grandma."

Savannah clicked on her MagLite. Grandma hung helplessly inside her cocoon of sleeping bag and rope. Her smudged glasses shone in the light, the lines around her eyes the deepening cracks of dry lakebeds. Her curly white hair lay matted in sweat on her forehead. Grandma looked at Savannah, and Savannah's heart cracked in two. There was no other face she had known longer, not even her sister's. And now she looked at it for the last time. For this *was* goodbye, Savannah realized. Goodbye for good. Because even if all did go well and Grandma found help, she wouldn't be coming back to join them. She might be badly hurt, but up there in the outside world she was a wanted criminal. Savannah had to assume that they all were.. And while she supposed there remained a chance of a reunion one day—inside a courtroom perhaps—Savannah felt about as certain of that as she did the idea of her father ever letting them surrender.

Grandma craned her head and gazed up. "Hold on, son. We should think again about—"

"Nope, no more thinking," Teddy said, peering down at her. "You asked to leave and so we're leaving. Everyone keeps crying to me about wanting more food and water and firewood, about their legs hurting. Well now that I'm doing something about it you can't go changing your minds." His head disappeared from over the hole and Savannah heard chains jangling—the bear trap being dragged away from the rim. Unseen he continued to talk, his voice echoey in the upper tunnel: "If you three have got anything more to say to one another, now's the time."

Mía came over and wrapped her arms around Grandma. Savannah did the same. Grandma lifted her arms higher out of the bag and, the canteen Teddy had given her still clutched in one hand, hugged the girls against her. Savannah couldn't even remember the last time she'd embraced her grandmother, but she was sure it hadn't felt like this. The woman was almost pure skeleton within her sleeping bag, bird bones. She trembled, and as she held the girls she whispered into Savannah's ear: "The pills. Hurry."

Savannah pulled away, not understanding at first. Grandma wagged her finger at something behind Savannah's back. Savannah turned around and shined her light on her father's duffel bag. Then it struck her. The film canister. *Suicide pills.*

Savannah took only a second to notice the greenlight of her father's headlamp emanating faintly from somewhere beyond the rim of the outlet. She leapt to the duffel bag and rummaged frantically through. The bag was lighter and more jumbled since Savannah had last searched it, and at first she worried her father had disposed of the pills. That or — the thought sending a shiver up her back — he had them on him now. But then Savannah's hand clasped the familiar smooth plastic of the film canister, and without a second thought she bounded over to her grandmother just as the green headlamp poured back into the chamber.

"All right, time's up," Teddy said. "Girls help me lift."

Savannah pressed herself against her grandmother one more time. Between their bodies their hands met.

"He won't make it back," Grandma whispered. "I'm sending help."

"Come on already," Teddy said. "Don't go pretending like you all of a sudden mean something to one another. Mom, all you did half the time was bitch about those girls. So c'mon, it's night up there and if we're going to get you out of here we need to do it now."

The ladder wobbled, leaned forward, and started to rise. Grandma snaked both her arms inside her sleeping bag, the canister and water canteen disappearing out of sight. Savannah and Mía each grabbed a post and lifted. Savannah wasn't sure how much good they did; both Grandma and the ladder elevating swiftly up as Teddy grunted above them. And just like that, she was gone.

The light of Teddy's headlamp bounced around above the skylight. Grandma moaned and there came the light clatter of the ladder laying flat. Teddy peeked his head back into the chamber.

"Be back before you know it. You two just sit tight and stay alive."

Without waiting for a reply, Teddy disappeared. The plywood slid over the top and the rock thudded down on top. The girls kept their heads turned up, following the sound of Grandma's muffled cries as the ladder thunked over the rocky floor above. Dust rained from the ceiling, drifting in the beam of Savannah's flashlight. She didn't know how her father was going to get Grandma out of the taller skylight in the tunnel above, especially by himself. There *had* to be a second exit, she thought.

"There's no sheep ranch," Mía said, barely a whisper. "He's not taking her for help."

"No. But Grandma might just find a way to get help herself."

"What if she doesn't? I'm scared, Savannah."

"She said she would send us help. That he wasn't coming back."

"What if *no one* comes back, though? If they both get.... If something gets both of them? We're stuck."

"Nothing's going to *get* them," Savannah said, "except perhaps the police. And then Grandma will tell them about us."

"But—"

"*But,* if something goes wrong, we're going to have to get out ourselves. I still say we wait a while, give him a head start."

Savannah didn't bother adding that she didn't see how they were going to get out with the ladder gone. They could pile everything in the chamber to reach the exit, but then there would still be the matter of somehow prying away the piece of plywood with the giant rock resting on top of it. And with the handle cut off the axe to make Grandma's splint, they didn't even have anything with which to pry.

The reality of the situation began to close in on Savannah, squeezing her with the cold truth that their only hope for escape relied on *someone* coming back for them. And no matter how much Savannah wanted to believe otherwise, deep down she *knew* that someone was going to be Teddy.

Mía must have seen it in her face. "If he comes back he'll never let us go."

"We're not going to give him the choice."

"What do you mean?"

Mía shielded her eyes and Savannah realized she was blinding her sister with the flashlight. She lowered the flashlight and ran it along the floor. She shined it on the shelves, the stove. "I say we do to him what he did to us."

"What?" Mía said.

"Trap him. I say it's his turn to be stuck and left behind in this...this *prison*."

Mía's brow furrowed as she appeared to consider this. After a moment she took Savannah by the hand, her little fingers icy in Savannah's palm. "We might hurt him," she said. "Will that make us bad? If we get to other people, won't they say we're bad?"

Savannah gazed into her sister's face, the girl's look of genuine worry. It was enough to make Savannah's heart ache. That this was still a concern for Mía: her innocence.

When exactly had Savannah stopped caring about her own? Or had she?

Tailypo appeared mewling from the shadows. He pawed up on Savannah's leg, digging his claws into Savannah's thigh like she was a scratching post. Savannah gasped and kicked her leg free. Tailypo continued to slink between her feet, unperturbed and Savannah rubbed her thigh. He took a seat on the ground and looked at her, jade eyes gleaming.

"And what about him?" Mía said.

20

Before she did anything else Savannah got to work on a bug-out-bag. She wasn't going to use the steel-frame backpack Teddy had given her—too cumbersome. Instead she went simple, efficient: a light JanSport daypack she found folded up on a shelf. It might not be prepper-approved, but it'd be easy to snatch if things got crazy. Or rather *when* things got crazy, Savannah thought. Not that there was much to pack; no food left anyway and only two liters of water. So she packed what she could, what her father would tell her to. Matches, paracord, compass. Space blankets, one of the smaller medkits, and a pocket makeup mirror that could be used for signaling. The girls would wear all the layers they could under their puffy winter camo outfits. Savannah gave Mía a working headlamp and a small Swiss Army knife she found in the bag. Mía strapped the light around her head and stuffed the knife into a coat pocket. Savannah let her own little flashlight dangle from its leather thong around her neck as she fit her utility knife in its case to her belt. The knife seemed heavy there all of a sudden. Like it was all Savannah could think about.

What else? What other thing was she forgetting to pack? Her gaze fell to the duffel bag, the long black steel she knew dwelled at its bottom. Without giving herself the chance to think twice Savannah reached inside the duffle bag and pulled out the first rifle her hands wrapped around: the shotgun. Except the moment its cold, dead weight was in her arms she wanted to drop it. A fresh terror seized Savannah, and with it she felt her very resolve chipping away.

Savannah jiggled the steel trigger lock, bulky and firm. She considered trying to smash the lock with something — perhaps the ax-head, which she noticed on the floor near the stove — but sensed she'd most likely just end up wrecking the gun itself in the process.

Savannah put the shotgun back where she found it and shoved the duffel bag back under the cot. Lock or no lock, it didn't matter: Savannah recognized she couldn't handle the weapon. Her fear of it rendered the gun's power useless in her hands. When she looked at the rifle she saw only trauma; trauma on display in the cloudy film coating her left eye. The vision of a curtain slowly descending.

She zipped the little daypack closed and handed it to Mía. "You're in charge of this," Savannah said. "Hide it somewhere, but make sure you can grab it fast if you have to."

Mía held the daypack against her chest and looked around the room. She went to a loose pile of vacuum-seal plastic pouches — now unsealed and mostly empty — and hid the pack inside. Tailypo meanwhile paced back and forth beneath Mía, crying madly, knowing something afoot. Savannah had never seen him so skinny, not even when he was younger. His shoulder blades jutted beneath his black fur in sharp, twin arcs, and the contours of his spine could be seen running all the way down to his nub of a tail.

Savannah looked around the room, her eyes going to the stovepipe — the ceiling hole through which the chimney poked.

The thought had crossed her mind before. She just hadn't been able to see where it'd get her.

Savannah walked over to the stovepipe and felt it. The metal was still warm, though the little clothing fire had died in the stove. The chimney was made of two tapered pipes inserted one into the other. Savannah found the connections to be loose and was able to yank the pipe apart at its center and slide the top portion out of the ceiling. She peered up through the empty chimney hole: about eight inches wide, she'd guess.

She had to pull the bookcase over to have enough to balance on, but ultimately Savannah was able to do it. She stood with one foot on the bookcase and the other denting the lid on the stove. Mía handed her Tailypo — mewling but for once unaggressive, complacent even — and Savannah pushed him through the small hole in the ceiling.

He ceased making noise the moment he was free. Through the aperture Savannah saw his nubby tail twitch back and forth for a moment. Then he was gone. It may very well be the cat would run smack into Teddy on his way back to the chamber. That or straight into one of his open bear traps. But somehow Savannah doubted both these things. Tailypo was resourceful — a lonely survivalist just like his master. He was also starving. Given the opportunity he'd find the way out if there was one. That or feast on bats.

It didn't matter where freeing the cat got her, Savannah thought as she climbed down. It didn't even matter that Tailypo never liked her nor she him. All that mattered was that the animal be given the same fighting chance the girls were going to get.

They put the chimney back together and rearranged the room. Savannah had started to feel light-headed, nauseous. She needed to sit down, think. The girls took seats next to each other at the edge of Savannah's cot, and Savannah took out her utility knife and began absentmindedly unfolding its blades. She could feel her sister looking at her and for a second thought she was going to ask what the plan was. But Mía only leaned against her, setting her head on Savannah's shoulder. Savannah looked into her sister's face — the girl's eyes weary yet still glistening with something Savannah could only call innocence. Savannah saw her mother in that face. She had always been able to find pieces of her mother in Mía. Aside from the obvious physical resemblances — their small physiques and richly dark hair — both possessed a quality of gentleness to them. Over the years, Savannah had alternatively admired and envied that gentleness. She remembered the three of them walking hand-in-hand in the yard once when all of a sudden their mother froze, gasped, and yanked Savannah back a step. Her mother had knelt then and picked up a crushed flower containing a bee that had been pollinating it. The bee was dead. Mía had cried and Savannah filled with shame. The walk that day had been ruined.

Mía and her mother shared a compassion that always seemed exclusive of Savannah. Whenever she felt jealous of it, Savannah liked to think of that compassion as naivete. She knew full well that's what her father would call it, and there was once a time this would make her proud. Of course, after spending more time with Teddy in this chamber than anywhere else — witnessing his transition from abductor to murderer, protector to sage, fabricator to suicidal captain of a sinking ship — Savannah wished to be nothing like him. Nowadays she recognized his qualities suspiciously, as one would precancerous moles.

But moles, much like many forms of cancer, could be surgically removed. The blood of your own father on the other hand, his influence? Savannah didn't know. How did she cut out the very spirit that made her?

Savannah considered this as she sat on her cot, fingering the utility knife her father had given her. She found the longest of the blades and thumbed its sharp tip.

After a while Mía returned to her own cot, and both girls curled up wearing their boots inside their sleeping bags. Savannah turned off the MagLite, and darkness washed over the room. She clasped the knife beneath the covers. Her nerves crackled. Her whole body shuddered. She tried to contain herself, hoping her sister wouldn't notice, while images played across her vision like jumpskips of a horror movie: her father's glistening head and bushy black beard; flames roaring from a hollowed-out building of twisted metal; smoke; the shard of oily red bone jutting from her grandmother's leg; a figure in flannel with the head of an antlered coyote. Savannah rubbed her eyes but the movie kept playing, and now it showed a thousand souls scurrying out of the earth like an evacuating ant colony as monsters clawed after them. Enveloped by darkness, entombed in stone, Savannah suddenly felt the presence of these monsters directly beneath her, as if they were trapped tenants in a foul room one floor down.

Sipapu, she thought. That was the name. A hole into hell.

She turned the flashlight back on. Mía immediately reached over from her sleeping bag and found Savannah's hand. They remained like this, quiet and hand-in-hand, for what could have been hours or merely minutes—Savannah would never know. She had entered a foggy half-sleep, devoid of dreams in which she could live forever.

All of a sudden, boots stomped overhead, and consciousness struck Savannah like a bolt of lightning. She heard him cough, the sound reverberating with a tinny buzz down the chimney. Something heavy and wooden dragged, clunking across stone. Savannah tore out of her sleeping bag, knife in hand and turned on her flashlight.

Mía stood up and switched on her headlamp. Rock scraped against plywood, thudded. Savannah motioned with her own light towards where Mía had stashed the backpack. Mía nodded. The plywood lifted and a green light shone down.

"Jesus," Teddy muttered from above. Savannah waited for his legs to plunge into sight and was surprised when instead the ladder reappeared. It slid down against the rim of the entryway until the base struck the chamber's floor. A second later the blankets that had once wound around the ladder to form a gurney dropped through the hole, landing at the bottom of the ladder in a heap. A messy coil of ropes fell down after it, followed by the steel canteen. The canteen rolled and tinked along the rocky floor. Empty.

"Jesus," Teddy said again, and this time his boots swung onto the ladder. He still had his backpack on and the rifle slung over one shoulder. He used only one hand to climb down as the other cradled what looked like a black bundle of cloth—his duster. Teddy slipped on the second-to-last rung, landed on his feet on the floor and yelped in pain. "*Jesus. Oh Jesus.*" He stumbled backward, seething, and as he turned Savannah gasped. Blood smeared the entire left side of his face, oozing from an open gash slightly above the ear. The wound was big, about the size of a grapefruit, and clearly fresh as blood continued to trickle down, matting his beard. The strap of his headlamp was pulled low to cover some of the lesion, and Savannah wondered if this hadn't been a feeble attempt at keeping pressure on it. It looked like he'd been struck with something, something hard and sharp.

"Where's Grandma?" Savannah asked.

Teddy leaned the rifle against the wall and tossed his backpack in a corner. He stooped over, put a hand on one knee and spat.

"Where is she?" Savannah said, her gaze darting to the uncovered exit above the ladder.

Teddy kept his head bowed to the floor. He closed his eyes and held up a finger as he tried to compose himself. The revolver was still attached to his hip but Shiloh's knife was nowhere in sight. The sleeves of his camo shirt were rolled up above his elbows, and Savannah could see the faint traces of blood coating his hands and forearms, despite there appearing no fresh injuries except the one on his head. Teddy rocked on his feet, breathing deeply. What skin wasn't covered in blood shined pale, almost ghostly in the beam of Savannah's flashlight.

He turned to Savannah and frowned. A string of drool hung from his lips. "What are you doing? It's just me."

She had no idea what he was talking about at first. Was he hallucinating, thinking her someone else? Then she followed his gaze to the blade she held out toward him in one hand. He cocked his head, waiting. Savannah eyed the empty canteen on the ground near his feet. After a moment she folded the utility knife and replaced it against her hip.

"What happened?" Savannah said.

"He's up there," Teddy said, staggering over to his cot and dropping the bunched-up coat next to it. He flopped onto the cot, the thin aluminum legs squeaking. "I'm sorry…. He got your grandmother. He just came out of nowhere and…and oh my god it was bad."

He put a hand on his stomach and winced. In addition to the blood glistening on the side of his head and shading his arms, Savannah noticed dark stains on his clothes. He looked like he'd just come home from a long day at the slaughterhouse. She could smell the coppery scent of it in the air.

"Almost got me, too," Teddy continued. "I'm lucky I got away. Your grandmother though, I'm sorry…. He came out of thin air."

"Tell us." Savannah said.

"God, those bats are not sitting right with me at all. I think I had a bad one."

As Savannah watched blood pulsed from the open gash above his ear. It was hard to tell how much of his present condition owed to the wound and how much might be attributable to something else.

Something, Savannah thought, like bad water.

He lay for while with his eyes closed, hands on his stomach. Finally Teddy opened his eyes and took a hard gulp. "We got up top, gone about, I don't know, half a mile, when this deer steps out of the trees. It was dark, but the moon was out and bright enough for me to see the deer easy enough. Everyone being so hungry and all, I set your grandmother down and took the shot. I got him. Wasn't a big deer, just a little doe, but good meat still so I start to butcher it." He hiccupped, put his fist over his mouth and became still. Then, "I figured I could get a few strips, take your grandmother the rest of the way down for help, and get right back to you. But as I'm working, all of a sudden I hear your grandma scream, and by the time I turn around it's too late. There's Shiloh standing right behind her. He...." Teddy started to quiver, tears brimming in his eyes. "There was nothing she could do, tied in like she was. He cut her throat. And before I could even get my gun up he was already gone, vanished into the forest." His eyelashes batted wildly for a moment, either in dizziness or memory Savannah could not tell. "You're not feeling it girls? The bats?"

"Where is Grandma now?" Savannah asked. "Where'd you leave her?"

Teddy turned onto his side, hiccupped and belched. A stream of bile splattered on the floor and he began to hack. Savannah stood over him, staring at the very gun he spoke of still attached to his hip. He lay on his side with the gun pressed beneath him. Only the handle stuck out, and Savannah wondered if she was even strong enough to yank it free. Whether she'd be fast enough and if the safety might be on. Or, most importantly, whether she was actually capable of pulling the trigger.

He continued to cough, his pale face flushing dark red as he fought to catch his breath. Then again, Savannah thought, perhaps she needn't worry. Perhaps all she needed to do was wait, give him time.

His breathing calmed but turned raspy. "I didn't just *abandon* her, don't even think that. She's buried safe in a ravine. A nice spot, peaceful. She'd have liked it."

"What happened to your head?"

He lifted it suddenly as if just remembering and touched a finger to his temple. He held the bloody finger in front of his face. "Hit me with a GODDAMN rock!"

Dizziness washed over his face the instant he shouted it. His eyes widened, bewildered.

"Shiloh?" Savannah said.

He shook his head and concentrated on the bloody finger. "Damn but I have bled though."

"Why'd you bring back the ladder?" Savannah said.

"The ladder? Oh…I don't know, why not?" He wrapped his hands across his chest and shivered. "Brrr. Start a fire, Savannah. It's cold."

"We don't have anything to burn."

"Find something. There has to be something. The ladder, there you go, that's why I brought it back. Burn the ladder. And eat what I brought you…."

"*Eat*? Eat what? What did you bring?"

"It's inside my coat," he said, flicking his hand at the floor beneath him "Wrapped up in my coat there…. The doe. Eat it."

Savannah inched closer beside him and shined her flashlight down at the duster, heaped in a messy bale with its arms tied over itself. She nudged it with the tip of her boot and felt something squish. "This is that…*deer*?"

Teddy reached toward the ground and fumbled his fingers across the coat. His eyelids drooped, and his speech started to slur. "You need to eat it…. Jusssst you, Savannah. Only enough for you. It is…*true* survival. I learned in those White Mountains. Thissss is the only way…that works."

His fingers succeeded in untying the sleeves, and he flung the coat apart. A ball of bloody t-shirt lay at the bottom. The shirt was wrapped around something else, something that soaked the once-white cotton a soppy crimson. It seemed to sparkle in the trembling beam of Savannah's flashlight.

Gently — like a fresh rosebud, a bow, a diaper — Teddy peeled open the shirt.

The second the wrapping fell away the glob of meat appeared to almost *sigh*, to loosen in the open air. It lay in a congealing glob, the ragged flesh cut into strips. The smell was sour, minerally, nauseatingly familiar like the cold scent of a package of hamburger being opened. A few of the strips slid off the heap. They looked like tiny cuts of bacon, so thin and pink with trace lacings of fat. And there were bits of skin attached, white and wrinkly with a few patches of stubble.

Like the hair Savannah used to shave from her shin, hunkered in a lukewarm bath.

"Start a fire and cook it," Teddy said. "Cook it good and through. Then eat it all."

Teddy pulled away, lay on his back, and ran a chalky tongue around his lips. Savannah peeked over at Mía who stared open-mouthed at the flesh. Savannah pretended to cough until Mía lifted her head, the headlamp swinging onto Savannah's face. Savannah nodded in the direction of the ladder. Mía began to move.

Suddenly Teddy shot up to his seat, clutching his head in both hands   and   screaming: "AAHHHHMMMMMMMAAAAAWWWWDDDD!"

The girls jumped, the scream bouncing off the stone walls of the chamber. Savannah grabbed her sister by the arm and prepared to run, but just as quickly something made her freeze. An icy chill prickled up her spine. She turned her head and saw her father looking at them. He sat bolt upright, head craned along his shoulder, eyes red and teary. His hand rest on the black handle of the revolver at his side. A fresh bead of blood trickled down the front of his ear to his neck. He tilted his head, confused.

"Your head," Savannah said, composing herself. "You're losing too much blood. We have to bandage it."

His eyes narrowed on her, and he began to teeter side-to-side. Finally he nodded, removing his hand from the revolver. "Yes. Thank you. But please.... Please eat when you are finished."

"Lay back on your side, like you were." Savannah said, helping him turn so that his back was to her and he faced the wall. Savannah shined the light down on the gash above his ear. "We can't let you lose any more blood. Here, I'm going to take your headlamp off."

"Thank you. Thank you." He wheezed in and out, but his eyes stayed open. "The med kit."

Savannah slipped the green headlamp from around his head, turned it off and slipped it in a pocket. She became aware then of Mía's own light beaming on her shoulders. She gestured with a hand behind her back, and the headlamp swiveled away. Savannah heard the crinkling of plastic, the shuffling of feet. She pushed Teddy's duster and its red contents aside with a foot and dropped down to her knees. Savannah slid the duffel bag towards her and felt around for the plastic med kit. She found it and was about to stand up when something else caught her eye.

The black, nylon case.

The camcorder.

Savannah set the med kit aside and pulled out the nylon case. She held it, listening to the steady wheezing of her father's breaths. Savannah aimed her flashlight behind her and illuminated Mia standing with the daypack on, one foot on the ladder. Savanah lifted her chin. Mía began to climb.

"No matter what I do..." Teddy said, trembling, staring at the rocky wall in front of him. "No matter what I do.... Everyone...."

Savannah slowly unzipped the case and removed the camera. She coughed as she pressed the on button, then again as she pressed record. Savannah stood up and set the camera on a shelf. The gleaming record light cast a soft red hue over their little spot in the chamber.

"Where's...? Huh...? Where's Tailypo? Where's my cat?"

He began to turn onto his back but Savannah caught him, kept him on his side. "I'm going to wrap your head so you need to stay still." She opened the med kit, discovering no more gauze but a little bit of tape and a handful of cotton balls. Savannah carefully lay the cotton over the wound, stretched out the tape and wrapped it around his bald head.

If Teddy felt anything it didn't show. His eyes were closed and he beckoned with his fingers. "Come here ol' gato. Come here big killer." His chest continued to swell up and down, the air sucking in and out through his teeth. "Come here Taily —"

"Shhhhh, save your breath, Dad. Just relax and breathe."

His eyes fluttered open a crack. Ever so slightly his face turned and he looked up at her. Savannah rest a hand on his shoulder. Blood spread and stained along the bandage. Teddy smiled, and in one fleeting moment Savannah saw in her father's face all the things that had led him here, to this place, to now. The misguided things he'd done just for a little compassion — for something like his own daughter calling him "Dad." And in this split second his pain became her own. She felt a wave of pity. Of sadness. Of fear she would be frozen forever, empathy-bound.

Teddy lowered his head back onto the cot and closed his eyes. The smile faded but not entirely, a slight crack keeping at the corner of his mouth. His breathing became soft, rhythmic. Savannah glanced behind her and saw the yellow wood of the ladder gleaming in the light of Mía's headlamp. Her sister peered down from the top, waiting for her.

Savannah let her own flashlight dangle around her neck, aimed at the floor. She still had one hand placed upon her father's shoulder, but she didn't immediately remove it. Instead Savannah let it stay there a moment. She imagined she felt the warm eye of the camera lens on her skin, on her face and on the back of her hand. On her father's body until he no longer shivered.

Innocence, freedom; Savannah couldn't say how much she still had. But if this was how she surrendered it all, then let it be known why. Let there be a record. Let there be a witness to watch over.

Savannah lifted her hand free and stepped back. She took one more look at him, then turned and made quietly for the ladder. Sparks swirled in her vision as she navigated through the shadowy chamber. A lump rose in her throat and she swallowed it back down. She'd imagined countless scenarios for how this would end. Not long ago she had steeled herself for her grandmother's death, to a certain extent actually accepting it, preemptively. Savannah had even tried to imagine what the death of her father would mean to her, telling herself that no matter what she would feel nothing.

But Savannah hadn't anticipated this. Not quite. And even if she had, anticipation and actual experience were two very different things. For how else could she explain the tears brimming in her eyes.

She no longer heard his breaths, but Savannah moved softly, silently all the same. She was almost to the ladder when she caught the glint of steel against the wall. Savannah raised her flashlight just barely to spotlight her father's 30.06 propped against the stone. The trigger open, unlocked.

Careful not to break her stride or allow any time for second-guessing, Savannah snatched the rifle by the barrel. She reached the ladder and started to climb.

Mía's head poked over the rim of the hole with her headlamp gleaming, and Savannah ascended into the shaft of light. The rifle was heavy in her one hand and Savannah felt it start to slip. She caught the stock on one of the ladder's rungs and struggled to reposition herself.

"Here," Mía whispered, holding one of her tiny hands down through the hole. Savannah raised the rifle and Mía pulled it the rest of the way out. With both hands firmly on the rungs Savannah continued to climb, her head breaching the outlet and a draft of cool air alighting her skin. Mía stood over her, the pack strapped behind her shoulders and the rifle propped on the ground beside her. She extended her hand again and this time Savannah took.

A set of fingers slapped around Savannah's ankle. She screamed, looked down to see Teddy's big veiny eyes — his blood-soaked face and sticky black beard.

"YOU CAN'T *LEEEEAVE*! THERE'S NOWHERE FOR YOU TO *GOOO*!"

He howled and squeezed her ankle tighter, pulling her down. She kicked wildly at him with her free foot, holding on to the top rung with both arms as hard as she could. Her arms began to loosen. She felt herself slipping. Mía shrieked as she dropped and snatched Savannah by the coat collar. She tugged but Savannah continued to slide down: back into the chamber, back into her father's hold.

He pulled harder. "I TOLD YOU IF YOU GO UP THERE — *ACK*!"

She kicked — hard, a solid shot into what felt like a nose, maybe his mouth — and his grip loosened. Savannah shook free and scrambled the rest of the way up and into the tunnel above. She pushed herself to her feet on the uneven floor and looked down. One after the other his hands grasped the rungs of the ladder, his bandaged head rising. The plywood board lay nearby. Savannah could flip it over, but she'd never be fast enough to get the rock on top.

She took up the rifle instead. She leveled the gun's sight on him, fear and doubt exploding inside her like a chemical reaction. Flashbacks:

Thunder.

Blindness.

Pain.

Her finger found the trigger, cold and curved. Paralysis struck. The barrel wavered.

"Move," said a small voice behind her.

Savannah turned to see Mía emerge from the shadows, something big and metallic balanced in her tiny hands.

The bear trap.

"YOU HAVE NOWHERE TO GO! YOU HAVE — "

His head popped out of the hole. Savannah stepped aside. Mía stepped forward, the steely jaws opened wide, and let the trap slide from her hands. It tipped over in the air, the plate landing smack on top of his bald crown. There was a thick, twangy *snap!* and the jaws swallowed his head whole, chomping down underneath his chin and catching the words in his throat. Teddy swayed, squeezing the top of the ladder. Teeth gritted, he let out a hard exhale, spattering the girls' legs with blood. He stared at them through his iron mask, stunned, refusing to fall.

But Savannah could see his grip loosening, his mouth falling slack. Blood welled in both his eyes and streamed down his cheeks.

Mía took hold of Savannah's arm. Savannah stepped forward, set the tip of her boot on her father's shoulder and gave him a push. Teddy released the ladder and dropped from sight, into the chamber's shadows.

The girls slid the plywood board over the hole and rolled the rock on top of it. They took off together down the tunnel, clambering over loose rock, making for the skylight. Along the way Savannah led them to the three remaining traps and the girls set them off by tossing rocks. The whole time Savannah might as well have been floating, the shock rendering her weightless, buoyant. She was keen for any sounds coming from behind them, below that plywood board. But the cave was silent.

They reached the skylight where a dull, grayish light streamed down. Savannah stepped under it, looking up to see a grim sky on the verge of daybreak or nightfall. She couldn't tell which. She slung the rifle over her shoulder, laced her fingers together and held them at her waist for Mía to step into.

"Here, you go first. I'll give you a boost."

Mía planted a foot in her hands and Savannah lifted her up. The girl felt fifty pounds heavier, which Savannah knew couldn't be true. Rather, it was the weakness in her own withered muscles as her arms trembled and her knees buckled. It was all she could do to keep her hands together and not drop Mía. Her biceps screaming, she lifted her cradled fingers as high as she could, desperate for her sister to find purchase.

Except Mía didn't seem to be moving. She'd gone rigid in Savannah's hands.

"Hurry up Mía. I can't hold —

Mía screamed.

Savannah dropped her and Mía collapsed on the ground as Savannah tumbled backward. But in the split second before she fell Savannah saw it: the thing that made her sister scream.

An arm dangled through the skylight. Flailing, *feeling* for them. The entire length of it was covered with scars, like suckers on a thrashing tentacle.

Mía, still shrieking, retreated back into tunnel. Savannah called after her. She climbed to her feet, grabbed the MagLite dangling around her neck and pointed it at the ceiling.

But the hand gone was gone from the skylight. Instead, something else peeked over from the rim. It was a face: round, disfigured and rotting. The face was feverish and shiny with burns, flakes of white skin peeling away in places as if diseased. At the center, where the nose should have been, were two bony nostril slits. And this time the figure wore no sunglasses. Now Savannah could see his yellow eyes, blinking in the beam of her flashlight. She actually saw the pupils shrink. Or rather *flatten*, it seemed, the black beads turning long and sideways.

Like the eyes of an animal.

Savannah bolted after her sister. She caught up to her, and the girls fled from the skylight. Into the black, uncharted depths.

21

They dashed over the loose stone — rolling their ankles, skidding their knees and palms, banging their heads. And yet neither girl looked back. As she ran, Savannah thought she heard a voice calling after them. The voice was gravelly, and it seemed to be calling the same word over and over: "*Baaaack. Baaaack.*" Savannah didn't dare ask if Mía heard it too. Delirious with terror, she couldn't even say for sure if the voice came from behind, from Teddy's chamber below, or from inside her own head.

It was only when the cave narrowed and the girls found themselves scurrying with their backs hunched and scraping against the jagged roof that they finally slowed. Savannah smacked her forehead hard into a sharp outcropping of stone and saw stars. For a second an intense wave of unconsciousness threatened to consume her. She stopped, put a hand to the spot and felt blood in her hair, sticky and warm.

"We're trapped in here, Savannah!" Mía said. "He's up there, it wasn't made up!"

"Shh, be quiet. Let me think."

"Is it true? Does he want *me*?"

Savannah felt her courage seeping away as if through a cracked bucket, and uncertainty rose within her. What were they doing running from the chamber, the one place they were safe? What had they done to the one man who could protect them?

"We have to keep going," Savannah said, unwilling to answer her sister's question.

"But where? There's no place to go. The way out is blocked."

Savannah aimed the light back the way they'd come, her heart skipping a beat when the beam flashed across what she at first thought to be the dark hair of a coyote pelt but was in fact a brown and bristly cluster of bats stuck to the ceiling. She hadn't thought about it when they first came this way — hadn't thought about anything but escaping those yellow eyes — but they'd run straight into the colony. She ran the light across the ceiling and walls, illuminating hundreds of them bunched into tiny brown balls and stuck to the rocky tube like splatters of mud. They surrounded the girls on every side — unmoving, a few just inches away.

Mía saw them too. She gave a little squeak and clutched Savannah's arm.

"It's okay," Savannah said. "They're sound asleep. And even if they do wake up they won't bother us." At least that's what she hoped. Once more she'd have to take her father's word for it.

Mía shook her hand out of Savannah's. "Where are we going then? How do we get out of here?"

"That skylight back there isn't the only way out. There has to be another way somewhere. If the tunnel hasn't collapsed it might be further down. We just have to keep looking."

"How do you know?"

"Because that's what Dad told me."

She hadn't even thought about it before opening her mouth, the name just came out. It surprised her, and yet it didn't feel wrong. Something about having said it once. That, and perhaps knowing she would never see him again.

Mía chewed on this, her little face tight with worry as she eyed the bats covering the walls and ceiling. She looked at Savannah and nodded.

They crept farther down the tunnel, crouched with their arms drawn in so as not to brush the twisting walls. The bats thickened the deeper they went, like fur growing from the rocks. Savannah kept both the flashlight and the rifle straight out in front of her. A part of her considered going back with the rifle, to see if the face was still up there, peering down. To see about taking a shot. But the horrible image of that face—the peeling skin, the yellow eyes and long, sideways pupil—instantly snuffed out the thought.

Besides, she'd already proven to be lousy with the rifle. She didn't trust herself with it. Chances were he'd duck away just as she brought it up to aim or that she'd miss if she did get the shot off. And then there they'd be, one less bullet out of how many Savannah didn't know because she'd yet to count, but certainly no more than four. Plus there was always the chance she'd happen to detach her retinas again. To once more go, as the saying went, blind as a bat.

She moved ahead slowly, pausing at the difficult spots to check on Mía behind her. Every time she turned her head Savannah couldn't help but also scan the darkness from which they'd come. Shiloh had been so close, could have so easily just dropped down and gotten them. So why hadn't he? Was he playing with them? Savannah didn't think he'd been lingering all this time—weeks or even months—just for sport.

So far at least one of Teddy's stories had turned out to be true, even if he hadn't known it at the time: Shiloh was up there. And if that was the case then Savannah had to assume it was—as her father also said—Mía that he wanted. The girl had been his bribe—a little sister pledged to replace the one he'd lost.

And since he hadn't dropped in and grabbed Mía back when he had the chance, then maybe Shiloh really *couldn't* enter the cave, this Sipapu with all its bad juju. And if that was so, then why was Savannah trying to escape the cave at all?

Because she had no other choice. Because it was find an alternate route of escape, or stay inside and starve.

"Do you smell that?" Mía said.

Savannah sniffed. The smell permeated the air, stirring in with the dust kicking up at their feet. It was the rich animal odor of the bats, their black stains on the rocks at the girls' feet, combined with something more pungent and fresh. Something familiar.

And then it came to her, the memory of the scent unfurling, peeling open with all its awful meaning.

It was the scent of flesh.

Savannah came to a stop, her eyes falling to a patch of dirt on the floor and, smack dab inside it, a boot print. Blood pooled on some of the rocks around it, dark and congealing. Savannah raised her flashlight beam. Her empty stomach twisted on itself.

A few steps ahead, the tunnel ended in a collapse of rocks. No, not quite ended. There was a small aperture between them about the size of a beach ball—too small for Teddy's big frame to have squeezed through. Blood streaked the bottom lip of the rocky mouth, spilling down it like drool. And sticking out of this mouth like a half-chewed meal was a foot. A bare foot whose skin had turned purple, the calf and shin all but carved away.

Mía screamed and turned to run but Savannah grabbed her.

"Shhh, I know. I know," Savannah said.

"That's Grandma!"

"I know, shhh."

"Let's go back. Let's turn around and—"

"No, we can't turn around. We have to go through. There's no other way."

It was the truth, and Savannah hated it. Out of the corner of her eyes she noticed the bats beginning to stir, unfolding their wings in sleepy agitation.

"I want you to just wait right here," Savannah said. "You don't have to look. Just close your eyes if you want. I'm going to go through and try and move...." She almost said *it*. "I'm going to try and move her."

Mía trembled in Savannah's arms. Savannah released her and handed her the rifle. She then turned and began to creep toward the hole between the rocks.

Why hadn't she anticipated this, stumbling upon her grandmother's body? *Because you had other things on your mind*, she told herself. Things like the feel of a giant hand wrapping about her ankle. The clacking sound of a bear trap springing shut. The sight of acid-burnt facial tissue. Nightmares all. And what were nightmares but twisty passages with one horror popping up after another?

A boot lay on its side beneath the foot. As Savannah approached the opening, she tried not to think about how many times she'd seen that boot at the foot of her grandmother's bed, side-by-side with its twin. Or else dipping its heel below the stirrup of Grandma's saddle. A slick-looking fabric, once green but now dark with blood, dangled from the rocks next to the foot, and Savannah recognized the bottom of her grandmother's sleeping bag. She had been cut out of it.

From the other side of the hole there came a wet smacking sound. Was something dripping, water perhaps? Blood? Or was it only the gushy natural sound of the body putrefying? Of gases releasing and fluids draining?

Savannah pushed at the foot. The leg pushed back at her with the stiff resistance of rigor mortis. The smell of flesh wafted across Savannah's face, making her eyes water as a hot rush of bile surged up her throat. She swallowed it down and held her breath, pressing harder on the foot, shoving it back onto the other side. Without hesitating Savannah followed it, diving through the hole. The rocks tore at her, ripping her shirt and slicing her skin, but she didn't stop wriggling until she was all the way through.

She landed flat on the corpse. There was a sudden squawking sound and something squirmed from under Savannah's belly. Savannah screamed and shot up, slamming her head hard into the ceiling. Now the bile did come up. She rolled off the body and began to retch, her stomach heaving and heaving in pain. The strange squawking noise sounded again, this time from farther down the tunnel. Savannah grabbed the MagLite hanging from her neck and aimed it. There stood Tailypo, yowling at her, his mouth and fangs coated in blood.

"*Savannnaaah!*" Mía called.

"Just hold on," Savannah said, pushing herself to her knees beside the body. "I'm going to move her. *Shoo! Get!*"

Tailypo crept back over to the body, and Savannah shoved him away. Something fell onto the ground between them, and both Savannah's and Tailypo's heads tilted down. The thing flapped its wings frantically, spinning. Tailypo pounced on it, stomping the little bat in his paws.

Savannah's breath caught in her throat. She raised her flashlight to the tunnel's ceiling. The entire rocky tube was all of a sudden *alive*. The walls and ceiling rippled with the flutter of a thousand little brown wings. The cave a deafening chorus of tiny screeches.

"SAVANNAH THE BATS!"

A gust of wind plowed over Savannah, the bats all at once launching from the ceiling and walls and whooshing past in the direction she had just come. Savannah herself tucked into a ball, making herself as small as possible, covering her ears with her hands to protect them from the piercing shrieks. She squeezed her eyes shut and tried not to think about all the leathery wings skimming her hair or the stiff form of the body nearby. She strained to put her consciousness in another place, to shut it somewhere it didn't exist, like death. But Savannah succeeded only in letting her mind drift overhead where it zoomed out to reveal the full and monstrous glory of her reality: fourteen years old and stuck inside a black wind tunnel of bats, the butchered corpse of her own grandmother laid out beside her.

Savannah screamed; screamed until her vocal chords threatened to tear.

Then everything became still. Savannah stopped screaming but remained as she was, catching her breath. Finally she removed her hands from her ears. From far down the tunnel in the direction of the skylight there echoed the retreating whine of the bats....

There were also the sounds of Tailypo chewing on his bat — completely unaffected it seemed, as well as Mía's gentle sobbing coming from the other side of the opening.

No more of this, Savannah thought, pushing herself up on all fours. Her nerves, her sanity, all of it was ready to snap. She took hold of her grandmother's cold hand and, willing herself not to look, dragged the body to a shallow crevice against the wall. She slid the body inside and covered it with rocks. She had Mía pass her the rifle and backpack before guiding her sister through the hole. Mía shined her headlamp on the ground, gasped and pointed. "What's *he* doing here?"

Savannah looked at Tailypo. He was almost finished with the bat and was already eyeing the crevice where Savannah had concealed the body. "Nothing," Savannah said. "But we're taking him with us. You think you can carry him?"

Mía frowned, and Savannah knew she was thinking about getting bitten and scratched. She observed her sister's eyes drift toward the crevice near the wall. The cat began to walk in that direction. Mía shook out of her puffy coat, lunged after Tailypo and flattened the coat on top of him. She wrapped him up in a bundle, then hoisted him against her chest. She held him tightly swaddled, the little black face poking out of the fabric, mewling.

"Let's go," Mía said.

Savannah slipped the pack behind her shoulders and picked up the rifle. She led her sister farther down the tunnel, away from the body. She was aware they marched in the opposite direction of the evacuating bats, but she refused to let this dampen her hope for a second exit. It was light out after all — or at least it was when she'd peered through the skylight. Last she saw the sky appeared on the verge of either sunrise or nightfall. If it was morning above ground, then the bats almost certainly wouldn't be looking to leave, and there very well could be a second opening further down the tunnel. If, on the other hand, it was nightfall…. If that was the case Savannah would prefer not to think about it.

The girls clambered along. At one point the tube broadened into an oval room just high enough for them to stand up in. But soon after the ceiling once more lowered, the tube narrowing, winding. Savannah thought of intestines, the guts of the earth.

Finally they turned a corner, and the tunnel abruptly stopped. This time there was no small aperture to wriggle through, only a solid wall of smooth, once-melted stone. Savannah padded her hand along it, feeling in vain for some hidden way out. Panic rose in her chest, denial stomping it back down until there was nothing left to deny and the panic gave way to surrender. Savannah put her back to the wall and sank to the floor. She pulled her knees up, dropped her face against them and started to cry.

"No, Savannah, don't. Please don't."

Tailypo yowled and was cut short as Mía squeezed her tighter. Mía's words had wavered and Savannah could hear her sister on the verge of tears herself. She knew the sight of her big sister giving up was too much for Mía, but Savannah couldn't help it. She *had* given up.

"All of this...all of this for nothing," Savannah said. "Why did we even stick it out this long? We should've just died a long time ago. When we first came down into this place we should have just killed ourselves and that way..."

"Stop, Savannah."

"...it could've already been over. Grandma had even told me how. She showed me those pills and said that—"

"Savannah, shut up!" Mía said, and this time Savannah did. Mía had her headlamp aimed at the ceiling. Her mouth popped open, eyes widening. "Do you hear that?"

Savannah listened, scanning her sister's face for clues to whatever it was she was supposed to be hearing. Mía looked back down the tunnel. Savannah heard it: a steady tapping from somewhere in the shadows. A tapping that also sort of plopped.

A dripping.

Savannah pushed herself to her feet and the girls crept softly towards the sound—back into the taller, oval-shaped room. Savannah shined the light around, trying to locate the exact source of the drips. Something gleamed and she swung the light on an icicle, a muddy one, the tip dripping into a half-frozen puddle of muck on the floor.

"Keep your light on it," Savannah said, letting her own light hang. Savannah propped the rifle against the wall, then felt along the ceiling around the icicle. Her fingers touched rocks, as well as something soft. She scraped away at it, wet clumps of soil dropping down and splatting. Her fingernails dug into what felt like a moist stick.

Not just a stick, Savannah realized. A root.

She clawed at the ceiling, showering herself with dirt, rocks, and then soggy pine needles. Fluffy white crystals sprinkled down last. They sparkled in the lamplight, dusting the back of Savannah's neck, melting down her spine.

"Snow." Mía said, a grin spreading across her face.

Savannah jammed her hands hard and as high up as she could. Her fingers burst through the icy crust of the earth, a laser piercing of radiant light striking her face. A light too warm and cosmically loving for any flashlight beam.

It was the light of the morning sun.

Savannah tore the opening wider. She grabbed the tree root in both hands, stuck her feet against the cave's wall and popped her head out. The sunlight felt almost painful, pressing like thumbs through Savannah's eyelids and into her brain. She could only squint at it. The air was frigid and crisp, but the morning rays encasing her cheeks were warm, nourishing. The woody scent of the forest was rich in Savannah's nostrils, invigorating to the core. She lifted her chin and forced her eyes to open a little wider. She was at the base of a massive juniper tree in a thick part of forest. Dazzling swaths of snow skirted the trees. The sun shone in brilliant slivers through the tree limbs, the few clouds drifting above it pink with azure outlines.

How long had it been since she'd last seen anything so beautiful? Had she ever? Peering at the sky, Savannah experienced a wave of déja vu. She couldn't place it. After all, when had she ever crawled from a hole in the earth into the rising sun?

She hadn't, but the Ancient Tonolans had. They experienced it while fleeing the darkness of their crumbling world for this one. Were they too met by this same early morning sun? Could it be *their* recollection of this sight, floating about in the greater collective memory of the universe, that came to Savannah now? Did it come to her as proof there would always be hells to escape, whether in this life or another?

Savannah burst into tears.

A hand tugged at her pant leg. "What's wrong?" Mía whispered from below. "Where are we, Savannah? What do you see?"

Savannah blinked a few times, sniffed and pulled herself together. She'd nearly forgotten what she was supposed to be looking for, forgotten that their escape was not yet complete. She looked around and saw only forest, heard only the chirpy songs of birds.

But just because she didn't see anything didn't mean something wasn't there.

Savannah dropped back into the tunnel. She held her arms out to Mía. "Here, give me the cat."

Mía took a step back, hugging Tailypo tighter in his bundle. He continued to cry.

"It'll make him shut up," Savannah said. "And if something is up there better it get him than us. Let's send him up and just see what happens. If it's nothing, and then we can go."

Mía swung her headlamp onto the cat, his grimy, yowling face in the coat. She handed the bundle to Savannah who quickly shoved it out of the hole. Coat and cat landed with a thump. There was a rustling of material and Savannah raised her head out of the hole again to see Tailypo paw himself free. He stood and shook. The rays of the sun gave his matted black coat an oily sheen. Just like Savannah, Tailypo scrunched up his face, his eyes struggling to adjust. The cat was quiet as he surveyed his new surroundings.

There came a loud chittering from somewhere in the trees. Tailypo tensed, his nubby tail standing at attention, and his face swung in the direction of the sound.

"Aw hell," Savannah said.

"What?" Mía asked.

"Squirrel," Savannah said.

The cat's eyes finally widened. Staying focused, he lowered slightly on his legs, the nubby tail twitching madly now. The chittering sounded again, the whole forest echoing with it. Tailypo tore after it like a rocket, leaving only a sprinkle of earth.

"Well, I think that's the last we'll ever see of him," Savannah said. "So long, demon cat."

"We can't go get him?"

"Why, you want to keep him? That cat has been nothing but a monster to you and me his whole life. Honestly I can't even picture anyone else taking care of him. Who else would Tailypo take for an owner? After the way he's been living, these open woods are going to be paradise. The best home he could ask for."

Mía clicked off her light, grabbed the tree root as Savannah had done and begun to pull herself up. Savannah had to help her, but soon Mía's head was sticking out of the hole.

Savannah held her sister up. "Besides, unless you still see him, I'd say he's twenty feet up some tree by now. And neither of us is going climbing."

Mía pulled herself higher, squirming herself out of the hole.

"Wait, Mía. We still don't know —"

"Let me go, Savannah. It's okay."

After a second, Savannah loosened her grip on her sister. Mía crawled the rest of the way out. Savannah's heart pounded the second her sister was on the other side, separated from her. Mía lay on her belly, and Savannah handed her first the backpack and then the rifle. Feeling suddenly naked and prone all by herself, Savannah said a silent goodbye to the stone tunnel, the darkness and the secrets it contained. In her mind's eye she saw a tiny red light. Still recording, perhaps, somewhere in the earth.

She pulled up and through, into the open air. Mía helped her to her feet, brushing the icy sludge off her sister's chest and legs. Savannah glanced for only a second at the surrounding forest before picking up the rifle and counting its cartridges. Four. She closed the bolt and slung the rifle over her shoulder. Mía put her coat back on, then the backpack. After that, they ran.

22

Their route out of the forest was not the same one they'd taken on the way in. This time there were no water crossings, no crow feathers or steady grade. Instead, after running what had to be close to a mile over flat ground — avoiding snow patches, cringing at every snapped twig or clattering rock, the sun all the while sailing overhead — the forest floor abruptly dropped and the girls found themselves at the precipice of an immense mesa. They must've come up its more gradual front side the night they rode the horses. Now it seemed like they'd reached the edge of a halved mountain. At least half a mile of sheer rock lay between them and the desert below. The land below was vast, rippling with gravelly mounds coated in brush and juniper. Red-soiled arroyos extended from the smaller mesas like capillaries. In the far distance the desert plane was broken by a butte the size of a low skyscraper, jutting magnificently up with a smooth, rust-red tabletop.

Savannah unzipped the backpack on her sister's shoulders and pulled out one of the two liter-sized water bottles she had packed. The girls drank from it, the water achingly cool along Savannah's parched throat. She returned the bottle quarter-full and retrieved the compass. Anxiety gnawed in her chest the longer they remained standing, the forest behind them unnervingly still, patient. But running aimless and exposed into a bleak desert wasn't going to do them any good. The girls' world had blown suddenly to infinite proportions. It was vital they keep some sort of bearings.

Savannah lay the compass flat in her palm and held it over the rim of the mesa. They faced almost due north. She didn't know the area well, but enough to know Albuquerque was still a good distance south, and that if they weren't careful they could wander all the way to Arizona without seeing a soul. Without many residences along this dry swath of the reservation, their best hope was reaching a road. She thought back to that gray afternoon eons ago when Grandma had driven them into this wilderness. After traveling for hours south along the highway, she remembered her grandmother turning onto the rough dirt road. She had turned right.

"We need to head east," Savannah said, pivoting her feet to face the rising sun.

They took off along the edge of the mesa, looking for a way down. After a few minutes search and just as Savannah started to debate making a go at scaling the walls — it was that or reenter the forest — they came upon a tree-lined fissure veining from top to bottom. Water had clearly once run down the path, although by the looks of it that had been long ago. The fissure cut at a more gradual, horizontal degree along the face of the mesa. The girls began their descent, plunging through great swaths of shale that cascaded around their ankles. They clung for balance to the same brush and tree limbs that scratched their faces and ripped out thick strands of their hair. Every little dart of a bird or strange shadow made Savannah's heart constrict, her hand grabbing instinctively for the rifle behind her shoulder. Halfway down Savannah remembered to turn off the MagLite hanging around her neck. The girls said little to one another as they hiked. Every so often Savannah would look back and catch Mía eyeing the path above them — doing what she herself was doing and refusing to believe it was this easy. That they were free.

The decline tapered, the trees growing farther and farther apart until the girls found themselves walking on flat ground. It was then that Savannah's weariness caught up to her. The true degradation of her muscles. After all this time living like some hibernating rodent she had atrophied. The plunge down the steep mesa had been an effort of adrenaline. But now that chemical force was fading, Now she ran on sheer will. Utterly fear-induced will.

The sun was directly overhead. Savannah felt it hot upon her crown, though the air remained crisp. The girls paused under the last of the tall trees and its protective cover. They had veered steadily west within the fissure, and Savannah rechecked the compass to get her bearings. She could only guess at how many miles away the highway might be from their current location. At least a dozen she'd say, recalling the long drive along the roughshod path to where they'd met Shiloh in his little black sheep truck and camper.

Oh God, *where they'd met Shiloh....* Why did she only remember this now? Would there be any reason for him to keep the same base camp? What had become of that black sheep truck?

"We need to go wide around this mesa," Savannah said, "get further out into the flats."

Mía looked down the base to the mesa, her eyes glossing over. She closed them for a couple seconds and then nodded.

"Ready?"

"Tired."

"I know, me too. But we have to keep going."

The girls took one last look behind them before breaking loose from the tree and then scrambling along spills of crumbled mesa. They ran with their backs hunched, weighed as if by the sudden exposure of the desert: a cold plane of red soil littered with sandstone that made Savannah think of Mars.

They were just a few minutes across it when Savannah heard a bellow behind her. The noise caused her to jump, spin around and in the process forget her footing. She tripped over a loose rock, pitched forward and fell. She landed flat on her chest, scraping her palms and the tip of her chin. The rifle rolled out into the dirt.

Mía bent down and helped her to her knees. "You okay?"

"Did you hear that?"

Mía's eyes widened. She held her breath, listening.

"I thought I heard something," Savannah said. "Like, someone shouting."

"Shouting what?"

"I don't know. Just...like a call."

They were quiet again a moment.

"I don't hear anything," Mía said.

Savannah grabbed the rifle and climbed up, brushing herself off. "Come on. Let's keep moving."

They resumed at a jog. Savannah picked at her grated hands while she moved, sucking out dirt and blood, peeling off dangling white slices of her palm. She was absorbed in this task when again she heard it: that same weird bellow. Only this time it was closer, almost directly behind them. Savannah skidded to a halt and dropped to one knee. She pulled Mía behind her, took the rifle off her shoulder and aimed.

A cloud of dust rose in the direction they'd come from. It angled toward them, fanning out, and Savannah followed it not through the scope but with the sight at the end of the barrel. She held the stock tight against her shoulder, unaware she was even doing it until the barrel began to droop—her arms, her whole body, her entire being too weak and tired and no match for the weight of this gun. The anticipation of its power.

Another bellow rose from within the gaining dust storm and Savannah watched as the first pair of eyes poked out, the glistening snout, the little ears on each side—green plastic ear tags dangling.

"You kidding me?" Savannah said. "Cows?" She stood and slung the rifle back behind her shoulder. She could still feel the depression of the trigger on her forefinger and was surprised by how close she'd come to shooting a harmless cow. Which, in this case, wouldn't exactly have been the worst thing she could do.

"I'd eat a ribeye right now, Mía. How 'bout you?"

She felt weirdly giddy, deliriously so. Maybe it was the sunlight, its very presence. The sky overhead instead of stone. Or was it the truth behind everything that had happened—her grandmother and father both dead—angling for acknowledgement as Savannah resisted?

When Mía failed to answer, Savannah looked to see her sister with her arms extended in front of her, bracing herself.

"What are you—"

"They're not stopping," Mía said. Savannah turned just as the first cow clambered into her, its nose jabbing hungrily into her chest, knocking her backward a step. Savannah shoved the cow's head away.

The others rushed in and circled, enclosing the girls in a bellowing ring of snot and saliva-dripping mouths, bulging and bloodshot eyes.

Savannah shoved at the first cow again but it kept shoving into her.

"Savannah, make them go away!"

"Relax. You can't really blame 'em. The only time these cows ever see a person is for hay or watering time. That or stock-trailer day, but no member of the herd ever comes back from *that* with any story to tell. Just slap 'em, push 'em away. They'll get the message."

Mía tried to push one of them but it only flubbed its lips searchingly over her small hands. Savannah pulled the sleeve of her jacket down over her hand and whapped the cow on the ears. It startled backward, eyeing Savannah in confusion. The other animals seemed to take notice of this sudden hostility and eased off. Savannah ushered Mía behind her and began prodding the cows aside with the rifle. She considered firing the rifle in the air to try and startle the animals away. The sound might even draw the attention of any nearby rancher. Then again, the sound could also draw some very unwanted attention. Or, at the minimum, simply be a waste of a bullet. A bullet she might just need.

Reluctantly the cows split to the side, a path opening between them. Savannah took Mía by the hand and led her through. The girls reached the edge of the herd. They froze. Savannah's eyes widened. Mía's hand tightened around hers.

There, lined in a neat row not twenty feet away, stood four horses. They stared at Savannah and Mía with blinking eyes — seemingly just as unsure of what appeared before them as the girls were. The sun shone lustrously upon their long winter coats. Each one was old, bony. Gray nubby scabs dotted their thin legs. One of them — dun-colored and taller than the others — was a stallion, and Savannah wondered if he wasn't a truly feral horse, born wild. Two of the others were geldings — one which stood awkwardly with what was clearly a bum right foreleg. The last was a mare: dapple gray with a tail cut short.

"Is that..." Mía said. "Are those —"

"Yep. Both of them. Looks like they found their friends."

The horses flared their nostrils and flicked their tails but otherwise did not come any closer. Savannah knew they were hungry though. Weary, but hungry. The stallion whinnied at them.

The cows continued to bellow but had already started to disperse, forgetting about the girls as their noses scoured the desert floor, blowing up dust. Savannah opened Mía's backpack again. "You're going to have to help me," Savannah said, slipping the backpack off her sister's shoulders.

"Help with what? What are we doing?"

Savannah took out a spool of blue paracord. "Getting a ride out of here."

She handed Mía the cord and told her to unspool half of it. Next she removed the water bottle and med kit from the pack but left in the smaller items, adding in a handful of pebbles for good measure. She shook the bag around, the contents muffled against the dense nylon. It might just work.

"We only need to get one," Savannah said. "That dun stallion looks like he's already about got us figured out, and if he runs they all do. We're best off with one of the others. I'm thinking the mare right there, the one who kind've looks like—"

She almost said 'Beeswax,' but something kept the name from coming out. Embarrassment? The fact the mare *didn't* look all that much like Beeswax, but she had the same *essence*. It was somehow personal to Savannah.

"What do I do?" Mía asked.

"As soon as she sticks her nose in this bag, throw the cord around her neck. Then hold tight and whatever you do don't let go."

Mía bunched a few feet of cord in one hand while the other held the remaining amount on the spool. Savannah shook the backpack enticingly out in front of her. Slowly the girls approached the horses.

The stallion flinched, stepped back. The others followed suit. Savannah kept shaking the could-be oat bag as she soothed the animals, assuring them that it was all right. The horses tossed their heads, nodding toward the bag as if trying to waft in its scent. The girls came to a stop shortly before the mare. Savannah held the bag low, almost to the ground. She shook it. The horse sniffed, extending her nose. Savannah lowered the bag a little more. The mare stepped forward and reached her nose into the bag.

Mía flicked the loose paracord over the mare's neck and clasped it together at the throat. The other three horses skittered back at the motion, but the mare remained calm. Her big head was heavy in Savannah's arms as her mouth pushed hungrily to the bottom of the bag. Savannah set the bag on the ground and grabbed the cord above her sister's hands. The mare inspected the limp bag some more, then ran its wet nose over Savannah's face. Savannah tied the cord in a knot around the neck.

"We need a bridle," Mía said.

Savannah gently tugged at the cord's knot, testing it. "Can you keep a good hold of her? I don't think she's going anywhere, but just in case she tries."

Mía wrapped the cord around her hands a few times and spread her feet into a ready stance. Savannah got out her knife and cut the remaining cord. She then went to work on a bridle.

While nothing fancy, it'd be simple to make. And, most importantly, it would do the job. Something about the mare told Savannah the bridle could be bitless, that a hackamore would be enough. She cut two short strips of cord. One she tied in a loop that would fit snugly over the mare's nose—a bosal, as her grandmother had taught her. She connected the other cord to each side of the loop to make a headpiece. Savannah then cut two longer lengths of cord. These would be the reins. If she had more time she'd braid everything first. But such a step would only be aesthetic; single extensions of paracord could support more than five hundred pounds. Savannah learned this while other fathers were teaching their kids how to catch fly balls or play Mario Kart.

She inspected her creation, feeling strangely proud. She had the strong desire to be *seen* in that moment. It was a yearning accompanied by a terrible sense of loss.

"Got her?" Savannah asked, letting the mare sniff the bridle.

"Yes. Hurry let's go. I don't like being out here."

Casually, as if it was something the two of them had been doing together for years, Savannah slipped the bosal over the mare's nose and tucked her ears under the headpiece. The animal threw her head only a little, and Mía was yanked a step. Otherwise she offered little fuss as Savannah twisted and knotted any bits of slack in the bridle. She gently tugged the reins in either direction, getting the feel. Mía removed the loop around the horse's neck. She collected the backpack and put it over her shoulders.

The other horses were all three whinnying, nervous about whatever was happening. A few of the cows bellowed in reply. The cacophony swept across the desert. Savannah ran her hand lovingly along the horse's flank, grabbed a fistful of white mane and hoisted herself up top. The mare spun the moment Savannah got her leg over, but she held on, pulling herself upright. The mare nickered and spun but Savannah talked to her, reminded her who she was. Who they both were. She caught a glimpse of the other three horses bolting into the desert, a trail of dust kicking up behind. The mare slowed to a stop. She turned to face her fleeing comrades. She whinnied, long and piercing. Her call echoed. She watched them, ears perked. Her flanks swelled out and she let out a deep sigh.

"It's okay," Savannah said, rubbing the mare's neck. "You have us."

Mía reached up and Savannah helped pull her on board behind her. The rifle pressed between them as Mía hugged her arms around Savannah's waist. It was awkward, and Savannah felt the horse totter a bit under their weight. She kept hold of the mane tight in one hand, the reins in the other. She asked Mía if she was ready and Mía said that she was. Savannah tapped with her heels and finally let herself think it.

They were getting away.

23

The sun dropped behind their backs, casting their shadows ever longer upon the red soil. The ride was uneven at first between the girls' shifting weights and the uncertain legs of the horse. For a long time the mare seemed capable of only a jagged trot, her old bones reacquainting with the weight on her back. But gradually a balance was struck between horse and riders, a pact of sorts. The mare found her stride, lengthening into a smooth gallop. She became self-perpetual in power, in rediscovery of her vitality.

Savannah was almost positive the mare had been abandoned, released to fend for itself along the harsh reservation. At least that's what her father had said. But there was the slim chance she *did* still have an owner somewhere, and at this thought Savannah couldn't help smiling. After all they'd done, after all they'd been made to do, here the two girls were committing one more act of degeneracy: horse thieving. In a different century they could have been hanged for this latest offense alone.

The wind picked up, scattering the dust behind them. But they remained exposed, and when a shallow wash opened before them Savannah steered the horse inside. The wash was dotted with sage as well as an occasional cottonwood. In between the vegetation the sand was firm, half-frozen. She kept the reins loose, the mare keeping her stride, finding her way.

Savannah's strength was fading fast. Mía slumped against her, and she knew her sister felt it too. Before long the mare's bony spine became painful against Savannah's crotch; she leaned increasingly forward, pressed her hands down in order to relieve the pressure. She knew the ache in her bones, the fatigue spreading as if replacing something vital in her body. Something like the desire to go on.

The mare's stride grew rhythmic, and the earth sped by underneath. The sand twinkled, hypnotizing. Savannah drifted into a daze. She didn't even notice the creaking sound until it was almost directly overhead.

A shadow fell over the girls. Savannah pulled back the reins. She looked up and saw a windmill.

The aluminum sails whirled in the breeze, rocking the steel tower gently and making it squeak in a way Savannah found lonely. The girls dismounted and approached the edge of the wash. A ruddy pond lay near the base of the windmill. The water was shallow and its perimeter glistened with ice, the banks a sloped mire of frozen hoof prints and manure. Savannah recalled one of her father's old stories about the sheriffs of the Old West staking out the local watering holes to catch outlaws. To Savannah, these two things alone — a dilapidated windmill and a mucky pond — contained enough civilization to look like an oasis.

Except there was more, much more. Beyond the windmill stood a house, round and no more than twenty feet in diameter. A tin chimney stuck out from the low edge of the conic roof. Such a house was called a hogan, Savannah recalled, although this one appeared only halfway completed with walls of exposed plywood that had turned brown and begun to peel. A single window had been cut, except instead of glass the frame was covered by what looked like rawhide tacked from the inside. A rust-red horse trailer sat parked next to the pen. The trailer tilted on a flat tire and weeds grew under it. A rough dirt road extended eastward from the hogan.

Next to the house stretched a large wooden pen containing a bustle of activity. About a dozen sheep milled about inside. Every so often one bleated out and Savannah could hear it under the creak of the windmill. Dust and mud clots clung to their wool. They appeared anxious, hungry perhaps. Unaware of the girls' presence.

"The sheep ranch," Mía said, dismayed. "He was telling the truth."

"It doesn't look like anyone's home."

"Why?"

"Because I don't see a car, do you? And...I don't know. It just *feels* that way, don't you think? It feels like we're alone."

But that wasn't all it felt like, even though Savannah wouldn't admit it out loud. The place seemed vacant. Yet, at the same time, it didn't.

"Do you think there's a phone?" Mía asked.

"I don't know. There's no telephone poles. You know what sounds really good right now? A lamb chop. All greasy."

"I just want to get out of here."

The attitude in her sister's voice surprised Savannah. She liked it. It said her sister still had some fight left. Because her drained and skeletal face suggested otherwise.

They climbed out of the wash, and Savannah let the mare drink from the pond. The sheep burst into commotion at the sight of them, pooling to get closer to them. Bleating. Pleading. A few angled their heads between the wooden slats as they called out, their long tongues hanging out of their crazed faces. The flock bunched together so tight that one of them — a black-faced ram with big curly horns — reared up and rested down on top his fellows.

The girls approached the hogan, Savannah's sense of unease thickening. Boot prints trailed about the property, running mainly between the home's front door and a parking area where a vehicle had — recently judging by the scattered dirt — flipped around and spun out of here.

"Look," Mía said, pointing to a tall butte in the eastern horizon. Savannah squinted at it. Nestled against the butte's flank and wavering as if a mirage lay a tiny strip of buildings. The few metal roofs glimmered in the late-day sun like fish scales. "If no one's here," Mía said, "then maybe that's where they are."

Three warped steps and a railing led to the front door. Savannah wrapped the mare's reins around the railing and knocked. They waited, listening, hearing only the persistent bleating of the animals behind them — desperate, Savannah thought by the scrawniness of the sheep, for food. She knocked one more time and when still there came no reply she tried the knob. The door was unlocked. She opened it. Cold and musty air whooshed across her face. She leaned her head in and uttered hello a few times before she and Mía stepped inside.

The interior was dark, the only light being what streamed through the opened door and what little filtered grimly through the lambskin curtain drawn over the one window. The place was a mess. Dirty laundry lay strewn about the uncarpeted floor, some of it quite old Savannah thought based on the way it remained in its same bunched shape when she kicked it aside. A wad of bedding draped against one part of the encircling walls, a pillow wrapped inside the blankets but no mattress and certainly no bed frame beneath. Everywhere lay objects typically kept outside, things like shovels, rebar, and even a couple truck tires. Trash—everything from food wrappers to glass bottles to crumpled up balls of tin foil—lay about as if rained down from the round roof. The only pieces of furniture were a faded pink La-Z-Boy with stuffing popping out from numerous splits, a small cabinet, and a square kitchen table with one chair pulled up to it. On top of this table sat a partially eaten Subway sandwich, still laid out on its logoed wax paper, along with a soda cup.

Without thinking twice Savannah grabbed the cup, pried off the plastic lid and the straw sticking through it and drank. The ice cubes had long ago melted, watering it down some, but the Dr. Pepper was nonetheless a sugary dream-come-true as it glided down Savannah's throat. She had to make herself stop before handing the rest of the soda over to her sister. Savannah picked up the sandwich—turkey by the looks of it—and sniffed. It smelled all right, despite the bread being soppy with mustard and tomato juice, and the wilting shards of lettuce sticking out....

Savannah chomped into it and if her hunger had been like a caged lion before, the sandwich not only swung open the cage but zapped the lion with a cattle prod on its way out. Handing the rest of the hoagie to her sister, Savannah searched the cabinet. The shelves were mostly bare save for some plastic cups, a few mismatched bowls and an assortment of basic utensils. But there, sitting the bottom shelf, glorious as a grail: a can of SPAM.

Savannah flipped the tab on the can, peeled it open, dug out a glob of the pink meat with her fingers and ate. Never in her life had she tasted anything so delicious. She dug her fingers in again, put them in her mouth and could cry it was so good.

Savannah wolfed down half the can, gave the other half to Mía, then went about inspecting the rest of the hogan. The livestock outside suggested that someone lived here at least some of the time, if not most—a bachelor by the looks of it. Savannah figured the resident might belong to a larger family or clan, situated somewhere else not far. She wondered if perhaps this was his retreat—a little plot of land, a house and a few animals he could call his own. She recalled the distant buildings her sister had pointed out. The penned sheep made her think that wherever the homeowner had gone he didn't intend on staying long.

Then again—the realization causing Savannah's anxiety to rise up anew—the unfinished sandwich and soda suggested that wherever he'd gone, he'd gone there in a hurry.

"What are you looking for?" Mía asked, finishing the SPAM.

"A cell phone, a radio, a…I don't know but *something* that can get us out of here."

"If whoever lives here has a cell phone he probably has it with him," Mía said.

Savannah kicked apart the bedding, finding nothing. She almost said something smart back to her sister, something biting and perhaps even hurtful, but stopped herself. Even if Mía's comment hadn't been helpful, turning on her right now would be even less so.

"We could just wait for the person to come back," Mía said, taking a seat at the kitchen table. She draped her arm across the table and rest her head on top of it. "Let's just rest here. Wait until someone comes back."

Outside the sheep seemed to be crying louder, their unrelenting wails swirling into a torrent of noise that could probably be heard for miles. She considered releasing the sheep, freeing them to the mercy of the wild as she had Tailypo. One more liberation from this whole ordeal. She didn't know what they could do about the sheep except leave them. Surely whoever owned them wasn't abandoning his property altogether. He knew he still had live animals penned here, that they'd be getting hungry....

Savannah watched the sky darken through the open door, clouds connecting. "Is that something you really want to do?" she said. "In here? Now? Just wait?"

Mía raised her head and looked around. Savannah could see the disquiet sinking into her as well.

Mía stood up. "I could keep going."

They returned outside. Something had changed in the air. A cold wind bit at Savannah's cheeks. The windmill sails whirled around in a blur, the vane twisting in all directions of the compass. A storm was coming. Savannah could smell it. It was the tranquilizing scent of winter wind, whisking with it the other smells of fresh manure and stale pond water, wool and dirt. It was the smell of despair.

She grabbed the mare's reins and walked to the road leading out of the property. Along the way Savannah checked the sides of the home for water jugs, having found none inside. She didn't see any, but she did find a chunk of salt lick in the brush. Savannah stomped on it and the girls put the pieces in their coat pockets.

They stepped onto the faint two-track road and Savannah peered at the butte in the distance. In the fading light the buildings at the base were indistinct dots. She couldn't be sure, but she'd guess them to be at least ten miles away.

She adjusted the rifle behind her shoulders and prepared to mount the horse. The mare's head swiveled, her ears perked. The yard reflected upside down in the animal's eyes—the hogan and the gray sky. It occurred to Savannah then how still everything had suddenly become. The wind had died. The sheep...had quieted. Silence....

Except for a single voice.... A strange moan that was animal but also somehow *pronounced*, vibrating with undeniable meaning.

Savannah turned around. The sheep huddled together at one end of the pen. Their legs trembled, their faces bowed in terror at the thing parading before them.

The ram walked on his hind legs. Staggering back and forth in the pen, his front legs bent in front of him, cloven hooves every so often clacking together. His long thin tail flicked spasmodically as he tossed his great horned head. The ram's long black mouth opened and closed, pink tongue lolling over big front teeth. Over and over he emitted the same unintelligible chant:

Bak!

It was as if he tried to spit something up. A blockage in his throat. A word.

Bak!

The mare whinnied, ears flattening on her head. The ram grew still. His voice quieted, mouth closing. He dropped to all fours. He turned his head slowly.

The ram looked at Savannah.

And in those eyes — those bright yellow irises and narrow sideway pupils — Savannah saw recognition. At no other time in her life had she looked at anyone, at anything, and ever felt so *known*.

24

A hole opened in the clouds. The last red rays of the sun streamed through, casting upon the magnificent butte like a beacon. The sunlight seeped down the stone flanks, flashed off the windows and metal siding of the structures situated at the bottom, and peeled out along the desert. The butte's shadow stretched ever longer. Then a great gloominess fell upon the land as the overcast reformed. Before long the sun dipped below the horizon. The air turned colder and the wind fiercer, sharpening its teeth.

All the while Savannah dug her heels into the mare's sides, fleeing as fast they could the hogan, the ram, the caverns, the vanishing sun, and everything else at their backs. Everything she refused to think about. It was a mad, bareback dash along a road so rough it was almost invisible, leading to what Savannah hoped were the structures at the bottom of the butte. They reached what looked to be a second path, similarly faint and branching off to the right. The mare slowed as they neared it but Savannah urged her past. For though the sky darkened the silhouettes of the buildings ahead became unmistakable. They were houses. A whole cluster of them.

Mía stayed balanced behind Savannah, legs squeezed, rising and falling in sync with the horse's long stride. She displayed a horsemanship Savannah never knew she had. And why not? Mía came up with horses just like Savannah, a bond in itself. And what good was such an upbringing when suddenly her life depended on it? Mía hunched low, her gaze dead ahead, second-guessing nothing. Neither girl ever looked behind them — they didn't need to; they had both seen it. What exactly *it* was Savannah didn't know, and she didn't care to find out. What she knew instead were the granules of sand grinding between her teeth. The first few tiny flakes of snow whipping in the wind and stinging her face. The sharp stab in her abdomen from eating too much too fast. The cold sweat trickling from her armpits. Her watery eyes and the structures in the distance.

They'd make it by nightfall, she told herself, before the snow grew any heavier. She tried to think of what they'd say once they reached the houses, where they'd even begin once a door opened and they found themselves looking into the first new face since this long nightmare began. She tried to think how they'd explain what they'd seen in the sheep pen, how they'd explain the man — the thing — still out there somewhere. Behind them in their tracks.

And then she remembered what her father had said about Shiloh, how he would come after them no matter how long it took, no matter where they might be. She remembered the terrible betrayal that had been committed — the acid, the screams, the fire. She recalled the debt — the little girl — still owed him. All at once these truths infiltrated Savannah, and for the rest of the ride she took on the steady job of convincing herself that what had happened in the sheep pen had been nothing but a funny act of nature as seen through tired, scarred, and untrustworthy eyes.

Eventually the mare's run slowed to a gallop, then an uneasy trot. Finally she fell into a lumbering, snorting walk. The animal's sweat soaked Savannah's pantlegs. Clouds and falling snow rendered the desert gray and spectral. She squinted at the buildings now slightly obscured — realization and, with it, fear bubbling up as it dawned on her that there were no lights.

Savannah swiveled around to look at her sister. But Mía only kept her stare dead ahead. They finished the ride in silence, refusing or unable to speak upon the cluster of buildings taking shape — no smoke rising from their chimneys, no lamplit windows, no cars. Just a few decayed, sepia-colored structures jutting randomly from the earth like fossils.

They'd come to a ghost town.

A barbwire fence stretched out before the girls, the wooden posts gray, twisted and deteriorated with some rotted through the middle and hanging uselessly by the strung wires. A dense levee of tumbleweeds had swept up against the opposite side. A steel gate, chained and padlocked, barred the road leading inside the town. Tires hung on either side of the gate with the words 'NO TRESPASSING' sprayed on in silver paint.

Getting off the horse, Savannah felt bowlegged, short on her feet and weirdly vulnerable. She stepped her boot down on a strand of one particularly deteriorated section of fencing and ushered Mía and the mare across. Neither girl even questioned whether or not to proceed. Night had fallen and a storm was underway. The sisters trembled, their teeth chattering, and Savannah knew that if they didn't take shelter soon exposure alone would kill them.

Besides, deserted or not, there was still a chance that some useable resources might be found in this old town. Despite the cramps in her stomach, Savannah was still hungry, not to mention parched. The girls each took a long swig of water from what remained in Mía's pack, leaving only a couple swallows. By the look of the gate and the NO TRESPASSING tires, the empty town was privately owned. Could it be that whoever owned it kept a piece or two of the place preserved, perhaps a little cabin to camp out in from time to time and feel nostalgic? A place where one might even keep a few cans of food for just such an occasion? And what had Teddy said about the ghost town — La Gloria, that was the name — and how sometimes mass was still held in the old church? Savannah wasn't Catholic but, starving as she was right now, she had no doubt a communion wafer would taste like God.

She remembered the chips of the salt block in her pockets. She and Mía put some in their mouths and sucked on them. The mare snatched up sparse clumps of yellow grass as they walked. There were about a dozen buildings in all, roughly half on either side of the road, which must have been something of a main street during the town's heyday. Most were small *jacale* homes of mixed clay and brush packed around wooden beams, stacked stones or, in some cases, chickenwire. The houses sagged — their walls crumbling, roofs slumped in the middle or else collapsed utterly with their beams angling skyward. The once-businesses appeared in the best condition, including the adobe post office with its white lettering faded but still readable, and a two-story clay general store with a pitched roof of rusted sheet metal, mostly-smashed windows and a hitching post out front. At the end of the street, next to the general store, loomed the church — equally old yet clearly maintained with windows intact, shingles on the roof and a steeple housing a brass bell.

Still, despite the apparent upkeep of the church, Savannah couldn't help but sense the *abandonment* surrounding the town, the lifelessness of it all. She didn't like places like this, places that had been given up on. It was a depressing feeling to recognize something that while perhaps not yet forgotten was also not exactly missed, like an old gravestone. It made her think of death — a thought punctuated by the grim sky, the cold, and a tiny cemetery behind the church.

She glanced at an all-wood building to her right, caved and looking like a tornado had struck it. *Every town will be a ghost town some day,* he'd said. *La Gloria just got it over with quick....*

They tied the mare to the hitching post in front of the general store and went to the church door. It was thick and padlocked. Savannah took the rifle off her shoulder, tapped the end of the barrel against the window.

"Do it," Mía said. "I won't tell."

Savannah smiled, wishing there was someone around *to* tell, then jabbed the rifle through the glass. It broke easily and Savannah swirled the barrel around the frame to clear any clinging shards.

They climbed through. The church was small, musty with the smell of dust and wax. Savannah turned on the MagLite but the beam was faint and nearly dead. She remembered then the headlamp she had removed from her father's head and took it out of her pocket. The tan headband was stained with blood. Savannah slipped the headlamp over her head and clicked it on. Green light washed over the interior of the church. Six pews sat before a bare altar. A wooden cabinet pressed against the far wall behind the altar. There was no aisle and the girls had to walk around the pews. Tiny wood carvings perched over their heads depicting the Passion. Reaching the cabinet, Savannah opened it but found nothing but stacked hymnals.

"Dammit."

"There's something under the table," Mía said. "Something shiny."

They scooted over and knelt behind the altar. Savannah lifted the thin cloth hanging over it to reveal a number of metal communion cups, saucers, a standing gold crucifix, and a brass, lamp-shaped object attached to a chain. Next to these lay some folded white fabrics and a bottle of wine. Savannah picked up the bottle and read its label, her mouth watering.

"Who's going to stop us?" Mía asked.

"You know, they say if you're stranded in the middle of the ocean in a life boat, and all you have to drink is a bottle of alcohol, the first thing you should do is throw the alcohol overboard."

"But isn't there juice in wine?"

Yeah, and sugar, Savannah thought. *Sugar and calories.*

"I'm hungrier I am thirsty," Mía said.

Savannah eyed the bottle, swishing around the purple liquid at the bottom. There was a little less than a quarter left, and while she'd never been drunk before she didn't think a quarter of a bottle of wine split between them would be enough to, as her school guidance counselor once put it, *impair* them.

The cap was a screw-on. Savannah twisted it off, tipped the bottle back and took a swig—her mouth bursting with the rich and bitter tang of the communion wine. She lowered the bottle grimacing, smacking her lips, and handed it to her sister. Mía drank and made the same face. They looked at each other, smiled, then finished the bottle.

"Come on," Savannah said, "let's go see what else this town has to offer. I think I saw a Chinese buffet when we first walked in."

Mía giggled and Savannah knew she was feeling it too.

They made their way past the pews, crawling back through the broken window into the street. The wind howled, the wooden buildings swaying and groaning, the snow blasting against Savannah's face. Yet none of it bothered her. She didn't feel cold and she didn't feel scared. She no longer hurt and all of a sudden didn't even feel all that tired. Best of all her mind had cleared. She forgot all about any troubles, past or future. Instead, walking with her sister beside her, holding hands and swinging them slightly without even knowing it, Savannah actually felt kind of — dare she say it — happy.

"Do you think we're the only people left in the world?" she asked, half-shouting it over the wind.

"That's *exactly* what I was just thinking," Mía said.

"I really hope we are, to tell the truth."

"Me too. It would be…. It would be—"

"A relief?"

"Yes!" Mia said. "It would be a relief."

"I think I could actually get used to this town," Savannah said.

"Me too."

They went back to where the mare waited, shivering, in front of the general store. The store appeared to be one of the few structures besides the church left with a door still in place. Although upon closer inspection Savannah found no lock hanging, just a simple brass handle. She grabbed it and pushed but the door didn't budge. She stepped back and kicked. The entire building shook, the old sheet metal on the roof buzzing. The door held and Savannah kicked it a second time, then a third — repeatedly until the door scraped open across the warped floorboards enough for them to peek their heads in. Savannah peered in with her headlamp.

The place looked like it had been abandoned reluctantly, and half-heartedly at that with much of the furniture still remaining. Rows of wooden shelves lined the floor, some of them toppled. The shelves were empty mostly save for a yellowing stack of old newspapers, scattered nails, some molded fabric, a faded box or two and a mess of black mouse droppings. There was a counter complete with an ancient-looking cash register and a chalkboard behind it with some of the old markings still legible. More signs lined the walls: tin advertisements for Coca-Cola, Marlboro, Purina, Winchester, Old Heddon Fishing Lures. A few chairs stood around a wooden table set in one of the corners, and Savannah noticed playing cards on the ground by the chair legs.

A gust of wind struck Mía, rocking her sideways a step. Snowflakes pattered against the building.

"I don't want to be out here anymore," Mía said. "Not tonight."

Savannah lifted her eyes to the second floor. "You want to go upstairs?"

They stepped inside, grinding the door open wider, leading the mare in behind them. Savannah tied the mare to a coat rack nailed to the wall and shoved the door shut again. The girls weaved through the shelves toward a second door behind the counter. The floorboards groaning beneath them, their boots shuffling through the decades-worth of dust that had swept in from the broken windows, Feeling a little bold from the wine, Savannah couldn't help banging her fist on the cash register as she walked by. It dinged and the drawer rolled out slowly.

The door led to a dark hallway with a staircase at one end and at the other a kitchen presided over by a massive cast iron stove. Savannah and Mía climbed the stairs with their hands firmly on the railing. The steps creaked, flexing beneath their feet all the way to an upper platform lit murkily by an intact window thick with grime. The platform led to a series of rooms, the first a bedroom containing a steel twin bed frame topped by a thin mattress that had been chewed and tunneled through by mice, along with a dresser and a floor that was littered with old clothes and blankets. There was a bathroom with a cabinet, mirror, and a long porcelain tub rimed brown. A second bedroom opened to reveal a queen-sized bed and a rocking crib, its red paint peeling off in flakes.

"I wonder what happened to them," Savannah said, walking over to the crib and rocking it. "I wonder if this baby is still alive today, an old lady now. Or else what if she never even made it past being a baby, and this crib is the only proof she ever existed?"

"I'm tired," Mía said. "And I don't like wondering about things like that."

"What? I'm just saying—"

"It sounds like something *he* would say."

In the dark, Savannah flushed.

"Let's just lay down for a while," Mía said, pointing to the bed. "Can we?"

Savannah moved over to the room's single window and crouched to look through where one of the glass panes had fallen out. Outside the snow accumulated in a thin sheet on the road. It built upon the roofs only to swirl away in quick gusts. There came a squeaking sound behind her and Savannah turned to see Mía crawling on top of the bed, lying down.

Savannah went to her. She turned off the headlamp and lay next to her sister, the old dust rising off the mattress and settling around them.

"I don't want to be the only ones left in the world," Mía said.

Savannah put an arm over her. "We're not."

Mía shuddered and Savannah held her tighter. She gazed through the window at the moon, tiny and faint behind the clouds. She felt her eyelids growing heavy. Almost experimentally, Savannah closed them and immediately experienced a moment of panic and confusion when she found herself back in the darkness of the chamber. In the darkness, an old-timey projector cast epileptic images across a screen made of smoke: flashes of blood and bear traps and rams with black faces. She reopened her eyes and the images disappeared, drowned by the murky light of the moon, the glimmering snowflakes drifting in through the broken pane.

She sank into the mattress. Sank and sank and sank. How long, she thought, could she resist the darkness? How long before her eyes could stay open no more and all that she'd left behind caught up with her?

25

Savannah dreamt of all sorts of things, but mainly she dreamt of animals. She had a vision of a lion named Mauricio, no stuffed toy but real and alive, king of beasts in his native Serengeti and known across Africa as the lion who walked through fire. One dream featured a turtle who lived grotesquely, threateningly, outside his shell, while another a garter snake who left its milky, rubber-smelling scent all over Savannah's fingers. She dreamed of owls more ancient and intelligent than any creature to ever live on the earthly plane, of featherless crows, of masterless horses. River trout, black flies, horny toads, tabby cats and salamanders.... There was more, she thought, to this weird collage of wildlife, including somewhere at the center of it all a man. And every single animal, in every form, carried within it a common element, a reoccurring presence, a distinct energy. The energy was dark, and in her dreams the darkness grew stronger as it drew nearer.

The mare whinnied downstairs, and Savannah bolted upright. It took her a moment to remember where she was, on top the bed in the abandoned store, and it shocked her to look out the window and see that it had not only stopped snowing but that it was light out.

Except the light seemed to be moving, beaming through the window and bending along the wall behind her. And then it dawned on Savannah that in the end Shiloh had come for them not on foot or hoof, paw or wing.

He'd come behind a wheel. He'd come with blaring headlights.

Mía lay next to Savannah, still asleep, and Savannah shook her. Mía's eyes fluttered a moment, confused, before she too registered the commotion of the horse and the light filling the room. She sat up.

"Savannah?"

"He's here."

The lights stopped moving and over the sound of the mare Savannah heard the transmission ratchet into park. A door opened. The headlights went dark. Keys jangled. For a brief moment Savannah tried to fool herself, imagining the town's caretaker rolling along — or, who knows, the local priest — and discovering the shattered window of the church. She swung her feet over the bed and ran to the window, willing this to be true, to thrust her head out above the street like some singing cartoon princess from a castle and call down to salvation. *We're saved we're saved we're saved....*

But the fantasy died the moment she got to the window. The vehicle looked different from this angle — long, black and silver like a winged beetle — but unmistakable nonetheless. How could Savannah fail to recognize the dingy sheeptruck with the camper in the back? The same camper from which this man-turned-monster had crawled into sight for the very first time that white morning now a lifetime ago? The same vehicle that had baked and killed a baby sister, a metal and glass death-box-turned-home, a penitence on wheels? No, Savannah knew the truck, just like she knew the ratty coyote pelt hanging atop the head directly below her — the head belonging to the man currently slamming his shoulder into the building's front door. Disappearing inside.

There came a terrible crashing downstairs, the mare ripping free from where she'd been tethered and rampaging about the bottom floor — banging against walls, kicking over shelves. Savannah grabbed the rifle and flipped the safety off.

"Hold on to me," she said, and Mía clutched the back of her coat. Savannah led them out of the bedroom. She kept the rifle pointed in front of her and her headlamp off, careful not to give away their position. A sooty moonlight seeped from the window above the second-story landing. The staircase was his only way up. The steps were narrow, creaky. Savannah knew that if he made it up them, their advantage would be lost.

Savannah swung the barrel over the railing. The staircase was empty, although the bottom half remained enshrouded in darkness. A cool draft wafted upon the back of her neck and she whirled around. Something wavered, a shadow, and Savannah nearly pulled the trigger. Only at the last second did she realize what she was looking at: herself. She peered into the bathroom, the moonlight silhouetting her against the facing mirror. Her gaze fell to the porcelain tub. It occurred to her then: what if, within the tumult below, he'd already made it upstairs? What if he was hiding?

Somewhere like in that tub....

Savannah took a step forward, into the bathroom. Just then a singsongy voice called out from below the stairs:

"GIIIIIRLS."

Savannah screamed, spinning around so fast she banged the end of the rifle against the doorframe. The voice was raspy, scarred, slithery, yet at the same time intimately familiar. Laced with memories of guns, tall tales and Savannah's own childhood. For one terrible moment she was sure of it: the voice was that of her own father.

Savannah rushed to the top of the landing and aimed the rifle down the steps. She still couldn't see anything at the bottom. Desperate for certainty, she clicked on her headlamp. The green light flooded the stairs, illuminating the thing standing at the bottom. She recognized the yellow eyes, the bony-white face, the narrow slits of nostrils. Strings of black hair fell around the sides of his head from underneath the coyote pelt on top. His teeth gritted together, lips no longer grinning but pulled back in a snarl.

Shiloh raised a hand out in front of him, a shield against the light or the rifle pointed at him or both. He lifted one foot and set it on the bottom stair.

Without thinking about it, Savannah curled her finger around the trigger and pulled.

The noise was deafening, no empty clack of a hollow chamber this time as the rifle boomed, knocking Savannah back, the staircase bursting alight with the orange blaze of the barrel. Straining not to drop the gun, she felt something bump into her legs. Again Savannah screamed — an image of him dodging her bullet, charging up the stairs into her — and raised the rifle in order to hammer it down onto whatever had just touched her only to restrain herself at the last second.

It was Mía, still holding onto her.

Savannah slid the bolt open, reloaded, picked up the flashlight and shined it back down. The staircase swirled with gunsmoke.

Mía muttered something.

"Huh?" Savannah said.

"Did you get him?"

The smoke began to clear. The bottom of the steps lay empty and Savannah scanned for signs of blood, tried to recall if she'd heard a shriek of pain, a scream other than her own.

The place was silent, motionless. Even the mare had gone quiet.

"I got him," Savannah said.

"Wait. Listen."

Savannah strained to hear through the ringing in her ears, a whine so loud it seemed palpable. She could hear her own heartbeat, feel it pulsing in her temples. Mía let go of her and put her hands to the floor. She slid them over to where the floor met the wall beneath the window.

"What are you —" Savannah said, and then she felt it, too. It reverberated through her boots, a light scraping that seemed to be coming from outside, on the other side of the wall....

Using her sleeve to wipe at a section of the windowpane next to her, Savannah turned the flashlight off and pressed her face to the glass. It was like peering through a brown bottle, the grime on the glass and the overcast night sky. Yet she could see him, his form long and insect-like as he scaled the crumbling clay exterior. Somewhere downstairs, amid the confusion, he had escaped back outside. Now, in an apparent attempt to surprise them on the second floor, he was climbing up to the window.

He ascended at a slight angle. Savannah took her headlamp off and set it on the floor. She crept down the steps with Mía behind her.

Dust fell from the wall where he kicked his toeholds on the other side, pulling himself up along the sheer wall whose dry clay was the only thing separating him from the girls. Savannah paused halfway down the stairs, pressed her ear to the wall, then her palm. She listened to his body sliding along the other side. She felt him....

Savannah stepped back, raised the rifle and pressed the muzzle against the wall. Mía put her hands over her ears.

Savannah found the trigger and squeezed.

An explosion of light, of debris, and the rifle blasted clean out of her hands. She tried to catch it and her foot slipped off the step. Savannah fell headfirst down the stairs, tumbling for what seemed like forever before somersaulting hard into the doorframe at the bottom. The rifle came clattering down behind her, followed by Mía. Savannah pushed herself to her feet. Dizzy, her head thrumming with pain, she picked up the rifle. She reloaded, took hold of Mía's hand and led them through the bottom floor.

Almost all the shelves lay toppled, the mare huddled and trembling in a back corner. Her reins dangled, still attached to the coatrack she had ripped from the wall. Savannah untied the reins from the rack and guided the horse to the front door. Mía wedged the door wide and the mare barged through, nearly yanking the reins from Savannah's hand. She held tight, keeping the frightened horse from rearing just long enough for her and Mía to swing atop. They burst off at a gallop.

Savannah hunkered low with her sister in her lap this time, one hand holding the reins and the other the rifle. The mare fled down the main street, leaving behind the forever-dark buildings. Without so much as slowing her stride she hurdled the barbwire fence, then opened into a hard gallop into desert. Behind them an engine roared to life. Savannah craned her head to see the truck peel a one-eighty, gravel clinking against its undercarriage. Twin headlights swinging around to flood the street as the truck barreled after them.

The mare veered left as if the beams were a powerful current she scrambled to escape. But the headlights turned with them, casting the horse's racing shadow long out front, piercing the dust and snow kicked up by her hooves. The vehicle rumbled closer.

Savannah knew they needed to weave somewhere the vehicle couldn't. In the light fanned out before her, she saw two options: an arroyo extending deep and sheer to the right, and the towering butte to the left.

The mare stumbled, almost crashing to the ground before regaining its stride at the last moment. She reached the bottom of the butte where instantly the soil cascaded around her hooves. Snorting, the horse heaved upward. Sinking. Slowing. There came the sound of wood cracking and wires twanging as the truck plowed through the barbwire fence and careened after them. The wheels struck the incline, headlights angling up. The engine revved, rear tires spitting dirt. A second later a thick clunking sounded as the truck dug into four-wheel. It fishtailed through the falling dirt, fighting its way after them, gaining fast.

"Take these!" Savannah said, and handed the reins to her sister.

"What are you doing?"

Savannah squeezed her legs tight around the horse and brought the rifle up in both hands. She nearly dropped it as the mare jerked to the side suddenly, avoiding a round sandstone boulder. The boulder slid in the cascading soil and began to roll. It plunged down the embankment, picking up speed. Savannah watched the truck veer to the side to try and avoid it but it was too late. The boulder smashed into the grill and then was sucked under. The truck pitched backward, headlights sweeping up to the sky, balancing there on its tail for one amazingly long moment—creaking, the tires spitting dirt—before finally tumbling over. The truck cartwheeled end over end, camper bursting free, all the way to the base where it crashed to a stop on its side. Glass tinkled. A door swung open. The one headlight that hadn't broken pointed straight up the butte....

Up to where Shiloh lunged after them....

On all fours....

His outline dark....

Swift....

And closing fast.

Blood pumped from a hole in the side of his belly as he charged hand and foot, panting. The incline grew sheerer the higher they climbed and the mare was slowing, her hooves burying deeper and deeper into the soil. Mía screamed and Savannah felt her sliding.

Shiloh was closing in on them. He leapt, one hand outstretched, and missed. He landing on his belly, picked himself up and lunged again. This time he grasped hold of the mare's ankle. The mare whinnied and kicked free. But in the process she lost her momentum. She began to slide

Shiloh crouched, preparing to jump.

Savannah aimed the rifle behind her. Her balance was off and the barrel swayed wildly. She fired. Shiloh yelped, the hurt bark of a stepped-on dog, and before the rifle fell from her grasp Savannah actually saw the bullet tear through the top of one of his shoulders. There was a spray of blood. Shiloh rolled down the slope and out of sight.

Mía fell. At the last second Savannah tried to catch her only to be pulled off the horse herself. She hit the ground hard on her back, the air punched out of her. She gasped, flopped over and sprang for the reins dangling above. She was too late; the mare gained her footing and rushed upward and out of reach—disappearing into the greater shadow of the butte.

"Here," Mía said. She was on her butt, half-buried in the falling dirt with the rifle in both hands. "You dropped it."

Savannah took the rifle and looked down to the bottom. She saw no movement in the darkness or within the one headlight beam illuminating the base. He'd been hit at least twice by now, Savannah was sure of that much, although she had no idea whether that would be enough to kill him. Or—an absurdity she shivered away—if such a thing was even possible.

"Come on," Savannah said. "Let's get to the top." She could see the cloudy night sky behind the tabletop summit. She didn't know what was on the other side of the butte, or whether they could even get down, but they needed to catch the mare before she escaped completely or fell off a cliff.

"Wait," Mía said, pointing. "Look."

Savannah followed her sister's gaze down to the truck and its one headlight. "What? I don't see anything."

"Someone moved, I saw it. Through the light...."

Savannah watched. The beam was long and perfectly conical in the dust settling around it. "I still don't—"

The beam wavered, wobbled slightly—not someone moving *through* the light, Savannah realized, but someone actually moving the light itself, rocking it.

"He's tipping the truck back over," Savannah said.

The headlight arched down and the vehicle banged as it fell onto all four tires.

He's getting back inside, Savannah thought.

He's hurt.

He's retreating.

Half-aware she was even doing it, she slid open the bolt on the rifle, ejecting the spent cartridge and loading a fresh one in the chamber.

The last one.

Sitting down, Savannah bent her legs and set the rifle's barrel between her knees. It was the driver's side light that shined. She found the light in the scope.

Savannah raised the crosshairs directly above it.

She took a breath, holding it. She listened.... Waited....

And just like that, there she was again, under the bright sun in the wide-open desert on the day she'd first met this gun. Just like that there *he* was again, arms wrapping around hers from behind, pulling the stock tight against her shoulder. His chest big and warm against her back. His beard alongside against her neck, breath faintly like mothballs and sweat a little sticky even though the sensations didn't bother Savannah so much as they comforted her. Empowered her. Urged her not to question him or herself or anything else in the world that might turn out to be false. A hallucination. A particle floating across an eyeball.

The car door slammed shut, headlight bouncing ever so slightly.

Savannah exhaled, her finger pulling so slowly, so steadily it surprised her when the rifle actually fired. The stock slammed into her shoulder, the shot ringing in her ears. But Savannah barely noticed. She held the rifle firm, watching through the crosshairs the headlight slowly retreat, the vehicle reversing. It curved slightly, and just when

Savannah feared it was going to brake, shift into drive and take off, once more the headlight swung straight up into the sky. The truck plunged into the steep arroyo, crashing onto its back end.

"You got him," Mía said. "You killed him."

The mare whinnied from somewhere above. Her cry swept across the night sky, carrying in the wind.

26

Savannah had to see him dead. She had no bullets left, no weapon except the menacing guise of the rifle itself, but she knew she'd never feel safe otherwise. If any air breathed through those slitty nostrils, if his heart had any beat left to it, then let it end here. Let it go no further than tonight. Be it barehands and blood, let there at least be certainty.

They discovered the mare trembling against the sheer stone flank of the butte. Mía took the animal by the reins, and half-falling half-sliding the three descended to flat land. They crept up to the arroyo and the flipped truck inside it. The wind softened, a few stray flecks of snow falling from the sky and spiraling in the vehicle's inverted headlight. Savannah saw where the bullet had entered the front windshield with a neat hole directly above the steering wheel, but it was too dark to see through the glass.

"Wait here," Savannah said, leaving Mía and the horse at the edge of the arroyo. She dropped in and, taking one last look up at her sister, opened the driver's side door.

He lay sprawled out in the tilted seat, the soft blue light of the dash glowing upon his limp form. Most of his jaw was missing from where the bullet had gone almost straight down his throat into the headrest. A powerful stench of flesh and urine wafted out from inside the cab.

"Is he dead?" Mía asked.

"As can be," Savannah said, not really knowing what she meant by that, only that his eyes bothered her. Everything from the loose limbs to the blood-spattered mess of teeth and cords that was now his lower face said he was dead. But inside those deep sockets his eyes still *looked* at her: yellow, unmoving, unavoidable.

She poked him with the barrel and his head drooped, along with his gaze.

The rest of the truck was a mess of clothing, trash, and shattered glass. Savannah spotted an unwrapped stick of jerky, as well as a plastic mesh sack of moldy apples — none of which she felt much of an appetite for. A part of her had hoped the truck would still be drivable, that somehow they'd be able to rev it free, but the arroyo was sheer and the truck more inside than out of it. Savannah didn't need to climb into that blood-soaked seat to know they weren't driving anywhere.

"There's something in his pocket," Mía said.

Savannah examined him. Indeed, something rectangular, slim and compact bulged in the front pocket of his jeans.

Something with the outline of a cellphone.

Savannah reached in the pocket, his lap wet and warm, and retrieved the object. She held it in her hands and examined it. Her sister asked her a question, but Savannah was suddenly too far away to hear it. She was lost in the photo in her hands, the framed portrait of Mía — so little at the time, sitting atop a bale of hay in her pink cowboy hat and matching boots. Savannah knew it to be the first time she'd ever viewed the picture outside the kitchen windowsill of their old house.

One final totem to filter through this nightmare and come out foul.

"What's wrong?" Mía asked.

"Nothing."

"You're crying."

"I know. I'm just really glad you're all right is all. You want this?"

She showed Mía the picture. Mía studied it, her eyes widening briefly before looking away. She shook her head. Savannah dropped the picture into the dirt and crushed it with the heel of her boot.

They rode eastward through the desert for miles, the moon sinking into the sky at their backs. The snow began to fall harder, accumulating into wind-blown swaths. The cold was bone-penetrating, razor-sharp against Savannah's skin. They passed a clump of junipers and Savannah thought about building a fire. Then she remembered that the pack containing all their gear, including matches, was still in that upstairs bedroom in La Gloria. And Savannah had no intention of turning back. At that point she wasn't sure the mare could make it back that far; her walk was slow, weary. Just like the girls, the animal needed rest. She needed food and water. She needed rescue.

Savannah decided then and that there she would never leave the horse. Whatever happened, wherever they ended up, the old mare had become hers. Savannah felt a sudden warmth spread inside her at the realization. It was not only the warmth of love; it was the warmth of certainty.

She rode for a long time still clutching the rifle, incapable of letting it go. Finally she asked herself why. Hadn't it done enough? Deciding the answer was yes, Savannah stopped the horse and hopped down.

"What are you doing?" Mía asked.

Savannah set her dad's prized 30.06 on the ground. She found a heavy rock and knelt before the rifle. Savannah raised the rock above her head and smashed it down onto the rifle. She smashed it again and again until the stock splintered, the trigger snapped and the barrel dented. As she smashed she grew aware of a knot untying itself within her chest. It was a knot she never knew existed until the moment it was gone.

She got back on the horse and they continued to ride. A few minutes later the coyotes started howling. What began as one voice was quickly joined by another and then another until all at once the wailing surrounded the girls. Savannah told her sister not to be afraid. Mía said that she wasn't. The cries were more mournful than threatening — imbued with loss. And soon they died just as abruptly as they'd begun. The night wore on, and before long Savannah grew as numb to the cold as she did the pain attached to her thoughts. It took her a long time to notice the light shining in the distance. Not just one light, Savannah realized as they crossed a barbwire fence and drew nearer, but two, each one sparkling in the snow. One shone brighter than the other — white and blaring like a porch light — while the second appeared fainter, flickering with a trace of color.

The mare whinnied and another whinny answered in reply. The mare picked up her step.

A mobile home took form in the darkness, metal, long and rounded at the ends like a submarine. Or a silver Twinkie, Savannah thought. Smoke drifted up from a narrow chimney in the roof to quickly dissipate in the night wind. A thin curtain was drawn across one of the windows and through it the flickering light emanated. Telephone wires extended from the home, and a satellite dish roosted on top. A pile of unstacked firewood rose a few feet from the edge of the home, half-covered by a tarp that flapped in the wind. There was a corral attached to a three-sided lean-to. A single white horse emerged from the lean-to. The two animals nickered back and forth at each other. A red pickup with a horse trailer attached sat parked beside the corral.

Savannah drew back the reins. They stopped.

"What?" Mía said.

"Hold on, let's just think about this."

"Think about what?"

Savannah wasn't sure how to say it. She wasn't even sure if she meant it since she hadn't even considered it until only now, just a few irreversible steps away from rescue.

"Before anyone knows we're here, let's see if the keys are in that truck," Savannah said.

Mía's clasp slackened around Savannah's waist.

"Let's just talk about it. Before we can't."

"I'm thirsty," Mia said. "And cold."

"There might be a spigot somewhere. And I bet that truck has a heater."

"I'm too tired. Please...."

"Plus there's something I didn't tell you, something you don't know. If we went back...you know, back up there, to the cave, there's cash. He had it hidden away, almost two thousand dollars. Not a whole lot but enough to get us someplace far. I won't even make you come in with me to get it. You can just wait up top while I go. I don't mind."

Mía gaped at her.

Savannah swiveled to better face her. "Think about it. Think about what other choices we have, what will happen to us. There's going to be cops and social workers following us around for years. We might even go to a juvenile hall, a jail for kids. They'd probably split us up, who knows. And if not that, then what, a foster home? An aunt or something we've never heard of? No matter where we go everyone's going to know who we are by our names. Think about that compared to hitting the road with two thousand dollars cash, free to go anywhere we want and do anything. Think about how we felt coming to that ghost town, back when we thought we had the whole place to ourselves...."

Mía looked off to the side, her eyes watering.

"Mía, I'm just saying —"

"Don't."

"It's at least worth talking about."

"Stop."

"Stop what? I'm only —"

"Stop talking like him."

Savannah's breath caught in her throat, her mouth hanging open. A tear fell down Mía's face and she wiped it away with a coat sleeve — her puffy camouflage coat sleeve, the one she'd started this whole ordeal in, filthy now. The white horse stood watching them with its head over the corral, black almond eyes blinking against the wind and snow.

Savannah no longer felt numb. Once more, she felt the cold.

27

The home was warm and smelled of woodsmoke, beans and red chile which the old woman heated on tortillas in a microwave. The girls ate ravenously while the husband made the phone call, then disappeared out onto the porch with a shotgun. He had helped Savannah put the mare in the corral with the other horse, giving them hay and water. He'd been disturbed by their story, scared even, whereas the woman didn't seem bothered in the slightest. She stood five feet at most with a braided gray ponytail and two of her front teeth missing. Like her home, she was warm and welcoming, and she appeared to only half-listen as Savannah did her best to explain who they were and what had happened. The woman nodded as if she'd heard it all before and was more interested in serving them the food so they could join her on the couch in front of the television.

A movie was on, a black-and-white western featuring actors Savannah didn't recognize and who were probably dead. As she watched, she found herself thinking of the vintage movie posters covering the walls of a 50's diner her grandmother once took the girls to. Savannah remembered sitting in the plush red leather seats of that diner, soaking in all those old posters and memorabilia, the mini jukeboxes on every table, and feeling a sort of sadness for how obscure it all was. How all this stuff could never have any other home except this diner, whose food wasn't even that good.

"That man's cows were stolen by the one you just saw," the woman said, pointing to the screen. "The one with the hat and mustache. That's why they are all going after him."

Savannah nodded and Mía sank deeper into the cushions beside her. Savannah's gaze went to the pictures hanging on the walls and the few propped in small frames beside the television. She recognized the woman and her husband in some of them, but not the young girl. She had long black hair and a pretty smile, and in nearly every photo was either on top a horse or on top a podium holding a blue ribbon.

"Is that your daughter?" Savannah asked.

The woman's eyes darted briefly away from the television, and Savannah thought she saw a shadow pass over her face.

"Yes," the woman said, brightening suddenly at the appearance of a wavy-haired girl on the screen. The girl was watching a cowboy—the good guy—attempt to mount a bucking horse inside a pen. "And that is the good guy's woman. Except she doesn't love him yet. But watch, she will."

"Does she race?" Savannah asked. "Your daughter I mean."

The woman was quiet a moment, crossing her arms, and Savannah could tell she was working hard to keep her eyes trained on the television. "No."

"Oh," Savannah said, and then because the expression on the woman's face seemed to call for it: "Sorry."

On screen, the cowboy hooked a boot into the stirrup and tried to climb up only to be thrown into the dirt. The horse ran wild around the corral as other cowboys laughed and jeered from the side.

The old woman shook her head. "Watch. He'll get on that horse, and it will be the fastest horse of them all."

Savannah glanced at Mía, fully asleep now and gently snoring.

The door swung open, snow and cold air whooshing in. The old man pointed out into the early morning. "Look."

Savannah leaned forward to see past him. A string of red and blue flashing lights approached in the distance. The whole desert was gray, blotted by the falling snow, and within it the emergency lights might well have been UFOs floating in the ether.

"Close the door," the woman said. "It's too cold."

The man propped the shotgun inside the doorframe and walked down the porch steps.

The woman *tsked*, pushed herself to her feet, moved the shotgun out of the doorframe and closed the door.

"He is always worrying," she said, returning to the sofa. "Always thinking about what happened, or else about what's going to happen. I tell him none of that matters."

On screen, the horse kept bucking but finally the cowboy made it over the saddle. He stayed on, reining the horse into a smooth, controlled gallop around the pen while everyone cheered.

The old woman clasped her hands against her chest in delight. "You see?"

"I see," Savannah said.

The End

About the Author

Adam James Jones is a writer and screenwriter living in New Mexico. He is the author of the acclaimed historical novel, *The Vendetta of Felipe Espinosa*, and has contributed articles and short fiction for *Backpacker Magazine*, *Wild West*, and *Darker Times* (UK). As a screenwriter he works on films with his wife, the director Catharine. E. Jones. Their most recent collaboration was the award-winning horror-short, *Hatchlings*, as well as their baby boy, Augustus.

Note from the Publisher

Word-of-mouth is crucial for any author to succeed. If you enjoyed *Prisoner's Cinema*, please leave a review online—anywhere you are able. Even if it's just a sentence or two. It would make all the difference and would be very much appreciated.

Thanks!